READING THE BRONTË BODY

READING THE BRONTË BODY

DISEASE, DESIRE, AND THE CONSTRAINTS OF CULTURE

Beth Torgerson

READING THE BRONTË BODY
© Beth E. Torgerson, 2005.

First published in 2005 by
PALGRAVE MACMILLAN™
175 Fifth Avenue, New York, N.Y. 10010 and
Houndmills, Basingstoke, Hampshire, England RG21 6XS
Companies and representatives throughout the world.

PALGRAVE MACMILLAN is the global academic imprint of the Palgrave Macmillan division of St. Martin's Press, LLC and of Palgrave Macmillan Ltd. Macmillan® is a registered trademark in the United States, United Kingdom and other countries. Palgrave is a registered trademark in the European Union and other countries.

ISBN 1–4039–6796–2

Library of Congress Cataloging-in-Publication Data

Torgerson, Beth E. (Beth Ellen)
    Reading the Brontë body : disease, desire, and the constraints of culture / by Beth E. Torgerson.
        p. cm.
    Revision of the author's thesis (Ph. D.)—University of
        Nebraska—Lincoln, 2001.
    Includes bibliographical references and index.
    ISBN 1–4039–6796–2 (alk. paper)
    1. Brontë, Charlotte, 1816–1855—Criticism and interpretation.
2. Literature and medicine—England—History—19th century.
3. Brontë, Emily, 1818–1848—Criticism and interpretation. 4. Brontë, Anne, 1820–1849—Criticism and interpretation. 5. Women and literature—England—History—19th century. 6. Body, Human, in literature. 7. Diseases in literature. 8. Desire in literature. I. Title.

PR4169.T67 2005
823'.8—dc22
                                                          2004065448

A catalogue record for this book is available from the British Library.

Design by Newgen Imaging Systems (P) Ltd., Chennai, India.

First edition: August 2005

10 9 8 7 6 5 4 3 2 1

Printed in the United States of America.

Transferred to digital printing in 2006.

For Patricia and Ken Torgerson

CONTENTS

ACKNOWLEDGMENTS

I am grateful for all of the support and encouragement I have received while researching and writing this book from colleagues, friends, and family. I am grateful to Linda Ray Pratt, Stephen Behrendt, Gerry Brookes, Ross Thompson, and Barbara DiBernard for reading the manuscript at the dissertation stage and for their insights and encouragement during the revision process. I am grateful to Farideh Koohi-Komali, my editor at Palgrave Macmillan, and Melissa Nosal and Lynn Vande Stouwe, her able assistants, for both their professionalism and their enthusiasm for the manuscript. I also want to thank Sheeba Vijayakumar for her wonderful work as copy-editor and Maran Elancheran for his work in production. I feel privileged to have had the opportunity to share my ideas with two writing groups, the first in Lincoln, Nebraska, in the early days of the project and the second in St. Augustine, Florida, as I worked through the final revisions. The members of these two groups—Judy Levin, Rene Meaker, Anne Whitney, Darien Andreu, Owene Weber, Kim Bradley Barzso, and Rosalinda Lidh—have all helped in ways that extend well beyond the actual writing. At crucial moments, other friends and colleagues have stepped forward to read a passage or a chapter, including Debra Cumberland, Anca Munteanu, Eric Sandberg, Ladette Randolph, and Todd Lidh. I am grateful to these individuals as well as to the larger University of Nebraska-Lincoln and Flagler College communities for their ongoing support. During my year in England, I developed an even deeper appreciation for Victorian literature and culture from working with Leonée Ormond, Paul Kenny, Max Saunders, Joe Phelan, and John Woolford at King's College London and with David Grylls and Elisabeth Jay during the summer program at Oxford. Looking back, I can see that the seed for this entire project grew out of a paper written while in Dr. Jay's class that summer.

I am grateful for the assistance of many wonderful librarians. Peggy Dyess, the Interlibrary Loan Librarian at Flagler College, was exceptional in her efforts to locate texts, including some fairly obscure Victorian manuscripts. Mike Gallen, the Director of Library Services at Flagler, was generous in his support, often offering to buy specific books to aid my research while building the library's collection. I appreciate Ann Dinsdale and her assistant Sarah Carr at the Brontë Parsonage Library, both for their help in person at Haworth and for their help via e-mail. At the University of Nebraska-Lincoln, I depended greatly upon the librarians in a variety of departments— Interlibrary Loan, Special Collections, and Microfilm Services. I am especially grateful to Tom McFarland, Kate Kane, Brian Zillig, Amy Heberling, and Carmella Orosco. The special collection librarians at both the Wellcome Library and the British Library have been extremely helpful. Thanks also to Samantha Cairns, the outreach librarian at the Wellcome Trust.

I want to thank the eleven Flagler College students who traveled with me to England on the study abroad program during the summer of 2004. Their enthusiasm for the Brontës and their novels was exhilarating. Our class discussions as well as our excursions in Haworth, York, Scarborough, and London all contributed to giving another dimension to this project. Special thanks also goes to the many Brontë Society members who lectured, organized, or led excursions for us. The knowledge of the Brontës shared with us by Ann Dinsdale, Andrew McCarthy, Jean Bull, and Margaret McCarthy was truly inspirational.

I want to thank Ann Dinsdale and Michael Hutcheon who were gracious enough to allow me to quote from their respective presentations. I want to acknowledge my debt to Sally Shuttleworth's work, *Charlotte Brontë and Victorian Psychology*, which has been used with the permission of Cambridge University Press. I am also grateful to Susan Hamilton, the editor of the *Victorian Review*, for permission to reprint as chapter 2 in this volume my article "Ailing Women in the Age of Cholera: Illness in *Shirley*," which appeared in *Victorian Review* 30.2 (2004): 1–31.

Friends, too numerous to mention by name, helped more indirectly with this project by ensuring my life remained joyful and balanced throughout it. A big heartfelt thanks goes to each of them.

I appreciate the love, encouragement, and support given to me by my family—my parents, Pat and Ken Torgerson, my brother, Lewis Torgerson, my aunt, Shirley Witt, and my husband, Bob Steinauer. Their love has made the journey worthwhile.

INTRODUCTION

The body, even when naked, is always a cultural construct.

Michael Hutcheon, M.D., "The Body Theatrical" (1999)

Representations of disease and illness pervade the seven novels written by Anne, Emily, and Charlotte Brontë during the years of 1847–1853. These representations include cholera, consumption, rabies, rheumatism, fevers, alcoholism, hypochondria, hysteria, monomania, madness, and more. Since medicine was not able to make any real advances in curing disease until after the mid-nineteenth century, with smallpox being the only exception, the Brontës' representations of ill-health may be a natural consequence of the prevalence of disease and death in early Victorian life.[1] Diseases that are now preventable through vaccination, such as influenza and rabies, and diseases that are now treatable with modern medicine, such as tuberculosis, malaria, and cholera, still took a toll on human life. Visibly present, death and disease were routine parts of life in Victorian England.

The health conditions specific to Haworth, the Yorkshire village where the Brontës lived, also brought issues of disease and death closer home to the Brontës. Out of concern for the high mortality rates of his parishioners, Reverend Patrick Brontë wrote numerous letters to London requesting a formal visit from an inspector of health. The Babbage report of 1850 was the result of Brontë's persistence. In *The Brontës*, Juliet Barker summarizes Babbage's findings, recording that "the mortality rates in Haworth rivaled those in the worst districts of London" (96). In general, the mortality rate was 10.5 percent higher than what the law considered needing special attention (Barker 635). The infant mortality rate was especially high with 41 percent of children in Haworth dying before their sixth birthday (96). These early deaths contributed to the fact that the average age of death in Haworth was only twenty-five years (96).

In addition to the state of poor health in Haworth in general, the Brontë family underwent personal tragedy brought about by early deaths of family members from diseases then considered untreatable. The deaths of Maria Brontë and Elizabeth Brontë, age eleven and ten from consumption contracted at the Clergy Daughters' School has become part of the Brontë legend, thanks largely to Charlotte Brontë's fictional portrayal of Maria as Helen Burns in *Jane Eyre*. Yet, by the time these two deaths struck the Brontë family, they had already suffered the premature death of their mother, Maria Branwell Brontë, age thirty-eight, to what is now thought to have been uterine cancer (Barker 102).[2] At the time of their mother's death, the Brontë children ranged in age from less than two to seven years.

Following the early deaths of their mother and their two eldest sisters to the ravages of disease, the remaining siblings' awareness of the ramifications of disease, not only on the sufferer but also those around her, would naturally affect the ways they perceived their world. Once they became authors, perhaps it only makes sense that they would repeatedly use representations and metaphors of disease in their writings.

Two ongoing health issues, Anne Brontë's lifelong affliction with asthma and Branwell Brontë's increasing addiction to alcohol, continued to plague them as they matured into adulthood. Both conditions were to play pivotal roles in the final family tragedy when consumption struck again, causing the deaths of Branwell, Emily, and Anne in succession within less than a year. Consumption worked most quickly on Branwell Brontë's constitution, which was already weakened by his addiction to alcohol.[3] Emily Brontë contracted the consumption from her brother and followed him rapidly into death. His death was in late September 1848, hers was in early December 1848, less than three months later. Anne Brontë's own health issues with asthma decreased her own resistance to the disease's influence. Her death by consumption followed five months later in May 1849. At thirty-three years of age, Charlotte Brontë was the only remaining sibling in a family of six children.

Because the Brontë legend is perpetuated by the magnitude of the family tragedy, it is important to place their deaths in perspective. By comparing the deaths of the Brontës with the statistics in the Babbage report, Barker notes, "According to Babbage's mortality rate tables, at least two of the Brontë children should have died before they were six . . . The average age at death was twenty-five, so Charlotte at thirty-eight, Branwell at thirty-one, Emily at thirty, and Anne at twenty-nine, all exceeded the statistical average" (852 note 23).

Assessing these statistical discrepancies, Ann Dinsdale, the current librarian at the Haworth Parsonage Library, asserts that the parsonage's prime location at the top of the hill insured cleaner water supplies and better sanitation and sewage conditions for the Brontës. Dinsdale makes the telling comment that "the surprise is not that the Brontës died so young but that they lived so long." Indeed, considering that during their mother's fatal illness, all six of the Brontë siblings came down with, but recovered from, a bout of scarlet fever, a disease often fatal in the Victorian era (Barker 103), it is remarkable that they were not victims of even earlier deaths, contributing to Babbage's statistics rather than contributing to our literary heritage.

After the death of her remaining siblings, Charlotte Brontë incorporates strong representations of illness into her later fiction writing, which seem infused with new wisdom gained through dealing with these multiple deaths. Consequently, representations of illness in Charlotte's final two novels are particularly insightful. Because Anne and Emily's awareness of the ramifications of the disease process are likewise insightful, these literary sisters' fictional use of illness deserves much more attention than that it has currently received. Among the possible functions such representations served the Brontës as authors, I am most interested in how illness provides them with unique ways to critique gender and class constraints inherent in Victorian culture.

While literary theory provides useful paradigms, such as feminist and Marxist theory, to analyze gender and class issues in literary works, cultural studies have encouraged literary critics to move outside of our home discipline to grasp larger cultural trends and themes at work. Cultural theorists working with the body, such as Michel Foucault and Judith Butler, have already helped to develop our awareness that the body itself is an ever-changing cultural phenomenon.[4] Thanks in part to their work, especially that of Foucault, medical anthropologists, medical sociologists, and others interested in the overlap between medicine, literature, and culture are currently developing a significant body of work structured around the idea that illness is also socially constructed. For this particular project, to analyze the representations of illness and disease within the novels of the Brontës, I am relying upon two interrelated fields, medical anthropology and the history of medicine. By its very nature, medical anthropology requires knowledge of cultural context. An in-depth look at the history of medicine in nineteenth-century England provides the necessary cultural context, giving modern readers a sense of how issues of health, illness, and the body were understood in Victorian England. Together, medical anthropology and the history of medicine offer a useful lens though which we can understand Victorian beliefs and knowledge concerning medicine, health, and illness. An application of this understanding calls for an analysis of the representations of illness and disease found in novels of the period, the Brontë novels among them.

The terms "illness" and "disease" need to be clarified. In *The Illness Narratives: Suffering, Healing, and the Human Condition*, Arthur Kleinman, a leading medical anthropologist who has helped to establish the field, distinguishes between them. In the biological terms of the biomedical model, Kleinman clarifies that "disease is reconfigured *only* as an alteration in biological structure or functioning" (5–6). In contrast, illness is understood as the "lived experience" of disease (4) and as such is "always culturally shaped" (5). Medical anthropology's idea that illness is "always culturally shaped" does not negate that illness is a very real bodily event, often having a particular disease as its origin. Yet, as Arthur Frank, a sociologist who researches illness, asserts in *The Wounded Storyteller: Body, Illness, and Ethics*, "no distinction between corporeal disease and illness experience can be sustained: a problem within the tissues pervades the whole life" (49). While I maintain the distinctions between the terms, the term "illness" is fundamentally more useful for the purposes of literary analysis since it can incorporate the concept of "disease" within it.

For example, Kleinman, Susan Sontag, and Judith Lorber give examples of how culture shapes the experience of having a disease, even affecting the resulting experiences of health care. While much of their work emphasizes current health issues in the American health system, their findings often include analyses of other cultures and other historical periods. As Kleinman points out, "In each culture and historical period there are different ways to talk about, say, headaches" (11), and he indicates that this is equally true of other diseases and their symptoms. For example, Kleinman relates that currently in China, decisions about an individual's health care are not up to the individuals, even if they happen to be medically trained experts, but to the other family members (155). Similarly, within Sontag's discussion of the cultural conventions concerning the concealment of cancer diagnoses in *Illness as Metaphor*, Sontag notes that as of 1978, "In France and Italy it is still the rule for doctors to communicate a cancer diagnosis to the patient's family but not to the patient" (7). In each case, the cultural context affects how the illness is understood and experienced.

Lorber's *Gender and the Social Construction of Illness* is a comprehensive work showing how "gender, race, class, ethnicity, and culture influence the experience of symptoms" as well as the treatment of those symptoms within the current American health system (ix). Lorber asserts,

> Social practices produce social bodies all through life and death—and beyond (consider how corpses are handled). Because gender is embedded in the major social organizations of society, . . . it has a major impact on how the women and men of different social groups are treated in all sectors of life, including health and illness, getting born and dying. (3)

Lorber's extensive examples, like the work of Kleinman, Sontag, and others, serve to highlight how people experience their illnesses differently based on a variety of external social and cultural factors. Examples of how illnesses are experienced differently, dependent upon the culture in which they occur, could be virtually endless. The primary point to gain is that illnesses need to be understood within their cultural contexts to ensure a full appreciation of each illness's significance. Medical anthropologists, medical sociologists, and theorists of the body together are providing examples and methodologies to understand the body and illness within cultural contexts. Their findings are not only of benefit to physicians and social workers who work directly with the body, but also of benefit to literary critics, historians, and others who are interested in how the interplay between culture and the body becomes embodied within literary texts and other cultural texts.

By placing the ill body within its cultural and social context, medical anthropologists aim to demonstrate that, quoting Arthur Frank, "illness is a social issue, not simply a personal affliction" (122). Medical anthropologists stress that bodies are always social bodies. They believe that the "body" can be seen theoretically as the bridge between the "self" and the "social world," making the body a battlefield for ideological conflicts. In such a position, the body carries wounds, the signs of conflict, when there are discrepancies between what the self desires and what the culture allows. In *The Illness Narratives*, Kleinman explores the conflict between cultural expectation and personal desire. According to Kleinman, where there is illness, there is "unresolved conflict" in the life between what one desires and what is expected, between what one desires and what is available, or perhaps between two conflicting desires (97–99). In a similar vein, in *The Body in Pain: The Making and Unmaking of the World*, Elaine Scarry asserts that the body embodies culture, which makes the body the necessary site to carry the scars and wounds of ideological warfare.

Throughout *The Body in Pain*, Scarry addresses the philosophical importance of understanding the body's role in embodying culture and cultural ideologies, whether they be religious ideologies or political ones. Scarry reiterates the body's position as "bridge" between the self and the social world (49). Even though Scarry's focus is predominantly on pain occurring from the trauma of torture and war, her insight on how ideology always depends upon inscriptions on the body to be made "real" to its believers is also applicable to illness and the pain attending it. Medical anthropologists, such as Arthur Frank and Byron J. Good, have made explicit the connections between Scarry's work and illness. Frank writes, "Chaos stories [a form of illness narrative] are told at the end of the process that Elaine Scarry calls 'unmaking the world" (103). In his essay, "A Body in Pain—The Making of a World of Chronic Pain," Good applies Scarry's description of "pain as 'shattering' language, as 'world-destroying' " to one patient's ongoing experience of chronic pain (35).

Another medical anthropologist, Paul Brodwin, clarifies the process by which cultural conflicts take place within the body in his work with a woman given the name "Diane." While Brodwin's in-depth description of Diane relates the pain of a living, suffering patient, his findings demonstrate meaningful ways in which symptoms of the body act as a language, a concept that can be easily transferred to literary analysis of how representations of illness function within literary texts. Considered a chronic pain patient, Diane suffers from an unspecified illness which has an array of physical symptoms, including headaches, stomach pains, hyperventilation, and the inability to see or breathe for brief periods of time. Brodwin emphasizes that the body functions on both private and social levels, even though our current biomedical model of medicine prefers to emphasize the former.

Brodwin develops the way "both the marker of troubling relationships and the attempts to change them appear in the internal spaces of the body—usually considered in our culture the ultimately private, nonsocial domain" (82). In Brodwin's depiction of Diane's body as a social body, interconnected to the people around her and the cultural expectations they have of her, he describes how Diane's physical symptoms of illness "convey, in metaphoric though inescapable terms, the frustration she experiences in her relations with friends and family" (82). Her symptoms become a nonverbal form of language. He continues, "To begin with, Diane feels condemned by virtually her entire social world for not meeting certain standards of behavior or achievement" (82). Brodwin stresses that she is acutely aware of "not conforming" to the images of *x*, *y*, and *z* that others hold up as the "ideal" (82). Brodwin comments that "Diane's world also seems unreceptive to direct protest or attempts to change it" and, thus, her symptoms "persist as one of the few legitimate forms of resistance" (82). He sees Diane's symptoms as "both a reaction to particular conflicts and a symbol of her general social discomfort—even more, a public symbol conveying that meaning to the people around her" (83). Brodwin's insight into the way that symptoms become symbols of resistance is important. However, Brodwin does not move beyond this insight to address the problems inherent in using illness as a "public symbol" of cultural conflict. Fortunately, both Kleinman and Diane Price Herndl do.

In Kleinman's "Pain and Resistance: The Delegitimation and Relegitimation of Local Worlds," he ends his discussion of pain symptoms as a form of nonverbal resistance to specific life situations by writing, "the bodily mode of resistance seemed to deepen personal crisis while not succeeding as a form of political protest or change" (194). What is true of pain is equally true of illness. Herndl makes this point specifically concerning illness in *Invalid Women: Figuring Feminine Illness in American Fiction and Culture, 1840–1940*. Herndl asserts illness, in both literature and life, may be seen as a type of resistance to cultural constraints, yet it ends by being ineffective in achieving political or social change. Herndl concludes, "When women are taught that illness and death offer them the best route to power, we all suffer the loss of possibilities. There is nothing empowering about victimage" (3). Thus, even though illness is often perceived to be a subversive attempt at gaining power over others around them, by its very nature, illness cannot, in fact, affect any positive change.

Kleinman is careful to clarify that cultural conflict is not necessarily the origin of disease. Nevertheless, he mentions that "a very substantial body of findings indicates that psychological and social factors are often the determinants of the swing toward amplification [of symptoms]" (7). In this way, social and cultural factors are at work even in biological disease. Even if one could theoretically put aside culture's ability to be a factor in the origin of disease or in the exacerbation of symptoms, culture is still always present within the realm of illness. As Kleinman declares, "Acting like a sponge, illness soaks up personal and social significance from the world of the sick person" (31). He feels "illness absorbs and intensifies life meanings" (32). Here, the sponge metaphor shifts to that of a magnifying lens. First, illness absorbs meaning from the interpersonal and social life in which it occurs, and then it acts as a magnifying lens, intensifying the life meanings of the person experiencing it.

An application of these ideas from medical anthropology requires us to pay greater attention to how disease and symptoms of illness point toward cultural conflicts, not only in life but also in literature. Wherever illness exists, it signifies tensions within the life or within the text. In order to appreciate fully the significance of what medical anthropology offers to an analysis of the Brontë novels, a closer look at the Victorian context of medicine will clarify how diseases were culturally understood and what medical, scientific, and technological advances were making Victorian medical history.

In itself, the fact that our current biomedical concept of disease was not yet constructed during the Brontës' lifetime is enough to emphasize the importance of an application of medical anthropology to the Brontë's novels. The biomedical concept of disease came about later in the nineteenth century when advances made in the medical knowledge of patho-anatomy led to the new field of bacteriology. In *The Greatest Benefit to Mankind: A Medical History of Humanity*, Roy Porter explores this historical shift from the traditional understanding of disease as affecting the entire body, that is, "the constitution," to the more modern understanding of disease as affecting a localized area within the body.

The shift occurred first when disease was thought to be localized at the level of organs, then at the level of tissues, and finally, at the cellular level. Porter summarizes, "Morgagni had highlighted the organ, Bichat the tissue; Virchow had now given pride of place to the cell" (331).[5] Each shift in thinking brought about a new understanding of disease, even if this lab-based knowledge of patho-anatomy was not yet advanced enough to make an impact on clinical medicine until Robert Koch's work with bacteriology later in the century.[6] Rudolf Virchow's book *Die Cellularpathologie* [*Cell Pathology*], published in 1858, could be considered the seminal text that breaks with prior disease paradigms and makes possible bacteriology, the germ theory derived from it, and ultimately our current biomedical model of medicine. Yet, even in 1858, Virchow's work was not widely available beyond Germany. It would take time before this new knowledge could make an impact on the general public throughout England and Europe. Patrick Brontë, who lived long enough to celebrate his eighty-fourth birthday in March of 1861, is the only Brontë to live long enough to be potentially aware of this new understanding of the diseased body. Our biomedical model, so familiar to us, would be a completely alien concept to Anne, Charlotte, and Emily Brontë as well as to other writers of their generation. Consequently, it is vital for us to understand their concepts of the body, illness, and medicine so we do not impose our own concepts and unknowingly make inaccurate assumptions based on this imposition.

In the nineteenth century, medical tracts written by physicians were becoming popular as advances in printing made such texts cheaper and more available to the lay public. William Buchan's *Domestic Medicine*, published originally in 1769, was the first success of this sort. This eighteenth century medical text was reprinted throughout the nineteenth century and found its way into many Victorian homes. Thomas John Graham's *Modern Domestic Medicine*, published in 1826, a second popular medical text, was owned by the Brontës.[7] In addition to being the source for Patrick Brontë's information on treatment for his son's symptoms of *delirium tremens*, Graham's text was also consulted for other familial health concerns, as Patrick Brontë's marginal annotations show.[8] Sally Shuttleworth details this marginalia, showing it covers such health concerns as Anne's consumption, Charlotte's facial tic (seen as a symptom of hysteria), Emily's dog bite as well as Branwell's *delirium tremens* (27). Both medical treatises, like the majority of medical texts available early in the nineteenth century, promote simple treatments, regarding diet, hygiene and temperance as remedies for most health problems.

Stressing diet, hygiene, and temperance as remedies made sense since medicine at mid-century had not made many advances in curing diseases other than smallpox. The contemporary work in pathology and anatomy that was taking place in French morgues and the scientific laboratory work that was taking place in German laboratories were not yet applicable to the clinical side of medicine.[9] While such advances would become central in medicine's ability to cure disease later in the nineteenth century, at mid-century, not much progress could visibly be seen in terms of scientific advancement.

Even though little change was occurring in curing disease in the early nineteenth century, new developments in technology were changing the face of medicine. Both the microscope and the stethoscope were making new knowledge possible. In *The Greatest Benefit to Mankind: A Medical History of Humanity*, Porter records, "With the aid of microscopes and the laboratory, nineteenth-century investigators explored the nature of body tissue and pioneered cell biology; pathological anatomy came of age" (10). Thus, for the first time since its invention almost two hundred years earlier, the microscope was beginning to make significant contributions to scientific advances.

Unlike the microscope, the stethoscope was a new invention. René Théophile Hyacinthe Laennec invented it in France in 1816.[10] The stethoscope was introduced to England by Thomas Hodgkin in 1825, who was also the first physician to lecture in London on the new ideas developing from French medicine's focus on pathology. The stethoscope made it possible for physicians to hear various internal bodily sounds, which helped them identify internal disease without having to wait until after the patient's death to perform a postmortem autopsy. As Porter explains, "At last, the living body was no longer a closed book: pathology could now be done on the living" (308). The stethoscope was common enough by mid-nineteenth century that it was used on Anne Brontë to confirm that she was suffering from consumption, the same disease that had resulted in the death of her siblings (Gaskell 285).

Thanks to the new technology, diseases began to be reconsidered and reclassified. The medieval humoral theory of disease, which was still prevalent at this late date, began losing more of its credibility. The practice of identifying diseases by their symptoms, started by the seventeenth-century physician Thomas Syndenham, continued in the mid-nineteenth century. However, once the microscope, the stethoscope, and other modern technology became available to aid physicians in classifying diseases by cause, the tradition of classifying by symptoms fell into disuse.

Yet, since the origins of many specific diseases were still not definable, the debate between "contagion" and "anti-contagion" continued. While purportedly being a scientific debate, this debate was also a political and economic one since supporters of "contagion" could demand quarantine sanctions to be put in place, thereby disrupting trade routes. Supporters of "anti-contagion" promoted the miasma theory, which held that effluvia and other environmentally polluting factors were the cause of various diseases. Thus, later, by extension, miasma could also target human agents of infection, a point taken up by many in the public health debates of the mid-nineteenth century.

External events and the external environment were assumed to play a key role in disease. For example, the effect of the weather, especially that of the wind, on the body consistently appears in early Victorian descriptions of a person's health. Throughout the Brontë letters, references occur concerning the impact that the "east wind" has on their nerves or on their bodily health in general; for example, Anne Brontë's letter to Charlotte's friend Ellen Nussey on October 4, 1847 details the three sisters' reactions to the east wind. Margaret Smith records the letter:

> Happily for all parties the east wind no longer prevails—during its continuance she [Charlotte] complained of its influence as usual. I too

suffered from it, in some degree, as I always do, more or less; but this time, it brought me no reinforcements of colds and coughs which is what I dread the most. Emily considers it a 'dry uninteresting wind,' but it does not affect her nervous system. (1: 544)

Since phenomena such as the wind was thought to affect both the mind and the body, it is important to understand that early Victorian concepts of medicine maintained a direct relation between the physiological and psychological. For example, increased or diminished "animal spirits" could affect the whole bodily economy, as could excessive emotions or lack of emotions.[11] Thus, since the body and mind were conceived as a closed system of energy, body could affect mind and mind could affect body.

In *Agnes Grey*, Anne Brontë routinely gives descriptions of specific events affecting her characters in terms of both mind and body. One is never mentioned without direct reference to the other. For example, Brontë's governess heroine narrates how "the task of instruction was as arduous for the body as the mind" (26), how her journey to Horton Lodge makes her "weary in body and mind" (57), how her sister Mary "will do her best to make them comfortable in body and mind" (73), and how Mr. Weston believes that close and constant study is "an injury to the mind as well as the body" (156). Anne Brontë is also in step with her time in her insights about how the mind can affect the body. Her narrator comments on the state of Mr. Grey's health, writing, "And thus the mind preyed upon the body, and disordered the system of the nerves, and they in turn increased the troubles of the mind, till by action, and reaction, his health was seriously impaired" (5–6). Later, Alice Grey tells her husband "there is nothing like a cheerful mind for keeping the body in health" (50). The interrelatedness of body and mind is much more prevalent in Victorian thought than it is with today's biomedical model of medicine, although much recent work in the mind/body connection is once again foregrounding the connection.

By the 1860s the advent of cellular pathology began to call into question, even to the point of negating, the role external events have on the body. Critiques of cellular pathology were based on the extremeness of the shift in belief. For example, Edwin Kleb condemned Virchovian cellular pathology, seeing it as "an extreme doctrine which regards all morbid processes as purely internal events and completely neglects the importance of external factors which provoke diseases" (qtd. in Porter 331–32). Prior to cellular pathology and the germ theory that derived from it, diseases were not easily categorized as being completely either physiological or psychological in origin. Hypochondria, now thought to be solely psychological in origin, was seen by the Victorians to be a legitimate disease that affected both the body and the mind. While we continue to use the same term, hypochondria has come to mean something quite different. According to Kleinman, "By definition, hypochondriasis is that disease in which there is no disease. In contemporary psychiatry it is classified as a chronic condition in which the patient persists in his nosophobia (fear of disease) in spite of medical evidence to the contrary" (194). Without any awareness of the future stigma that such a medical understanding of the disease would put in place a century later, Charlotte Brontë was just one of many Victorians who confidently claimed hypochondria as an ailment from which they suffered. Her letter to Margaret Wooler in November of 1846 records in detail her own year-long bout under the "tyranny of Hypochondria" (Smith 1: 505). In Charlotte Brontë's first novel *The Professor*, the narrator, Arthur Crimsworth, suffers twice from hypochondria, once in his youth and once again as the novel reaches its *dénouement*. Similar to hypochondria, hysteria was another disease comfortably understood in the Victorian era as being both somatic and psychological, which now is seen as being psychological in origin.

George Frederick Drinka, Elaine Showalter, and Sally Shuttleworth all explore the changing concepts of psychology in Victorian England. While both Drinka's *The Birth of Neurosis: Myth, Malady and the Victorians* and Showalter's *The Female Malady: Women, Madness, and English Culture 1830–1980* provide wonderful surveys of the developments in the field, Shuttleworth's *Charlotte Brontë and Victorian Psychology* provides the most in-depth look at psychological beliefs in the early nineteenth century. Shuttleworth's work explores the changing concept of self, writing, "a new interiorized notion of self-hood arose and, concomitantly, new techniques of power designed to penetrate the inner secrets of this hidden domain" (3). No longer did the straightforward theory of physiognomy which grounded the eighteenth-century idea of character apply. In the eighteenth century, external facial features were thought to equate to the inner being. In the nineteenth century, the new theories of "physiological psychology" began to explore what external features could and could not reveal about the person's hidden inner psychology. The need to be able to tap this hidden self resulted first in the emergence of phrenology and then of psychiatry as fields of inquiry. Shuttleworth develops how nineteenth-century psychiatry "broke down earlier absolute divides between the normal and pathological, insisting that disease arose merely from an excess or deficiency of elements integral to normal functioning" (12). This shift mirrors a complementary shift in medicine's new understanding, thanks to patho-anatomy, that health and disease of bodily tissues were not polar opposites as earlier thought, but rather that health and disease occurred along a continuum.

Consequently, for the first time in history, sanity and insanity, as well as health and illness, were seen as an ever-shifting continuum which depended upon self-control for management of health. In terms of psychological health, Shuttleworth shows that madness, which had functioned in earlier times as a marker of "social division" by creating an outcast group which did not fit the established criteria of normality, had to be rethought (35). Shuttleworth concludes,

> in the nineteenth century it [insanity] became increasingly an internal, psychological divide. The border to be policed was not so much between self and other, as between the conscious and unconscious self. If all individuals were liable to eruptions of insanity, the only visible sign one could cling to that one was not insane would be one's capacity to exert self-control. Social conformity thus became an index of insanity; the only measure available to the individual fearful of his or her own normality would be a willing obedience to designated social roles. (35)

The consequent need for self-control in efforts to conform to rigid social roles based on class as well as gender placed a new emphasis on excess, especially for members of the middle classes. As a result, Victorians, professional medical people and lay people alike, seemed obsessed by the shift from "normal functioning" to that of excess, such as excessive emotion and excessive desire. Shuttleworth explains, "Excessive activity in one sphere might engender physical or mental breakdown; valuable qualities might turn into agents of pollution if developed to too high a degree" (12). The result was a desire to regulate the health of both the individual body and the social body through what Shuttleworth terms, "organized management of resources" (12). For the individual, this management of resources was always understood to mean rigid self-control.

Shuttleworth points out that much of the cultural conflict in the Victorian period stems from issues of self-control. She writes, "The question of whether the individual is a self-determined agent, or merely part of a larger machine, hinges on the crucial issue of self-control— that sacrosanct principle of Victorian culture" (23). The problem, especially for Victorian women, with the concept of self-control meant "without an external field to exercise her harnessed energies, repressive self-control became a goal in its own right, and internal pain a source of pride" (24). Self-control was seen positively as leading to social opportunities, that is, opportunities of social control, since it allowed for an individual's merits to determine his or her social standing. The early Victorians are much more optimistic than later Victorians about the benefits of self-control in controlling the psyche. Shuttleworth correlates this shift with the changing patterns of industrial prosperity. She writes,

> The brash confidence of early Victorian optimism which gave rise to theories of moral management and the infinite malleability of the human psyche, gradually shades into the increasingly pessimistic visions of inherited brain disease and social degeneration propounded by Maudsley and other post-Darwinian theorists writing in the era of economic decline in the latter part of the century. Against [Charlotte] Brontë's mid-Victorian belief in her protagonists' ability to determine their own destiny we must set the imprisoning biological cycles of Hardy's later fiction, where all attempts to assert control are thwarted by the cumulative forces of history expressed through familial and racial genealogy. (37)

While I agree with Shuttleworth's point in general about the historical shift from optimism to pessimism, my chapter on *Wuthering Heights* indicates that the pessimism she locates in Hardy's later fiction is already present in terms of Emily Brontë's own work. Charlotte, Emily, and Anne Brontë all work through this issue of individual agency versus social forces beyond the control of individuals in their respective novels. As Shuttleworth asserts, "All three explore the experience of social marginality, and the constraining effects of gender ideology" (5). Nevertheless, I see each of the three sisters resolving the question of how to work with the prevailing social constraints differently, often moving beyond a focus on only gender ideology.

By applying medical anthropology's idea of the body as site for ideological conflict to the Brontë novels, I explore the various illnesses represented in order to arrive at the cultural critiques implied by these illnesses. I read the Brontës' representations of illnesses first and foremost as a result of their critiquing of cultural issues, interpreting the texts' signs of individual and cultural dis-ease; however, in certain novels, such as *The Tenant of Wildfell Hall* and *Villette*, illness is also read as a possible remedy for these cultural constraints since Anne and Charlotte Brontë's use of illness works in these two texts to create new possibilities of identity for their characters.

The first chapter, " 'Sick of Mankind and Their Disgusting Ways':
Victorian Alcoholism, Social Reform, and Anne Brontë's Narratives of
Illness," develops the youngest Brontë's use of representations of
illness in *Agnes Grey* and *The Tenant of Wildfell Hall*. Of the three
sisters, Anne Brontë is the most direct and straightforward in her use
of literature as social critique; thus, her use of representations of illness
for these purposes is the most overt. For this reason, it makes sense
to start with her two novels since they provide literary critics new to
medical anthropology relatively easy access to such an application.
In her novels, Brontë uses representations of illness, including alcoholism as the Victorians understood it, to critique social issues
inherent in a culture based upon hierarchies of power. Brontë explores
the interrelations between abuse of power, intemperance, and other
illnesses in both *Agnes Grey* and in *The Tenant of Wildfell Hall*; however, the latter novel's extensive focus on intemperance—a condition
which we now understand to be the disease of alcoholism—provides
an in-depth commentary on hierarchies of power based primarily on
both class and gender.

The next two chapters address Charlotte Brontë's novels, *Shirley*
and *Villette*. My decision to work specifically with Brontë's final two
novels is based on the fact that they were written after she experienced
the illnesses and deaths of Branwell, Emily, and Anne. Even though
illness is used as a literary motif throughout all four of her novels,
Brontë's personal experience of illness as both caretaker and survivor
enriches her use of illness as motif in these final two books. Her
insights into the psychology of illness in *Villette* in particular are
highly sophisticated.

The second chapter is entitled "Ailing Women in the Age of
Cholera: Illness in *Shirley*." While the apparent focus of *Shirley* is class
conflict—with the Luddite Rebellion as the focal point of this class
conflict,—Charlotte Brontë's use of illness suggests that the central
focus of the novel is gender issues. I explore how *Shirley* is a novel of
displacement, with the Luddite Rebellion displacing contemporary
concerns with the Chartist Rebellion; with gender issues displacing
class issues; and with a range of diseases, from consumption to rabies,
displacing the contemporary concerns about the 1848–1849 cholera
epidemic.

The third chapter, "Hysteria, Female Desire, and Self-Control in
Villette," analyzes Charlotte Brontë's use of hysteria in *Villette*. Of the
Brontë novels, *Villette* looks most unflinchingly at the instability of
human identity, looking at the self, both at the self in isolation and in
relation to others. Brontë explores the role of illness, in the re-shaping

of identity, taking us through a step-by-step process of illness which allows Lucy Snowe to rethink first the Protestant ideology at home and then to challenge the Roman Catholic ideology of her adopted country. Chapters 1, 2, and 3 all follow a pattern in being shaped primarily around one Victorian illness. In Anne Brontë's two novels, Victorian alcoholism becomes her symbol of societal ills. In *Shirley*, while many illnesses appear, Charlotte Brontë develops cholera as her primary metaphor for social change. In *Villette*, the use of hysteria predominates, showing Brontë's new emphasis that change must come from within the individual. Because Emily Brontë's use of illness is so dramatically different from her sisters' more realistic representations of illness, the fourth chapter on Brontë's *Wuthering Heights* does not follow the same one-to-one correlation with a specific Victorian illness. Because Brontë's extensive use of illness metaphors throughout *Wuthering Heights* build toward her concept of a larger metaphorical disease affecting civilization, the chapter's title "Vampires, Ghosts, and the Disease of Dis/Possession in *Wuthering Heights*" does not include the name of a specific Victorian illness but rather focuses on the metaphorical disease of "dis/possession."[12]

In *Wuthering Heights*, illness becomes a dominant metaphor for the flaws within a land-based patriarchy since Brontë views the patriarchy as a system where power perpetuates itself no matter what, preying upon the life-energies of those caught within it. To highlight the unnaturalness of a cultural system that ultimately drains the individual's life blood, resulting in illnesses such as consumption, intemperance, monomania, and madness, Brontë metaphorically creates two supernatural creatures—the vampire and the ghost. Brontë's representations of vampires and ghosts provide her readers a clearer view of her rejection of culture, especially since Brontë's alignment of the supernatural and the natural together point toward the unnaturalness of culture. Developing how male vampires and female ghosts are two sides of the same coin, Brontë explores how women become ghosts through the life-denying and blood-draining qualities inherent in such a self-alienating cultural system, vampiric in its very nature. Brontë's images of vampires underscore patriarchy's emphasis on "possession" while images of ghosts render visible "dispossession" and the powerlessness of the dispossessed. Together these three interrelated metaphors—illness, vampires, and ghosts—signal Brontë's critique of her culture's disease of dis/possession.

My conclusion contrasts the differences of approach to illness taken by the three Brontë sisters. While all three are concerned with a critique of patriarchal culture and all three use representations of illness to explore the cultural constraints faced by their characters, each sister's individual beliefs shape her use of illness as cultural critique.

This study aims to illuminate similarities and differences between each of the sisters' individual cultural critiques while participating in the larger theoretical conversation concerning the interplay between body and culture. By working with the interrelated fields of medical anthropology and the history of medicine, this study aims to contribute to a deeper understanding of the ways in which Victorian ideas of the body, including ideas concerning health, illness, disease, and medicine, inform literary texts of the time period. The interdependent concepts that ideologies need the body to be inscribed and made "real" and that the body thereby becomes the site for all ideological conflicts provide powerful tools for a cultural analysis of literary texts. By applying these concepts in a focused analysis of the Brontës' use of representations of illness and disease within their novels, I illuminate each of the sisters' individual cultural critiques, as well as provide theoretical and historical backgrounds to suggest possible application of these concepts to other Victorian writings.

CHAPTER 1

"SICK OF MANKIND AND THEIR DISGUSTING WAYS": VICTORIAN ALCOHOLISM, SOCIAL REFORM, AND ANNE BRONTË'S NARRATIVES OF ILLNESS

In an unsigned review of *The Tenant of Wildfell Hall* from *Fraser's Magazine*, now attributed to Charles Kingsley, the reviewer describes the author "Acton Bell" as a satirist performing the functions of a surgeon or contemporary sanitary reformers, since all three—the satirist, the surgeon, and the sanitation reformer—operate for the health of the larger community. The review reads:

> It is true, satirists are apt to be unnecessarily coarse. Granted; but are they half as coarse, though, as the men whom they satirise? That gnat-straining, camel-swallowing Pharisee, the world, might, if it chose, recollect that a certain degree of coarse-naturalness, while men continue the one-sided beings which they are at present, may be necessary for all reformers, in order to enable them to look steadily and continuously at the very evils which they are removing. Shall we despise the surgeon because he does not faint in the dissecting-room? Our Chadwicks and Southwood Smiths would make but poor sanitary reformers if their senses could not bid defiance to sulphuretted hydrogen and ammonia. Whether their nostrils suffer or not, ours are saved by them: we have no cause to grumble. And even so with "Acton Bell." (qtd. in Allott 270–71)

This review places Anne Brontë in the middle of the health reforms of the mid-nineteenth century. While Brontë herself never uses the specific metaphors of "surgeon" or "sanitary reformer" to refer to her work, she is forthright that her goals for writing are for social reform. She asserts in the preface to the second edition of *The Tenant of Wildfell Hall*, "Let it not be imagined, however, that I consider myself competent to reform the errors and abuses of society, but only that I would fain contribute my humble quota towards so good an aim . . ." (3). Stressing her understanding of the realist novelist's truth-telling as being more desirable than the "delicate concealment of facts" favored by polite society (4), Brontë proclaims, "I wished to tell the truth, for truth always conveys its own moral to those who are able to receive it" (3). Elsewhere, declaring herself to be "Sick of mankind and their disgusting ways," Brontë probes society's wounds in order to heal them and writes to educate rather than simply to entertain.[1]

In her endeavor to bring social ills to light, Anne Brontë readily adopts representations of illness as her dominant metaphors for social critiques in her two novels, *Agnes Grey* (1847) and *The Tenant of Wildfell Hall* (1848). By the time Brontë writes the second novel, she has honed her technique of using illness as a metaphor for cultural disease by focusing on one specific illness, that of "alcoholism"—or rather "intemperance," since that is the term which the early Victorians applied to the condition we now know as alcoholism.[2] In *The Tenant of Wildfell Hall*, Brontë's critique of alcoholism is extensively developed, but scholars have overlooked the fact that issues concerning intemperance are already in place in *Agnes Grey* through Bronte's development of the drinking habits of three male characters. Rivaling intemperance, other illnesses used in Brontë's first attempt at a novelistic social critique include Mr. Grey's depression, Nancy Brown's inflammation of the eyes, Mark Wood's consumption, and Agnes Grey's own experiences of illness, such as when Agnes catches a cold or feels nauseous riding in the carriage. By comparing both novels' overall treatment of intemperance, we can arrive at fuller appreciation of Anne Brontë's final choice of alcoholism as the one illness best suited for a depiction of Victorian societal ills.[3]

Brontë's novels enlarge the scope of the Victorian debate on the "drink question" through their focus on middle- and upper-class drinking. In contrast to Brontë's novels, much of the contemporary writing on temperance of the 1830s and 1840s, either political or literary, focused on the impact of drinking on the working class, due largely to the perceived impact of the Beer Act of 1830.[4] In the political world, for example, as Richard Valpy French records in

Nineteen Centuries of Drink in England: A History, the report written by the Parliamentary committee of 1834 specifically addressed "the extent, causes, and consequences of the prevailing vice of intoxication among the labouring classes of the United Kingdom" (352). This parliamentary report represented the first attempt to look at the national scope of the drinking problem, but the report not only focused on, but was limited to, the working classes.

Similarly, in the literature of the time, intoxicated characters were from working-class backgrounds. In the 1830s, for example, Charles Dickens includes two pieces in *Sketches by Boz* about working-class drinking. Dickens's "Gin-Shops" appears in Volume One (1836), and "The Drunkard's Death" appears in Volume Two (1837). In the first story, Dickens's description of the gin-shop frequenters includes two old washerwomen, a group of Irish laborers, and a group of children.[5] In "The Drunkard's Death," the protagonist, who ends his miserable life through suicide, is also of the working class. Of these two early pieces, Dickens more directly connects drinking and working-class poverty in "Gin-Shops." He comments, "Gin-drinking is a great vice in England, but wretchedness and dirt are a greater; and until you improve the homes of the poor, or persuade a half-famished wretch not to seek relief in the temporary oblivion of his own misery . . . gin-shops will increase in number and splendour" (1: 217–18). In the 1840s, Elizabeth Gaskell creates the character of a female working-class alcoholic in *Mary Barton* (1848).[6] Mary Barton's aunt Esther is a fallen woman who depends upon alcohol to see her through the day. Esther declares, "I must have drink. Such as live like me could not bear life, if they did not drink" (192). Writers such as Dickens and Gaskell are understandably tapping into a larger cultural fear held by the middle class about the excesses of the lower class. Even later in the century, literature dealing with alcoholism remains focused on working-class drinking.[7]

The magnitude of such middle-class fears about the potential dangers of working-class excesses motivated the early temperance movement, which started as a middle-class movement, aimed specifically at working-class reform. As such, the movement was often led by church leaders. The Haworth Temperance Society, founded in 1834, was itself led by the Reverend Patrick Brontë for approximately three years.[8] Rather than follow the more common cultural trend of focusing on working-class drinking, Brontë's novels bring the issue of alcoholism much closer to home, showing how alcoholism was already affecting middle- and upper-class homes without distancing these fears and projecting them onto the lower classes.

In *Agnes Grey*, Brontë develops the drinking habits of two well-to-do middle-class males, Mr. Bloomfield and Mr. Robson, and a member of the gentry, Mr. Murray. All three are shown as habitual drinkers. Mr. Bloomfield drinks, by constant sipping, a "considerable portion every day" of gin and water (43). Mr. Robson is described as follows: "Though not a positive drunkard, Mr. Robson habitually swallowed great quantities of wine, and took with relish an occasional glass of brandy and water" (43). As a man of the gentry, Mr. Murray suffers from gout, an affliction of luxury linked in Victorian thought to alcohol, according to Victorian medical texts, such as Thomas John Graham's *Modern Domestic Medicine*.[9] In "The Drinking Man's Disease: The 'Pre-History' of Alcoholism in Georgian Britain," Roy Porter includes the historical shift in the understanding of gout as part of his overview. Porter notes that whereas eighteenth-century physicians, such as Dr. Peter Shaw, thought "wine was a 'grand remedy,' as good for prevention as for cure and that drinking 'the strongest white wines' were particularly excellent specifics [remedies] for gout, hypochondria and venereal infections" (qtd. in Porter 387), nineteenth-century physicians, starting with Thomas Trotter in 1804, recognized that alcohol actually *causes* gout in the first place.

Even with the new knowledge, many physicians, rather than promote abstinence from alcohol as a preventive measure, only recommended abstinence from alcohol as the after-the-fact cure for gout. Thomas John Graham is among these nineteenth-century doctors.[10] Yet Brontë makes the connection between gout and alcohol explicit in *Agnes Grey* when Rosalie Murray tells Agnes that even though her papa's gout "made him very ferocious," that "he would not give up his choice wines . . . and [he] had quarrelled with his physician, because the latter dared to say, that no medicine could cure him while he lived so freely" (178). Brontë thus implies until Mr. Murray abstains from wine, his gout will continue.

In *Agnes Grey*, all of Brontë's representations of illness, particularly those of intemperance or alcoholism, call into question issues of inequality within a culture based upon hierarchies of power, such as hierarchies based upon distinctions of class and gender. In her social critique, she explores the interrelationships between power, abuse, and illness. Brontë attributes cultural symptoms of abuse inherent in such hierarchies of power back to a misguided societal need for hierarchy and a sense of superiority over others. Consequently, within *Agnes Grey*, Brontë explores a variety of abuses, each of which opens up not simply the possibility of overt violence but also, more subtly, the possibility of illness for her characters. Illness, like violence, is a natural consequence of abuse based on hierarchies of power, but of the two, illness is a much more hidden reality, needing more authorial probing to be brought to light for the benefit of her readers. Brontë develops the interconnections between abuse and illness by connecting four variations of abuse, all based on hierarchies of power, to the illnesses represented in the text. Brontë explores abuse fourfold—abuse based on hierarchies of class, gender, age, and species. Brontë best captures the essence of abuse through her depiction of the dynamics between Mr. Robson and Master Tom as represented by Mr. Robson's intemperance and his willingness to insure Master Tom is caught at an early age by this same disease. By focusing on Victorian alcoholism, Brontë successfully brings together all four manifestations of abuse.[11] Alcoholism encapsulates adult abuse of children through Mr. Robson's inconsideration for Tom's health, male abuse of women through Tom's treatment of his sisters and through his uncle's pleasure that Tom is "beyond petticoat government already:—by G—, he defies mother, granny, governess, and all!" (45), man's abuse of animals through Tom's violent antics with the nestlings, and lastly, abuse of those of a lower class through both Mr. Robson's and Tom's treatment of Agnes. In addition, whereas other illnesses only capture the effects of the abuse within the hierarchies of power on the victims, alcoholism can go beyond this to show the effects of such a system on the perpetrators, that is, those in power, as well. As a symbol of social disease, alcoholism can articulate the resultant self-centeredness as individuals who are caught up within the hierarchies of power withdraw from being in healthy, reciprocal relationships with others and become increasingly self-alienated as they begin to lose touch with themselves. Alcoholism becomes Brontë's focus since it is the one illness best suited to symbolize the isolation and alienation that are experienced by all members living in a society based on hierarchies of power.

Even though Tom is only seven years old, Mr. Robson teaches Tom to "imitate" his drinking habits and "to believe that the more wine and spirits he could take, and the better he liked them, the more he manifested his bold and manly spirit, and rose superior to his sisters" (43). Not willing to see how alcoholism can affect even a fully grown man's health, Mr. Robson potentially threatens Tom's health since an addiction to alcohol obtained at such a young age could prove quite difficult to cure. Mr. Robson falsely equates manliness with drinking, a leftover belief from the eighteenth century which ascribed displays of masculinity with quantities of alcohol consumed.[12] Mr. Robson's idea that drink gives a sense of superiority over others has the potential to prove unhealthy not only for Tom himself but also for all of those in positions subordinate to Tom as he grows up. Here, hierarchies of power again link abuse to its partner, open violence, and to its more hidden counterpart, illness.

Although neither *Agnes Grey* nor *The Tenant of Wildfell Hall* explores female intemperance, the true equivalent of male intemperance, each novel's exploration of a culture which educates its young men to grow up to become drinkers looks at the issue in terms of both genders. In *Agnes Grey*, the perverse education given by Mr. Robson to his nephew Tom is paralleled by that given by him to his niece Mary Ann. Whereas Mr. Robson's influence on Tom leads to his youthful drinking of alcohol, his influence on Mary Ann heightens her vanity. Agnes records, "He was continually encouraging her tendency to affectation . . . talking about her pretty face, and filling her head with all manner of conceited notions concerning her personal appearance . . ." (42). Mr. Robson is not alone in his focus on female beauty since Mrs. Murray educates her daughter Rosalie similarly. Brontë's insight that female vanity is the female equivalent of male drunkenness is clearly articulated in Agnes's description of Rosalie Murray's heartless machinations in keeping Mr. Weston's attentions to herself. Agnes narrates,

> but when I saw it with my own eyes, and suffered from it too, I could only conclude that *excessive vanity, like drunkenness, hardens the heart, enslaves the faculties, and perverts the feelings*, and that dogs are not the only creatures which, when gorged to the throat, will yet gloat over what they cannot devour and grudge the smallest morsel to a starving brother. (italics added, 142)

Female vanity and male drunkenness both result in the same outcome—selfishness and inconsideration of others. Both happen when adults educate children falsely so that the faculties are "enslaved" and the feelings "perverted." Both result in "thoughtlessness" and a "thoughtless temper," terms that Brontë reserves respectively for Rosalie, the female flirt, in *Agnes Grey* (154) and for Arthur, the male drunkard, in *The Tenant of Wildfell Hall* (140).

Within her second novel, *The Tenant of Wildfell Hall*, Brontë's development of the complexity of the issues brings new depth and new dimensions to her cultural critique. While alcohol and the assumption of male superiority were already linked in the first novel, their interconnection dominates the social critique in the second. Male alcoholism is repeatedly connected to the same four varieties of abuse resulting from society's hierarchies of power. For example, Arthur Huntingdon's alcoholism results in class abuse toward his servant Benson. Arthur's verbal abuse of Benson occurs after Arthur's return home following months of dissipation in London and specifically after Arthur has partaken of a "bottle of soda-water mingled with brandy" as well as "a tumbler of wine and water" (242). Similarly, Brontë stresses that the night when Arthur abuses his dog, Arthur has taken "an unusual quantity of wine" (200). Likewise, Brontë emphasizes how Arthur's abuse of his wife and child also are closely related to his intemperance. Because Brontë's exploration focuses largely on the impact Arthur's drinking has on the family dynamics, the last two arenas—male abuse of women and adult abuse of children—are developed in the most depth.

Abuse based on hierarchies of gender is highlighted primarily through Arthur's alcoholism leading to his abuse of his wife. As his wife Helen herself expresses it, "When he is under the exciting influence of these excesses, he sometimes fires up and attempts to play the brute" (309). However, in the early stages of the disease, Arthur's wife abuse existed only in the form of neglect. Yet, in time even Arthur's neglect of Helen places her in danger. Once Arthur's drinking friends began to perceive Helen as a "neglected wife," she is open to insult in the form of Mr. Hargrave's making unacceptable sexual advances to her (218). Brontë specifies that Arthur's own improper sexual advances to a woman other than his wife happen when Arthur is "obviously affected with wine" (222). When Arthur kisses Annabella Wilmot's hand in front of his wife and their house guests, Helen herself "felt ill" and is asked "if [she] felt unwell" by Mr. Hargrave who then offers to "get [her] a glass of wine" as medicine (221–22). While Helen's being offered wine follows the common Victorian belief that wine was medicinal, within the larger framework that Brontë is developing which links alcoholism, abuse, and illness, this offering of wine seems ironic.

Arthur's drinking friends also reinforce the hierarchies of power, especially that of gender. His friends' attitudes toward women and marriage parallel and reinforce Arthur's own attitude. Arthur's drinking friends are known for their own abuse of women. Several of the novel's subplots develop these men's abusive treatment of women. For example, the subplot concerning Hattersley's courtship and marriage to Millicent Hargrave largely revolves around his verbal and physical abuse of Millicent. Hattersley admits his own ill-usage of Millicent, saying "I positively think I ill-use her sometimes, when I've taken too much—but I can't help it, for she never complains, either at the time or after" (277). His consequent "reform" halts both the excessive drinking and the wife abuse since the two are so intimately related.

Brontë develops the abuse of children within the novel's hierarchies of power by showing how Arthur's alcoholism results in his abusing his son almost from birth. Similar to the progression of abuse with Helen, at first the abuse is simply neglect. Later, Arthur Huntingdon encourages his young son Arthur to excesses with alcohol and to abuse towards those seen as subordinates. Connecting wine, masculinity, and abuse, Helen records how "the little fellow . . . learnt to tipple wine like papa, to swear like Mr. Hattersley, and to have his own way like a man, and sent mamma to the devil when she tried to prevent him" (335). Tom was already seven years old in *Agnes Grey*, but here young Arthur is only age five, an even more vulnerable and impressionable age. In both cases, Brontë emphasizes the laughter and foolish amusement derived by the men present from watching each young boy being initiated into manhood through alcohol and abuse to women and animals. In *The Tenant of Wildfell Hall*, Brontë's heroine can openly condemn such men intent on educating her son in such "evil habits" as being "human brutes" (335).

Although the social critique found in *The Tenant of Wildfell Hall* includes all of the four previous forms of abuse already articulated in *Agnes Grey*, its thorough exploration successfully allows Brontë to develop in depth another dimension of alcoholism—the deterioration of the self through the abuse of one's own physical and emotional health. Not only does Brontë track the progression of the disease over an extended period of time through her detailed analysis of Arthur Huntingdon's drinking life, she also tracks the disease's progression through other male characters, such as Arthur's drinking companions, Lord Lowborough, Mr. Hattersley, Mr. Hargrave, and Grimsby, as well as drinkers of the older generation, such as Helen's father, old Mr. Lawrence, who dies of alcoholism, and Helen's uncle, Mr. Maxwell, who suffers from gout. Through the combined descriptions of all these male characters, the toll alcoholism takes upon each individual drinker and on society becomes much more visible.

Arthur's case is given in the most depth. Brontë includes the precise moment when the physical effects of Arthur's self-abuse become noticeable on his return home from London. Helen records the change, writing, "he is come at last! But how altered!—flushed and feverish, listless and languid, his beauty strangely diminished, his vigour and vivacity quite departed" (213). Originally, when Helen first met him, Arthur's alcoholism was invisible to Helen's inexperienced eye but not to her aunt's greater experience. Helen's aunt is aware of Arthur's reputation as a man "destitute of principle, and prone to every vice that is common to youth" (128), and she readily condemns him as a "thoughtless profligate" (141). Mrs. Maxwell's fears for her niece grow out of her own marriage to a man whose excessive drinking habits have resulted in gout. Once Mr. Maxwell is seen as a long-time drinker suffering from gout, Helen's comparisons between Arthur being a "bit wildish" and her uncle having been "a sad wild fellow himself when he was young" furthers the connection between the two men's youthful drinking and their oncoming symptoms of disease with age (128).

Within the course of *The Tenant of Wildfell Hall*, three of Brontë's male characters—old Mr. Lawrence, Grimsby, and Arthur Huntingdon—die because of their alcoholism. Helen's and Mr. Lawrence's father is the least developed of the three characters and the first to die. Brontë gives the cause of his death as parenthetical information when she writes, "(Now it was generally believed that Mr. Lawrence's father had shortened his days by intemperance.)" (38). Although he is a minor character whom we never meet, the legacy of old Mr. Lawrence's drinking casts a shadow over the entire novel since Brontë uses his drinking to raise questions about the familial role in intemperance. Without clarifying the more modern debate of whether it is "nature" or "nurture," that is, a genetically biological trait or psychological response to a maladaptive environment, Helen and her brother Mr. Lawrence both believe that drinking can be passed down through the family line.[13] Acting out of this belief, Helen decides to give her son tartar-emetic to counteract his being "inordinately fond of them [intoxicating liquors] for so young a creature" (354). Helen's rationale is specific; she writes, "remembering my unfortunate father as well as his, I dreaded the consequences of such a taste" (354). Mr. Lawrence also refers to the familial logic of intemperance, telling Mr. Millward, "But don't you think, Mr. Millward . . . that when a child may be naturally prone to intemperance—by the fault of its parents or ancestors, for instance—some precautions are advisable?" (38). In addition, Brontë develops the ramifications of her father's drinking by showing how the shadow of Helen's father's drinking contributes not only to Helen's beliefs that she can save Arthur but also to her choice of a potentially alcoholic husband in the first place. As much of today's literature on alcoholism attests, the pattern where the daughter of an alcoholic ends up marrying an alcoholic man, or a man who often reaches his potential as an alcoholic later within the marriage, is quite common.[14]

In terms of Grimsby's demise and its relationship to his alcoholism, Brontë asserts, "that low scoundrel, Grimsby, . . . went from bad to worse . . . and at last met his end in a drunken brawl!" (440). Brontë's development of Grimsby's drinking is important in three ways. First, in Brontë's presentation of Grimsby's denial of the severity of his disease, Brontë indicates how many Victorian men could view their drinking habits as being within the norm. Second, Brontë uses Grimsby to point out the faulty logic of a contemporary idea about the masculine nature of intoxication. Both of these points are manifested in the scene where Grimsby is one of "three 'bold, manly spirits' " showing their masculinity through the amount of alcohol consumed (265). Already Grimsby's actions have pointed out his extreme intoxication; now his theory on drinking successfully points out his denial of the effects such drinking has on him. Grimsby declares,

> they can't take half a bottle without being affected some way; whereas
> I—well, I've taken three times as much as they have to-night, and you
> see I'm perfectly steady . . . you see *their* brains . . . *their* brains are
> light to begin with, and the fumes of the fermented liquor render them
> lighter still, and produce an entire light-headedness, or giddiness,
> resulting in intoxication; whereas *my* brains being composed of more
> solid materials will absorb a considerable quantity of this alcoholic
> vapour without the production of any sensible result—. (italics in
> original, 264)

Finally, Grimsby's drinking is significant in how it promotes his selfishness, leading him to turn upon Lord Lowborough, someone who considers him a friend, in using Lowborough's gambling addiction against him for his own personal gains. Grimsby becomes Brontë's least likeable character due to the fact that throughout the novel Grimsby is most overtly concerned only with his own gains and his own well-being.

Arthur Huntingdon's death is the most developed alcohol-related death in the novel. Arthur dies due to complications when his drinking causes a fatal relapse following what would have been a minor accident for a nondrinking man. While Arthur's death is not a given from the beginning, his downward slide into alcoholism becomes unstoppable once he has passed a certain point. Brontë's portrayal of Arthur's being past reclamation may have its primary source in Branwell Brontë's inability to arrest his downward slide into alcoholism. Yet this portrayal also reflects the more general belief in early Victorian England that few "drunkards" were reclaimable. According to temperance historians such as Brian Harrison and Lilian Lewis Shiman, the temperance movement underwent several evolutions in terms of how the leaders perceived intemperance and their goals

toward solving the problems of intemperance. Both Harrison and
Shiman indicate that the early temperance movement of the 1830s
stressed "temperance," that is, moderation of drinking in order to
prevent intemperance rather than working toward the reclamation of
known drunkards.[15] Because Brontë chooses to have Helen's journal
start in 1821, Helen's hopes to reform her husband appear to be at
odds with the contemporary cultural belief that such "drunkards"
were past hope. However, since Brontë was writing the novel in 1846
and 1847, Helen's hope in her husband's reformation is, in fact,
backed by new beliefs in the temperance movement. The temperance
movement of the 1840s challenged the earlier belief that prevention
through moderation was the only solution for intemperance. With the
new beliefs, which initiated a shift from a pledge of moderation to a
pledge of complete abstinence, any drinker could be reformed as long
as he or she abstained from drinking. Such a shift in understanding
intemperance had political and social ramifications. As Shiman
explains in *Crusade Against Drink in Victorian England*, within this
new teetotalism framework, a large number of working-class men who
had taken the pledge "reformed" and began taking a larger role in the
temperance movement, which shifted the movement's power from
the early middle-class reformers of the 1830s to the working-class
reformers of the 1840s (23–25). Even with the shift in the power base
of the temperance movement, the new awareness that reformation
was possible affected drinkers of all classes.

Brontë's decision to have two male characters, Lord Lowborough
and Mr. Hattersley, become "reformed" in their drinking habits needs
to be more fully explored in the context of Victorian ideas of alcoholism in order to discover whether or not "recovery" as we understand it today is indicated. Thormählen has already pointed out the
connection between Brontë's description of the difference between
Lord Lowborough's pattern of drinking and Arthur Huntingdon's
pattern of drinking with its historical source, in Robert Macnish's *The
Anatomy of Drunkenness*. Macnish's treatise describes two types of
drunkards:

> Some are drunkards by choice, and others by necessity . . . The former
> have an innate and constitutional fondness for liquor, and drink *con
> amore*. Such men are usually of a sanguineous temperament, of coarse
> unintellectual minds, and of low and animal propensities. They
> have . . . a flow of animal spirits which other people are without. The
> delight in the roar and riot of drinking clubs . . . The drunkard by
> necessity was never meant by nature to be dissipated. He is perhaps a
> person of amiable dispositions, whom misfortune has overtaken, and

who, instead of bearing up manfully against it, endeavours to drown his
sorrows in liquor. It is an excess of sensibility, a partial mental weakness,
an absolute misery of the heart, which drives him on. (qtd. in
Thormählen 832)

Using such a description, it is easy for readers to conclude that Arthur
is the drunkard "by choice" and Lord Lowborough is the drunkard
"by necessity." Yet once the issue of recovery is considered, the terms
are misleading since Lord Lowborough, if a drunkard "by necessity,"
should not be able to be successful in his quest to give up his addiction to drinking, and yet he does, in fact, succeed. Similarly, Arthur, if
a drunkard "by choice," should not lose his ability to choose whether
or not to drink, yet he does lose this supposed choice. This interesting
twist is designed by Brontë to help her readers understand that, no
matter what motivates the drunkard's drinking, abstinence from drink
is his only option for reformation.

Brontë's descriptions of Lord Lowborough's attempts to break his
addiction to drinking (as well as his addiction to gambling) are psychologically accurate in their portrayal of the difficulties of breaking
such addictions on one's own.[16] Part of the temperance movement's
attraction was, like support groups of today, that it helped create a
counterculture for people who had given up drinking and thus no
longer felt comfortable participating in the culture of drink found in
the mainstream culture. The universal nature of the culture of drink
during the Victorian era is best described in Harrison's *Drink and the
Victorians*.[17] Choosing not to drink meant a man cutting himself off
from all of his known companions and all of his previous habits.
Harrison summarizes, "to abandon drink was to abandon society
itself" (50). Without having access to people with similar values of
temperance, abstaining drinkers would often find themselves returning to their old habits. Lord Lowborough's returning again and again
as a "ghost" and as a "skeleton at the feast" to the club where his
friends drink and his relapses into drunkenness make sense psychologically since he has acted alone without putting more healthy companions in place of his old drinking companions (181).[18] When
Lowborough himself realizes the nature of his dilemma, he proclaims
his decision to find a wife since he believes that a wife would help him
to reform and he calls Arthur to account for not supporting his efforts
to reform, saying "Yes, but you wouldn't let me [reform]; and I was
such a fool I couldn't live without you. . . . I can't live with you,
because you take the devil's part against me . . . all of you do,—and
you more than any of them, you know" (184). Arthur, like Grimsby,

is guilty of promoting Lowborough's addiction to drink out of his own self-interest. In fact Arthur justifies his and the group's actions of encouraging Lowborough's drinking habits by saying, "they were obliged, in self-defence, to get him to drown his sorrows in wine" (183). Again, Brontë uses irony, since even Arthur's recommendation to Lowborough to "take a little wine for his stomach's sake" is problematic for the cure he offers is, in reality, the source of Lowborough's health problems (182).

In contrast to Lord Lowborough who reforms his drinking habits on his own initiative, Hattersley reforms through Helen's direct intervention when she shows him his wife's letters which reveal Millicent's true sentiments concerning her husband's drinking. Although Hattersley has already reformed prior to Arthur's death, the death provides a "lesson" for him to refrain from returning to his earlier habits (440). Brontë writes, "the last illness and death of his once jolly friend Huntingdon, so deeply and seriously impressed him with the evil of their former practices, that he never needed another lesson of the kind" (440). Since the descriptions of both Lowborough's and Hattersley's "reformation" (as well as the lack of reformation on Arthur's part) indicate that recovery from alcoholism is simply a question of willpower, Brontë should be understood as still working under the more traditional view of drunkenness as being a moral crime, with its attendant idea of willpower being necessary to stop drinking. Thus, even though Brontë's work is published later than the medical treatises, such as Thomas Trotter's *An Essay, Medical, Philosophical, and Chemical, on Drunkenness and its Effects on the Human Body* or Robert Macnish's *The Anatomy of Drunkenness*, it incorporates some, but not all, of the new medical insights into the narrative.[19]

Helen's direct intervention with Hattersley is quite different from her direct intervention with her son Arthur. Her actions with her son aim at more than a psychological rethinking of his youthful habit of drinking. In preventing Arthur from progressing any further in the "vice" of drinking, Helen takes the more radical step, as mentioned earlier, of using tartar-emetic to make him physically ill from the effects of the wine. As Thormählen notes, tartar-emetic was proposed originally by an American physician, but it was advocated in England by Dr. Robert Macnish and Ralph Barnes Grindrod, a temperance writer, among others concerned about the dangers of alcohol.[20]

Not convinced that a physical aversion to alcohol will be enough to save her son from his father's "corrupting intercourse and example," Helen decides to take her son and leave her husband to live a secret life in exile (312). Helen literally breaks Victorian laws by leaving her

husband, refusing to return to him, and claiming her right to protect
the child from the father through her removal of the child from the
father's presence. Since children were seen as the legal property of
their fathers, Helen's fleeing with young Arthur is radical. Helen's
first choice for a life of exile is America, but she stays in England for
financial reasons. While this preference for America may be seen
simply as Helen's desire to put distance between herself and her alcoholic husband, the preference for America may relate to the historical
fact that, as Brian Harrison notes, "Americans helped to establish the
British anti-spirits movement" and, thus, America itself was seen
as a "land of liberty" to some British temperance members (101).
America's strong temperance movement offered a vision of freedom,
of a new life without the social ills connected with intemperance, a
vision that Brontë could be trying to invoke for her readers.

Helen Huntingdon's attempts to address issues of alcoholism by
working a reformation, by fleeing its effects, or by attempting to prevent alcoholism in the first place are only sometimes successful, but
the very fact that Helen's words and actions have the potential to
affect the people around her signals a remarkable change from the
portrayal of the heroine in *Agnes Grey*. In Agnes's marginalized position as governess, she has limited power both within the family and
within the larger society. As a governess, Agnes Grey is an outsider to
the social circumstances she observes in each family. She knows that
she has no power to affect change within each of the families because she
is not recognized as their equal. She can only attempt to correct the
budding vices she perceives in her young charges, such as the two
correlating issues of male alcoholism and female vanity. At best, she
can address these vices by re-educating her charges with what she
perceives to be more health-promoting values. Agnes's limited power
ultimately means she will have limited success. Agnes learns that her
only power consists of her consistency in maintaining her spiritual prin-
ciples since she has no socially sanctioned power to reward and punish
her pupils. Although the older Agnes who narrates the novel gains
some power through her ability to comment on her earlier sense of
powerlessness, her power is still relegated to commenting on earlier
events. She can only point out the injustices of the system after the fact.

Significantly, Brontë's second novel not only focuses more exclu-
sively on the illness of alcoholism but also re-positions the heroine so
that she can do more than just stand on the sidelines of society and
comment on its vices and social ills. In contrast to Agnes, Helen is
much more intimately involved in the drama that unfolds around her.
She is not simply an outside observer but an active participant within

the family drama of alcoholism. In contrast to Agnes, whose interaction with children is based upon her job as governess, Helen's role as mother allows her to have a much greater impact on her son's development. Also, Helen's incentive to leave her alcoholic husband finds its source in her maternal instincts to protect her child. Helen's duty to her son gives her the courage to take action, even though great risk is involved. Helen's new position in relation to the nexus of power also expresses a new dimension in Brontë's exploring the female counterpart to male alcoholism.

The earlier idea of female vanity being equivalent to male alcoholism is still present throughout *The Tenant of Wildfell Hall*. However, the idea of female vanity does not receive the same degree of primary focus as it did in the first novel. Instead, Brontë shifts focus to an exploration of how female gender roles and the ideals of femininity contribute toward actively encouraging male drunkenness. This shift extends Brontë's social critique since female vanity is basically another gendered version of self-centeredness on par with male alcoholism, whereas by developing the idea that Victorian ideals of femininity are based on one gender sacrificing their own needs for the other gender, Brontë highlights a cultural situation which by its very nature perpetuates hierarchies of power based on gender. Catherine Gilbert Murdock links issues of male alcoholism with Victorian ideals of femininity.[21] Murdock argues that by Victorian standards,

> The mother, daughter, or wife of a drunkard could thus be considered a failure, for she had failed to perform the most important duty assigned her by society and ultimately by God: to keep her family pure and temperate. Yet to admit this failure would upset the entire structure of nineteenth-century femininity. (25)

While Murdock's insight that the woman's "failure" to keep her family temperate would "upset the entire structure of nineteenth-century femininity" is helpful to understand what is at stake in failing, an even deeper appreciation of how that structure of femininity was in itself responsible for promoting male alcoholism is needed. In much of today's literature, which focuses on alcoholism as a family disease, an awareness of the role that traditional concepts of femininity has played in alcoholism is growing. For example, Ruth Maxwell asserts that "Natural 'wifely' responses that a traditional marriage calls for only further the progression of alcoholism" (37). Claudia Bepko's study on gender development in alcoholic families indicates that within the alcoholic family, the gender roles are intensified. Bepko claims that "the daughter is often expected to become even more understanding, more nurturing and more oriented to meeting others' needs than are daughters raised in non-alcoholic families," a situation which promotes an unconscious pattern of self-sacrifice continuing when the daughter takes a partner or spouse (qtd. in Ackerman 33). Yet, as early as 1848, Brontë critiques the Victorian cultural system to show that the interconnected ideals of femininity and masculinity become pathological when taken to their extremes.

Brontë's critique openly equates excessive masculinity with male drunkenness because in Victorian terms moderation was seen as the key to good health—for eating, for drinking, and as Brontë sees it, for gender roles. Taking this common Victorian belief in moderation as a sign of health, Brontë shows how excessive male drinking should no longer be seen as a positive attribute of manliness, but a sign of unhealth that needs to be moderated, as a sin that needs to be reformed. Similarly, Brontë shows how the feminine ideal with its excessive focus on someone other than the self can no longer be seen as a positive attribute of femininity, but a sign of unhealth that needs to be moderated, as a sin that needs to be reformed. It is no accident that in the preface to *The Tenant of Wildfell Hall*, Brontë addresses her goals of reform at readers of both genders. Brontë writes, "if I have warned one rash youth from following in their steps, or prevented one thoughtless girl from falling into the very natural error of my heroine, the book has not been written in vain" (4). Both Victorian masculinity and femininity are under the microscope, with alcoholism being Brontë's lens.

By showing Arthur Huntingdon's inability to reform from his alcoholism, Brontë simultaneously stresses his inability to grow through his personal experience of illness and Helen's own growth in response to Arthur's illness. Through Helen's growth, Brontë indicates that, at least, the parallel vice of excessive femininity which encourages such excessive masculinity could be addressed. Through the events in Helen's journal, Victorian readers learn about how Helen rethinks her own position vis-à-vis Arthur's increasing alcoholism. Helen's naive beliefs that "whatever I do, or see, or hear, has an ultimate reference to him; whatever skill or knowledge I acquire is some day to be turned to his advantage or amusement" are part and parcel of the self-sacrificing ideal of Victorian femininity which would play into her blind belief that she has the power to save Arthur (143). Helen tells her aunt of her position in strong words, in such statements as, "Then, I will save him from them [his friends]" (142), "I shall consider my life well spent in saving him from the consequences of his early errors" (142), and "I would willingly risk my happiness for the chance of securing his" (142). Helen's diary traces her own growth as the discrepancies between the reality of her marriage and her ideals force her to let go of her illusions. Helen moves from her initial position of wanting to "save" Arthur to realizing it is not within her power to save someone other than herself.[22] At first, she can only articulate the foolishness of her presumptions, saying "Fool that I was to dream that I had strength and purity enough to save myself and him!" (251). Finally, she breaks free from her self-blame. She sees that she is not responsible for his health and his salvation, declaring, "he may drink himself dead, but it is NOT my fault!" (309). Elsewhere in the text, Brontë uses italics to emphasize her main ideas, but the emphatic use of all capital letters in "NOT" is used only here, indicating the amount of weight Brontë places upon Helen's realization that she is not at fault, that no matter what she does or does not do, she is not responsible for Arthur's health and salvation.

The cultural script of traditional femininity as self-sacrificing is learned by both genders. Helen is not alone in her original illusion that it is her role to save her husband since Arthur also sees Helen as his saving angel. He never outgrows this belief. During his last illness, he begs, "Helen, you *must* save me!" (italics in original, 425). Arthur's exclamation, "I wish to God I could take you with me now! . . . you should plead for me" indicates that he dies still thinking only of himself and that his wife's role should be to intercede on his behalf and save him, even in death (430). It is important that Helen moves from using language that illustrates her desire to "save" Arthur to language that acknowledges that Arthur must be responsible in saving himself; it is equally important that Arthur does not make a similar move. By not having Arthur make a reformation on par with Lord Lowborough's or with Hattersley's, Brontë encourages readers to question an outdated cultural script for such extreme forms of femininity and masculinity.

Helen's return to Arthur during his illness highlights again the problems inherent in the extreme gender roles. In her efforts to be available to Arthur in her role as his nurse, Helen allows Arthur's excessive demands upon her to undermine her own health. Even Hattersley, who has been known throughout the majority of the novel for his desire to have a subservient, submissive wife who puts his needs above her own, tries to intercede on Helen's behalf, stressing the importance of her taking an occasional break from the sickroom. In response to Hattersley's command, "Look at her, man, she's worn to a shadow already," Arthur replies, "What are her sufferings to mine?" (427). Helen's complete collapse from exhaustion after Arthur's death is an indication of how demanding he was and of how giving, albeit detrimental, she was in her attentions. The final days in Arthur's sickroom emphasize the interrelatedness between Arthur's alcoholism, his abuse of Helen, and her collapse into illness from exhaustion. Even within Helen's return to the traditional feminine role of sacrificing herself for Arthur, her new growth is apparent in her requiring her husband's written agreement to her terms before she allows him to see their son. In " 'I cannot trust your oaths and promises: I must have a written agreement': Talk and Text in *The Tenant of Wildfell Hall*," Catherine MacGregor places Helen's demand for a written agreement in the novel's larger context, arguing that here, as elsewhere in the text, the written word offers fixity in a world where alcoholism has rendered oral language unreliable. MacGregor defends Brontë's choice of the imbedding of the diary within the outer narrative framework in terms of the psychological dynamics of addiction. She writes that Helen's offering of the journal to Gilbert Markham is not a "Richardsonian gimmick" but rather that "[Brontë] knew that those who live inside a world of addiction cannot or will not talk about it, just as those who live outside that world too often cannot or will not listen to representations of it" (32).[23] Helen's decision to let her diary speak for her to Gilbert rather than a face-to-face telling of her story is repeated in the larger narrative framework where Gilbert writes the story to Halford rather than tell him in person. Helen's and Gilbert's reticence in sharing Helen's story of life with an alcoholic husband in an oral telling speaks to the cultural silences around the issue of alcoholism that still exist even today. Within the double narrative framework, Helen's diary provides lessons for Brontë's female readers to educate themselves to become strong women and Gilbert's letters to Halford provide lessons to educate Brontë's male readers how to be receptive to strong women such as Helen. Both narrative frameworks depend on Helen's growth and newfound ability to challenge the Victorian ideal of femininity since this knowledge will ultimately have an impact on the Victorian ideal of masculinity, thereby threatening all of the hierarchies of power, not solely that of gender.

Through Brontë's exploration of the hierarchies of power in both *Agnes Grey* and *The Tenant of Wildfell Hall*, readers can arrive at a deeper awareness of the value systems behind Brontë's depictions of illness and her sense of what constitutes a remedy for social ills inherent in a cultural system based upon hierarchies of power. Ultimately, both of Brontë's novels portray the conflicts between two competing value systems in Victorian culture. Brontë herself espouses a spiritual value system. Through her depiction of spiritual conflicts with worldly values, which espouse money, status, power, and difference, Brontë demonstrates how a spiritual belief in God can provide the means of healing the breaches and ruptures in a hierarchical society. Seeing God as the Healer, the Physician who can cure society's sickness and seeing herself as His instrument, Brontë asserts in her preface to *The Tenant of Wildfell Hall,* "when I feel it my duty to speak an unpalatable truth, with the help of God, I *will* speak it . . ." (italics in original, 4). Whereas alcoholism becomes Brontë's primary symbol for "the unpalatable truth" of the unhealthy state of a hierarchical society, Brontë's primary symbol for her characters' ability to connect with each other—and her own ability to connect with the larger world—is through writing. The healing power of writing is called upon to offset the isolation and abuse of the world of alcoholism. A quotation from the 1851 temperance reformer Benjamin Parsons mirrors Brontë's own understanding of the interrelationship of the disease of alcoholism and the health of writing. Parsons writes, "The only rational way of dealing with erroneous opinions was to talk and to write them out of people" (qtd. in Harrison 98). Anne Brontë would agree that both of her books are written with just such a purpose in mind.

CHAPTER 2

AILING WOMEN IN THE AGE OF
CHOLERA: ILLNESS IN *SHIRLEY*

Charlotte Brontë's novel, *Shirley*, is a novel of displacements. Even the novel's title is an indication of the novel's penchant for displacement since the title character, Shirley Keeldar, does not appear until the end of Volume I, long after readers' sympathies are attached to Caroline Helstone. Within the text, the displacements happen on three levels, two of which have already been explored by scholars. Terry Eagleton explores the first level of displacement in *Myths of Power: A Marxist Study of the Brontës*, showing how Brontë displaces the contemporary events of the 1848 Chartist Rebellion onto the earlier Luddite Rebellion of 1811–1812. Eagleton contends, "there can be no doubt that Chartism is the unspoken subject of *Shirley*" (45). In the second level of displacement, *Shirley*'s overt concern with class conflict hides Brontë's primary concern with gender issues. Feminist critics, such as Susan Gubar and Juliet Barker, have explored how *Shirley*'s class issues cover for Brontë's protest against conditions for women. Gubar notes, "this book about the 'woman question' uses the workers' wrath to enact the women's revenge against the lives of enforced emptiness, of starvation" (233). Barker agrees that "the whole story [*Shirley*] was an exploration of the 'Woman Question' " in light of Brontë's omission of the "question of the rights and sufferings of mill workers" (603).

In the third level of displacement, a level that has not previously been explored by Brontë scholars, cholera serves as yet another "unspoken subject" of *Shirley*, with women's health as the focus of Brontë's concern. Instead of *Shirley* being written to look at issues of starvation, poor health, and conditions affecting the lower classes, Brontë's primary goal is to educate her male readers on how important female health is to the nation. She uses references to cholera to intensify her readers' response to her pleas for reforming female health. For example, Caroline Helstone's long soliloquy on the life of English women reads like an authorial address, serving to focus readers' attention on the core issues of *Shirley*: women's ailing health. Within this address, Brontë's choice of the "plague" metaphor ties into this final level of displacement in *Shirley*. This metaphor is not simply rhetorical. Rather, it indicates a hidden concern in *Shirley*. The "plague" metaphor gains both urgency and credibility in times when countries are dealing with plague epidemics. Significantly, *Shirley* was published in 1849, the year of the second nationwide epidemic of cholera in England.

Throughout Caroline's impassioned soliloquy, Brontë makes explicit the connection between societal limitations for women and illness:

> Men of England! look at your poor girls, many of them fading around you, dropping off in consumption or decline; or, what is worse, degenerating to sour old maids,—envious, backbiting, wretched, because life is a desert to them; or, what is worst of all, reduced to strive, by scarce modest coquetry and debasing artifice, to gain that position and consideration by marriage, which to celibacy is denied. Fathers! cannot you alter these things? . . . You would wish to be proud of your daughters and not to blush for them—then seek for them an interest and an occupation which shall raise them above the flirt, the manoeuvrer, the mischief-making tale-bearer. Keep your girls' minds narrow and fettered—they will still be a plague and a care, sometimes a disgrace to you: cultivate them—give them scope and work—they will be your gayest companions in health; your tenderest nurses in sickness; your most faithful prop in age. (392–93)

By saying that "they *will still be* a plague" (italics added), Brontë implies that these daughters already *are* a plague. Brontë stresses that the lack of opportunities for middle-class women to lead fulfilling lives results in a lack of health, not just for individual women but for the nation. If women's desire for fulfillment is not taken seriously, consumption, decline—at another point in the novel, Brontë adds "slow fever" to this list—will be their futures (191).[1] And the plague will continue.

With a cholera epidemic sweeping England in 1849, why does Brontë choose not to work more overtly with cholera references in her novel? Several reasons seem probable. First, cholera must be displaced onto other less dramatic, less disgusting diseases, ones that will suit Brontë's purposes of making her characters ill, but with the likelihood of recovery. Not only is cholera a "bad" literary choice since it is often fatal,[2] but also cholera is a nasty disease that does not make for good reading. William H. McNeill in *Plagues and Peoples* gives a picture of the devastating impact of cholera on its victims. McNeill writes,

> The speed with which cholera killed was profoundly alarming, since perfectly healthy people could never feel safe from sudden death when the infection was anywhere near. In addition, the symptoms were particularly horrible: radical dehydration meant that a victim shrank into a wizened caricature of his former self within a few hours, while ruptured capillaries discolored the skin, turning it black and blue. The effect was to make mortality uniquely visible: patterns of bodily decay were exacerbated and accelerated, as in a time-lapse motion picture, to remind all who saw it of death's ugly horror and utter inevitability. (261)

Second, Brontë's need to make the book historically accurate to 1811–1812 excluded the option of writing overtly on cholera. Cholera cannot be directly referred to in *Shirley* since the disease was unknown in Europe until 1831.

Asiatic cholera first arrived in Western Europe in 1831, coming from India via Russia. Cholera's second visitation to Europe was in 1848. Remembering the first epidemic, which had found them totally unprepared, the English watched and waited in horror as cholera revisited Russia in September 1847, wintering there and proceeding early the following year to Germany, then to England, reaching London in September 1848.[3] By the time Brontë finished writing *Shirley* in the summer of 1849 and recopying the manuscript of Volumes II and III to be delivered to London on September 8, 1849, cholera had hit England nationwide for the second time, including Brontë's beloved Yorkshire.[4]

By choosing to place *Shirley* in the historical past, Charlotte Brontë cannot explicitly use the metaphor of cholera in her novel. Nonetheless, indirect references to the 1848–1849 cholera epidemic occur. Although cholera historically attacked the lower classes in much greater numbers (now known to be due to the larger concentration of people using a contaminated source of water supply), again following the thematic displacement of class issues onto gender issues, the disguised cholera references in *Shirley* are to two middle-class female characters, Caroline Helstone and Mrs. Yorke. Brontë describes Mrs. Yorke as a potential cholera nurse since she "would nurse like a heroine a hospital full of plague patients" (563). Brontë describes Caroline as a potential cholera patient. In the Chapter entitled "The Valley of the Shadow of Death" which opens Volume III, Brontë links Caroline Helstone's illness to the "taint of pestilence," "the poisoned exhalations of the East," and "the breath of Indian plague" (421).[5] All three references occur within the opening paragraph. Brontë expands on the connection, writing, "So long as the breath of Asiatic deserts parched Caroline's lips and fevered her veins, her physical convalescence could not keep pace with her returning mental tranquility" (444). Caroline's body continues ailing until the east wind is replaced by the "pure west wind," which results in the "livid cholera-tint" vanishing "from the face of nature" (444). The phrase "livid cholera-tint" is the most direct reference Brontë makes to the cholera epidemic since the word "cholera" appears, but it is relegated to the status of an adjective. Brontë's various references to the "wind," "breath," "exhalations" relate to the early idea that cholera was an air-borne disease. This assumption tied in with the prevalent miasma theory, which held that disease was the result of "foul air," of gaseous emissions coming off decaying matter.[6]

Contemporary readers would have appreciated Brontë's references to the cholera epidemic.[7] For them, Brontë's cholera references would reinforce the novel's theme of class conflict because, in the eyes of her contemporary middle-class readers, the political revolutions of 1848 and the 1848–1849 cholera epidemic interrelate. Both events stirred up similar middle-class fears concerning the impact the lower classes could have on the status quo. As Linda and Michael Hutcheon note in *Opera: Desire, Disease, Death*, cholera and the contagion of the revolutionary ideas of 1848 are often linked since the contagious natures of both were calling into question the very structure of society (129). While political revolutions overtly question class structures, cholera questioned the class structure by threatening an epidemic unaware of class distinctions. Margaret Pelling writes, "cholera must have had much to do with establishing in the minds of the prosperous, the reality of their interrelationship with the poor" (5). Cholera reinforced how interconnected the classes were.

Just as revolutionary ideas suggested a shift in thinking away from monarchy, cholera marks a paradigmatic shift in thinking about disease. In earlier centuries, disease was seen as punishment from God, striking certain individuals needing divine chastisement. However, the unclear correlation between sin and cholera helped many rethink this idea. As R.J. Morris notes in *Cholera, 1832: The Social Response to an Epidemic*, "the sins of the individual were being replaced by sins of omission on the part of the nation. By 1848, Providence and public health went very nicely together" (203). The significance of this change indicates that, with the advent of cholera, health was no longer seen as the domain of religion, and that, as Morris explains, for the first time, "health was a secular matter" (214). Thanks to the research done on the 1831 cholera epidemic, the British were the first to be aware that social forces were at play in deciding who became infected with cholera. This change in awareness of the social role in disease made an impact on perceptions of why disease occurred in the first place and on perceptions of people's ability to prevent disease.[8] Charles Rosenberg asserts in *The Cholera Years*, due to cholera, "Disease had become a consequence of man's interaction with his environment; it was no longer an incident in a drama of moral choice and spiritual salvation" (228). New ideas concerning social reform as prevention of cholera, and then, by extension, all disease, began to be implemented. Working with the prevalent miasma theory of the day, social reformers and sanitary reformers went to work ameliorating conditions in London and other areas.[9] By the time Brontë relinquished the manuscript of *Shirley* in September 1849, the newly altered perceptions of disease as stemming from social conditions to be addressed through social reform were prevalent.[10]

Consequently, Brontë's references to cholera would tap into her contemporary readers' awareness of both this new idea of illness as being caused by social conditions and of this new approach in the prevention of illness—social reform. Thus, even though cholera cannot be an overtly addressed subject in *Shirley*, the new paradigm for understanding illness that it has created in Victorian England by the time of its second visitation in 1848 informs the text in very fundamental ways. Thus, it is significant that in Caroline Helstone's soliloquy, as throughout the novel, Brontë identifies her targeted audience as male,—first directing her authorial appeals to the "Men of Yorkshire" and then broadening the scope to "Men of England"—since Brontë perceives they have the power to make the necessary social changes.[11]

Cholera's displacement onto other illnesses named in the text,—Brontë adds cancer, rabies, and hysteria to the list of consumption, decline, and slow fever—asks us to rethink these illnesses as being caused by social forces rather than being seen as punishments from God for moral failings. In *Shirley*, Brontë's female characters suffer from illness, not because they are weak, evil individuals, but because they are caught in specific social circumstances. Thus, Brontë's novel becomes a call for social reform to address the disease-producing circumstances that these Victorian women face.

In *Shirley*, Brontë focuses thematically on conflict between external reality and internal desire. Brontë's choice to have both heroines, Caroline and Shirley, become ill within the narrative emphasizes her desire to explore the cultural tensions for women expressed within the novel. Thus, in its desire to tap into the contemporary fears fed by the current cholera epidemic and its dependence upon the new resultant paradigm in understanding illness, *Shirley* explores illnesses as social constructs, subject to change given necessary social reform.

In Brontë's exploration of social conditions, her characters face social constraints, often in terms of class and gender expectations. While Caroline and Shirley are affected by both issues of class and gender, Brontë indicates that gender, not class, is the determinant factor in their lives and in their relationships to others. To provide a contrast between lives of middle-class women and lives of middle-class men in Victorian England, Brontë tells her heroes' stories of the sickroom as well. Unlike the female characters, Robert and Louis are principally affected by issues of class. Brontë's presentations of the male lapse into illness serve more to clarify the intensity of the cultural tensions for women than to develop the cultural tensions for men.[12]

Caroline's illness is the most fully developed example of illness in the novel. As a result, the critical work on *Shirley* which addresses Caroline's illness rarely comments on the other illnesses in the novel. Miriam Bailin, Susan Gubar, Deirdre Lashgari, and Athena Vrettos have all explored how Caroline's illness is brought about by her compliance with a patriarchal code of feminine conduct which results in her silence, self-erasure, and consequent illness. Vrettos notes, as one of Brontë's most conventional heroines,

> Caroline seems trapped in conduct book codes of proper feminine behavior. Even her illness serves as a proof of her femininity, as she responds to her lover's indifference through a process of self-starvation. Faced with the choice of whether "to pursue him, or to turn upon herself," Caroline chooses a suitable maidenly decline. (39)

Caroline moves into illness when a crisis threatens her ability to fulfill the culturally prescribed destiny for a woman as wife and mother. It is important to recognize that Caroline's illness is not a result of her wanting something different from what her culture deems appropriate for her. She wants the same life of wife and mother that her culture expects her to fulfill. For Caroline, it is the discrepancy between this desire and her inability to achieve it, which will lead to her illness. Robert's withdrawal of affections first triggers Caroline's stay in the sickroom.

Caroline fears that life as an old maid equates automatically to ill-health, saying of the old maids in the community, such as Miss Ainley or Miss Mann, "this stagnant state of things makes them decline in health: they are never well; and their minds and views shrink to wondrous narrowness" (391). Marking her vested interest in the class issues of *Shirley*, Brontë continues, "Old maids, like the houseless and unemployed poor, should not ask for a place and an occupation in the world: the demand disturbs the happy and rich: it disturbs parents" (391). Here, Brontë openly equates the rights of single women to the rights of the "unemployed poor," an overt indicator of how gender issues have thematically displaced class issues within the text.

Miss Ainley, who lacks both a husband and a brother, spends her time helping the poor and nursing the sick of the community, and thus, she represents the option of self-abnegation through good works. Miss Mann, who has lost her health in nursing members of her family, takes the option of self-abnegation one step farther than Miss Ainley—into illness. Miss Mann's movement from nurse to invalid is a fairly common one since, as Bailin points out in *The Victorian Sickroom*, the feminine positions of nurse and patient were often interchangeable (26). Many Victorian women who were nurses, including Florence Nightingale herself, ultimately became patients. In their role as caretaker, they were to put the patients' needs before their own, which ultimately undermined their own health, making them patients as well.

Brontë's description of Miss Mann as "a cankered old maid" relates to the lack of fulfillment available to her in a culture that allows single women few options and little freedom (177). In an authorial address concerning Miss Mann, Brontë attributes an added element of destructiveness to the spinster's need for concealment of this unhappiness. Brontë writes, "Reader! when you behold an aspect for whose constant gloom and frown you cannot account, . . . be sure that there is a canker somewhere, and a canker not the less deeply corroding because concealed" (180). Brontë's choices of the words "cankered" and "canker" relate Miss Mann's position metaphorically with "cancer." Etymologically, "canker" and "cancer" are from the same Latin source and were, in fact, the same word until the 1700s.[13] In *Illness as Metaphor*, Susan Sontag gives the OED's figurative definition of "cancer" as "Anything that frets, corrodes, corrupts, or consumes slowly and secretly" (10). Sontag stresses that "cancer works slowly, insidiously" (14). Whereas Miss Mann never identifies her illness specifically as cancer, Brontë metaphorically describes it as such, reminding us that the conflicts and the silences involved in the

culturally undesired position of old maid slowly and unobtrusively
corrode and corrupt a woman's sense of self and undermine her
health. With circumstances denying spinsters the only culturally valued role for women, they are de-sexed, unnaturally shaped by culture
into female men. Literally, Miss Mann is a "Miss Man"—culturally, an
irreconcilable position for a woman.

Caroline does not feel that either option represented by Miss
Ainley or Miss Mann is acceptable to her. While Caroline confesses to
prefer the philanthropic model presented by Miss Ainley, her own
illness implies that she chooses a path similar to Miss Mann's. Brontë's
metaphoric comparison of Miss Mann and Caroline to phantoms,
ghosts, and spectres deepens the connection. Miss Mann is a
"spectre" who has a "starved, ghostly longing for appreciation and
affection" (180). Caroline's "dim shadow on the wall" is compared to
a "pale phantom" (173).

Just as Miss Ainley and Miss Mann represent Caroline's potential
future as an old maid, Brontë includes Mrs. Pryor's history as a governess to represent Caroline's potential future as a governess.
Mrs. Pryor's story also builds upon the possible slippage between
illness and insanity first hinted at in Caroline's fears that she may be
"dreaming or delirious" (438). Brontë uses Mrs. Pryor's story to
explore the overlap between illness and insanity, how physical deterioration may first result in illness, but fears of insanity can follow quickly.

Mrs. Pryor's decline in health begins when working as a governess.
Her insights concerning her ill-health take into account what Arthur
Kleinman refers to as "unresolved conflict" in her position as governess, which places her outside of established class lines (97). In
response to this isolating experience, Mrs. Pryor first mentions its
effects on her physical health, saying "The dreadful crushing of the
animal spirits, the ever prevailing sense of friendlessness and homelessness consequent on this state of things, began ere long to produce
mortal effects on my constitution,—I sickened" (376). Mrs. Pryor
then mentions her own fears of insanity, as well as telling of her
employer's insinuations that she might "die an inmate of a lunatic
asylum," a fate commonly expected of governesses (376–78). This
expectation is historically supported by *Fraser's Magazine*'s
November 1844 article, "Hints on the Modern Governess System,"
which reports "The statistics touching lunatic asylums give a frightful
proportion of governesses in the list of the insane" (573).

The *Fraser's Magazine* article explores the lack of options available
to women needing work, which limits them to being underpaid
governesses. The article reports, "The governess must endure all things,

or perish. A low marriage or a slow death are her only loopholes of escape" (578). Since Mrs. Pryor admits, "if I had not been so miserable as a governess, I never should have married" (380), and since the consequent story of her marriage is one of abuse, we can intimate that Mrs. Pryor's "loophole of escape" was her "low marriage" to James Helstone.[14] Unfortunately, this escape into marriage only increased her fears of insanity. Instead of lessening the unresolved conflicts in Mrs. Pryor's life, marriage increases them since the distance between the reality of marriage and what she expected of marriage has been too great. While she successfully escapes from a bad marriage, the resultant tragedy is that she must live her life under an assumed name and for years remain unknown to her daughter.

Once Mrs. Pryor reclaims her status as mother, in her advisory roles as governess and mother, she influences both of the heroines' lives. Because both Shirley and Caroline look to her for guidance, Mrs. Pryor's allegiance to the Tory government and the High Church gives them less opportunity to question the impact of the dominant culture's values on their own thinking. Even though Mrs. Pryor's escape from marriage demonstrates her ability, of necessity, to lead an unconventional life, her proclaimed values conflict with her lived experience. Not strong enough to claim her reality, Mrs. Pryor remains attached to the dominant ideology. Mrs. Pryor's need to transmit cultural values wholesale overshadows the value the two heroines could gain through her lived experience. But, even in this respect, Brontë is providing a realistic portrait. For Caroline and Shirley, there are no ideal models. Every female character has seemingly been compromised by the reality of few positive alternatives. In complicating the picture with the character of Mrs. Pryor, Brontë enables readers to reach a fuller understanding of women's situations both in and out of marriage.

In contrast to Caroline's situation, Shirley's relationship to the patriarchal culture in which she lives is more complex since her money and status entitle her to more options than those offered Caroline in her dependency. In developing the contrast with Caroline, Shirley's "perfect health" is emphasized (350). For example, one manifestation of Shirley's "perfect health" is her ability to sleep soundly after the excitement from the attack on the mill, whereas Caroline's nervousness will not let her sleep at all.

Through Shirley's "perfect health," as readers we can see more of the externals of the conflict between women and the male power structure, whereas through Caroline's lapse into illness, we are shown internal struggles which cannot progress to the point of action. We hear Caroline's thoughts, but her actions are limited. We are not privy to Shirley's thoughts, but Shirley's actions speak. Through Shirley's actions we learn that while she does have greater freedom of action, she is still limited by her gender in some fundamental ways. While Shirley's better health provides this contrast between female agency and female illness, the conflicts Shirley faces will also manifest themselves in terms of health.

For example, when the working-class Joe Scott wants to assert his male dominance over Shirley in spite of her class superiority, the weapon he calls upon is concern for her health. Refusing to talk politics with women, Joe Scott asserts, "The dews at this hour is unwholesome for females" (328). His concern for Shirley's health masks a deeper desire to control women by keeping them cut off from venues of power such as politics. Here, if he cannot keep Shirley ignorant of political facts, he will at least silence her. Her retort, "If you make that remark out of interest in me, I have merely to assure you that I am impervious to cold" (328), shows Shirley's awareness that male self-interest is behind Joe Scott's sudden concern for her health.

While Shirley will not let Joe Scott use illness to control her, she will feign illness as a weapon to get her own way. In both scenarios, illness-as-idea, not illness-as-fact, is being used to limit or open up possibilities for Shirley as a woman. When illness-as-idea carries this much cultural power, we need to realize how much more cultural force is behind illness-as-fact. If Shirley were truly ill, she would have little to no control over her world. Yet, through Shirley's recourse to feigning illness, we recognize the very limited nature of Shirley's control—in full health—over her world. For example, during the Whitsuntide picnic, Shirley is unable openly to declare she is keeping the seat next to her available for Robert. Instead Shirley complains of "want of air and space" and announces she "expected to faint" in order to be rid of Sam Wynne (309). Similarly, once Timothy Ramsden appears to replace the unwanted Sam Wynne, Shirley makes a commotion expected of the "most delicate and nervous of her sex" by intimating "her intention to 'give way' and swoon on the spot" (309). Not once, but twice during the picnic, Shirley has been reduced to pretending illness to keep a limited degree of control over her world. Yet, while Shirley may sometimes use fainting as a ploy to get her way, in times of real crisis, fainting is not an option. When the mill is attacked, Brontë indicates that neither Shirley nor Caroline responds to the crisis by fainting.

In terms of courtship, Shirley has veto power, but she does not have the ability to speak her love prior to the man's declaration, even when that man happens to be her tutor Louis Moore and, thus, her social inferior. Shirley's silence on this point, even to Caroline, her confidante, shows the severity of this societal mandate for silence. When Louis and Shirley confront each other about who will be the first to declare love for the other, it is a battle between Louis's pride of class and Shirley's pride of gender. Their exchange reads,

Louis: "You look hot and haughty."
Shirley: "And you far haughtier. Yours is the monstrous pride which
         counterfeits humility."
Louis: "I am a dependant: I know my place."
Shirley: "I am a woman: I know mine." (617)

Their entire dialogue is laced with tension concerning who can break the silence imposed upon them by their cultural locations. Louis's being the first to break out of this stalemate indicates his class-based need for repression is deep, but Shirley's gender-based need is deeper. Even though he can be taunted "with being a tutor" and "with being poor," his gender gives him speaking privileges capable of overcoming class constraints (619). For Shirley, the strictures on repression of female emotion are too great; as a woman, she is condemned to silence. Similarly, when Caroline is disappointed by Robert's withdrawal of affection, she too is condemned to silence by her gender: "A lover masculine so disappointed can speak and urge explanation; a lover feminine can say nothing" (105). This well-known passage with its bread-turned-stone and egg-turned-scorpion metaphors attests to the severity of the mandate on women's silence in Victorian courtship to maintain their propriety (105). Here in the interchange between Louis and Shirley, Shirley's higher status, which provides her more say in most matters, still falters, since in this situation, her gender ensures her silence.

Elsewhere in the text, Brontë's insight that female silence results from a feminine need for propriety is reinforced, most intriguingly when Shirley is confronted with the life and death threat of rabies. Rather than tell her family and friends of her fears that Phoebe's bite may have infected her, Shirley laments, "the best thing that could happen to me would be to take a good cold and fever, and so pass off like other Christians" (503). In voicing a desire for a specific mode of death, Shirley supports the idea that some fates are worse than death, hydrophobia among them. Significantly, "cold and fever" are attributed to Christian deaths; rabies is not. Sontag's description in *Illness as Metaphor* of the prevalent fear that rabies transformed people into "maddened animals" includes the idea of "unleashing uncontrollable sexual, blasphemous impulses" (127). As Sontag notes,

> The most terrifying illnesses are those perceived not just as lethal but as dehumanizing, literally so. What was expressed in the rabies phobia of nineteenth-century France . . . was the fantasy that infection transformed people into maddened animal—unleashing uncontrollable sexual, blasphemous impulses—not the fact that it was indeed, until Pasteur's discovery of a treatment in 1885, invariably fatal. (126–27)

While Sontag is speaking of rabies in nineteenth-century France, this quotation is equally applicable to nineteenth-century England where the incidence of rabies was also common.

To understand fully the implications behind Brontë's choice of rabies in connection with Shirley and the cultural mandate for silence for women, we need to be aware of how contemporary readers would have understood rabies. Not knowing what caused rabies, several theories existed. For our purposes, the most important theory linked rabies and hysteria. In "Nineteenth-Century Treatments for Rabies as Reported in the *Lancet*," K. Codell Carter asserts, "some physicians connected hydrophobia with hysteria either because of symptomatic similarities or because both diseases seemed to involve sexual abnormalities. For example, several writers attributed rabies either to inadequate sexual release among dogs or among men . . ." (70). To nineteenth-century readers, since both rabies and hysteria were understood as a repression of sexuality, that is, "inadequate sexual release," their reading of Shirley's hydrophobia would include this sexual dimension. Shirley's comparison between Louis and her beloved canine companion Tartar would have reinforced this sexual reading. Louis himself comments on Shirley kissing Tartar, saying "It is dangerous to say I am like Tartar: it suggests to me a claim to be treated like Tartar" (620). Thus, we must realize that Shirley feels threatened by hydrophobia, not only because she has been bitten by Phoebe, but also because of her gendered inability to voice her feelings for Louis, a repression of emotion and sexuality which results in hysteria. Given Shirley's earlier reliance on the hysterical symptom of fainting when keeping a seat available for Robert, there too, her hysteria was the result of her gendered inability to voice an emotional preference for a specific man.

Throughout the section where Shirley deals with her fears of hydrophobia, the connection between rabies, hysteria, and the need for emotional and sexual repression is emphasized. Rather than voice inappropriate emotional or sexual desires through the disease-medium of rabies, ever the proper woman, Shirley would rather die in appropriate Christian silence. Stoically facing the crisis alone, Shirley, strong and independent as she is, tells no one of the encounter with the rabid dog and denies to all who ask that she is ill. Alone, she cauterizes the wound with an iron, just as her real-life counterpart Emily had done before her (Barker 198).[15]

If the dog bite starts the process of Shirley's "abdication of personal power" as Lashgari asserts, her confiding to Louis deepens it (149). Louis declares, "I believe confession, in your case, would be half-equivalent to cure" (507). Yet, his desire to be Shirley's confessor is not based solely on his belief that talking would relieve Shirley's mind. It also stems from his desire to shift the balance of power between them—she is a rich heiress, he is the Sympsons' family tutor. Shirley's confession does not indicate a position of agency; rather, it marks her dependence upon Louis. Consequently, when Shirley finally confesses her fears of hydrophobia, she asks Louis to promise that if her worst fears do, indeed, come true, that he will "Lock the chamber-door against the surgeons—turn them out, if they get in . . . and lastly, if I give trouble, with your own hand administer to me a strong narcotic: such a sure dose of laudanum as shall leave no mistake" (512).[16] Louis's vow not only frees Shirley's mind momentarily of her fears of dying a mad animal but also serves as a pledge that successfully breaks down the social barriers of class between them (512). Through Shirley's illness, Louis can claim the active male role earlier denied him because of his class. Even though the fears of Shirley's hydrophobia prove unsubstantial, Louis retains his new status within their relationship. Thus, Louis's pledge of honoring Shirley's desire for a humane death ultimately sets the stage for their later marriage pledge.

Significantly, the changes in health of both heroines correspond to moments of transition in their status as women. As Kleinman indicates, "illness involves rites of passage between different social worlds" (181). Caroline sickened when she moved from her Elf-land idea of herself as wife and mother to her vision of herself as an old maid. With Caroline's marriage, since it follows the societal dictates that guide her own desires, Caroline no longer feels any of Kleinman's "unresolved conflict" and thus, her health is fully restored (97). In contrast, ironically, Shirley's health changes when she gives up her independence to claim the status of a married woman, subservient to her husband. If Brontë's main point has been that the lack of options for *single* women leads to lack of health, Shirley's lapse into ill-health would not make sense thematically. Shirley's ill-health enlarges Brontë's focus to encompass not only the lack of options for single women but also the lack of options for women even within marriage. Shirley's unresolved conflict indicates that even if the marriage pairing starts out unconventionally, the marriage will end traditionally with the man being the dominant partner, having the power within the relationship. Legally, in Victorian England, a woman's rights and property became her husband's. Without ever alluding directly to this fact, Shirley's loss of stature, once aligned with Louis, addresses Brontë's awareness that all women, no matter how high their standing or how original their abilities, once coupled must submit to their husband's rule. Brontë demonstrates that marriage does not offer the strong, independent Shirley much room to be herself. Shirley herself realizes this and ultimately chooses to abdicate her power to her husband, confessing Louis "would never have learned to rule, if she had not ceased to govern" (638). In the struggle between love and self-determination, Shirley cannot find a way to reconcile the two, and in deciding to give up her agency, she forces herself to fit a prescribed role that does not suit her.

Shirley has successfully out-maneuvered the cultural script, which requires a woman to marry a man above her socially, yet her unconventional marriage still remains problematic on some level. While many readers see Brontë's ending the novel with a double wedding as indicative of her endorsement of marriage, Shirley's plight at the end of the novel calls this interpretation into question. Through the contrasting impact of marriage on her two heroines, Brontë indicates that marriage is not necessarily ideal: while it may bring health and happiness to Caroline, it may not necessarily bring it to Shirley. Yet since it is the only culturally accepted route available for women, it is the best option available. All other options are second-best, to be considered only by default. Through her exploration of women's lives, Brontë questions how to make life more meaningful to middle-classed women. Her call for reform is to make more options available to women, whether single or married.

Because Louis and Robert Moore serve as foils to Caroline and Shirley, their illnesses demonstrate how Brontë perceives the difference in degree between constraints placed on middle-class men and women. While Louis and Robert are both middle class, Robert's running of the mill gives him greater status in the community than Louis, who is a tutor in a private home.

Similar to Caroline's location in society, Louis's social position is one of dependency. Yet Louis has the gendered advantage over Caroline of being male. His gender gives him the option of work that affords him some economic independence and thus some independence of thought and of action. Because his position is similar to Caroline's, Louis's illness is a masculine mirroring of Caroline's. In both cases, lovesickness does not seem to be the full picture. Caroline and Louis both have a sense of their dependent status resulting in impotence and inability in taking effective action to change their situations. What Gubar writes of Caroline is equally true of Louis, "Her illness is a result of her misery at her own impotence" (244).

When Louis and Caroline are sick, they choose not to communicate the true nature of their health condition with their respective lovers. Caroline's desire to keep her decline from Robert leads her to write to Hortense that she only had a "severe cold" (424). Robert, not realizing the severity of her illness, never comes to visit her. Louis's pride causes him, like Caroline, to equivocate about the nature of his illness, leading him to reject Shirley's offer to be his nurse. For both Caroline and Louis, regardless of gender, their social status as dependents affects their presentation of their illness. Pride isolates them in illness, whereas for Robert and Shirley, pride isolates them in health.

While many similarities exist in Caroline's and Louis's positions of dependency, because of the gender difference, Louis nevertheless has more opportunities—of work, of travel, of being active in the world—at his disposal. This difference in gender leads not only to the contrast in the duration of their illnesses—Louis is ill only a short time whereas Caroline's illness is of long duration—but also to the contrast in the severity of their respective illnesses. When Brontë describes Caroline's illness, she uses metaphors of pain and torture; however, in the description of Louis's illness, these metaphors of torture are absent. Consequently, while impotence may be the source of both characters' misery and ill-health, Louis suffers less because he is less dependent and, thus, less dis-empowered.

A conversation between Shirley and Caroline touches on what Brontë perceives to be the most fundamental difference in how gender affects a person's life. Shirley asks Caroline the question, "Can labour alone make a human being happy?" Caroline responds, "No; but it can give varieties of pain, and prevent us from breaking our hearts with a single tyrant master-torture" (229). Even before living through the experience of her illness, Caroline already knows why illnesses affect women with such intensity. Women, denied other outlets for their energy, only have the "single tyrant master-torture" of love (229).[17] For women, if love is denied or withheld, illness will replace this "master-torture" with its own potent version of torture.

In already having "varieties of pain," men will not suffer tortures to the same degree if love is denied or withheld. Robert survives Shirley's rejection of him without incurring illness, and even at the period of Louis's greatest fears of losing Shirley, when he fears she will marry either Robert or the newest suitor, Sir Philip Nunnely, he is sick for a very short period of time.

In Robert's position of relative independence, he is similar to Shirley. Even with his financial dependence upon Shirley's generosity to keep his mills open and producing, Robert's gender makes his position superior to hers in its greater freedom of action. As a man with his status, Robert has a much greater option to act than any of the female characters in *Shirley*. Robert explains, "I am quite cheerful: so long as I can be active, so long as I can strive, so long, in short, as my hands are not tied, it is impossible for me to be depressed" (291). Significantly, Robert's illness differs in its source from those suffered by the female characters in that his illness is caused by an external event. Linking Shirley and Robert's greater positions of power within their respective genders, Shirley is bitten by a mad dog and Robert is shot by a mad-worker. Robert's gunshot wound is the most overt sign of the class conflict in the novel since broken machines have been replaced by the broken human body. Robert's body carries the wounds of the battle between the two classes. His overt wound, open and bleeding, contrasts with the silent, unseen, cankerous or consumptive wasting away of the women's bodies. Part of his greater power even in illness lies in the fact that his wound can be acknowledged publicly and can become a source of pride and honor, whereas the women's wounds must remain private and unacknowledged if they want to retain their self-respect. It seems that women's culturally enforced silence deepens, rather than lessens, their suffering.

Brontë's treatment of the lower-class characters who represent change through rebellion and revolution is another indication that her true empathy is with the plight of the middle class, not the lower classes.[18] Nonetheless, in order to educate Robert, it takes the violent action of a disgruntled worker. Robert first becomes vulnerable in the text when gender difference is excluded, and the confrontation is between men. Michael Hartley's firing of a gun voices the discontent in the novel loud enough to be heard, whereas the women's silent suffering through illness has not had any impact on the dominant power structure.

Instrumental in Robert's emotional growth is the suffering he endures in the sickroom. Athena Vrettos notes, "it is through Robert's own feminizing convalescence that the 'romantic' half of the text emerges as the dominant genre; as Robert comes to terms with his own abstract feelings, the love story supersedes the narrative of labor unrest, educating the hero in the gestural nuances of emotional expression" (43). While this is clearly true, part of Robert's education ties back into the narrative of labor unrest. Part of Robert's reason for not being present in Caroline's sickroom stems from his absence from the community. Robert has spent time educating himself in Birmingham and London about the lives of the poor. Using Brontë's thematic idea of the necessity of looking at reality that grounds the entire novel, Robert tells Mr. Yorke, "While I was in Birmingham, I looked a little into reality, considered closely, and at their source, the causes of the present troubles of this country; I did the same in London . . . I went where there was want of food, of fuel, of clothing; where there was no occupation and no hope" (542). Robert's "looking" into reality will, of course, be heightened by his heavier dose of "reality" in the form of his being shot and spending time convalescing in the sickroom.

Robert's decision to visit the poor echoes the public health reformers' decisions during the 1848 cholera epidemic to visit the dwellings of the poor. Their motivation was not charity but to grasp a larger sense of the social reality behind the contagion. With the health reformers, "contagion" is disease; with Robert, "contagion" is the fear of revolution. Robert's actions reflect the social response to the second cholera epidemic of 1848, whereas Shirley's earlier aid to the poor reflects the social response in the first cholera epidemic in 1832. Voluntary subscriptions for relief of the poor were set up long before a deeper awareness of the disease could lead to social reform. Morris explains that "in 1832, the middle class organized and acted as a class at local and provincial level but rarely operated on a national basis . . . At the local level their most characteristic response was to raise and distribute a voluntary subscription for the relief of the poor during the epidemic" (119). The voluntary funds were significant as an "expression of class feeling" since, as Morris explains,

> They were a result of the middle-class adoption of the paternalistic values of the eighteenth-century aristocracy as they consolidated their urban power. Their privilege and authority were legitimised, at least in their own eyes, by their ability to defend the "rights," as they saw them, and protect the living standards of poorer classes. An ideal of duty and responsibility guided the actions of many individuals during the epidemic. (119)

Shirley's chosen technique of philanthropy to ameliorate the conditions of the lower-class people is inadequate as a cure; at best, it operates as a temporary bandage. Charity was not enough to solve the problems of the cholera epidemics, and Brontë suggests it will not be enough to solve the class issues—or, by extension, the gender issues in *Shirley*. If her male readers settle for such measures, the "plague" will continue. Robert's going to the source of the problem and using this newfound knowledge to change his own understanding and behavior gives a more favorable reading of the potential for social reform.

Robert's look into the source of the rebellion results in his admitting, "I saw what taught my brain a new lesson, and filled my breast with fresh feelings" (542). He clarifies, "Something there is to look to, Yorke, beyond a man's personal interest: beyond the advancement of well-laid schemes; beyond even the discharge of dishonouring debts. To respect himself, a man must believe he renders justice to his fellow-men" (542–43). Once ill and placed in the feminizing role of being an invalid—Robert himself describes it as being "unmanned" (584)—Robert's desire to "render justice to his fellow-men" is further broadened to rendering justice to his fellow-*wo*men as well.

Consequently, by the novel's end, Robert has a new vision of his role within class relations and within relations with women. *Shirley* ends with Robert's dreams of making the Hollow into an ideal industrial world that benefits workers as well as owners. Robert's dream is based on his desire to implement reform thanks to his new social awareness. In hearing Robert's plans to benefit the working class, because his new plans are also aimed at benefiting the women in his life, once more working-class issues are displaced by those of middle-classed women.

Robert's time in the sickroom most distinctly improves his relationship with Caroline, the reclaimed lover, and with Mrs. Yorke, the newly claimed surrogate mother. His illness also influences his relationships with other women, including Mrs. Pryor, Shirley, Miss Ainley, and Miss Mann. Mrs. Pryor is to be given a home with Caroline and him. Both Shirley and Miss Ainley are to be given jobs as Sunday school teachers, along with Caroline, for the children of the workers Robert is to employ. Miss Mann has already been given a plant. While a gift of a plant is of less significance than the gift of a home or of a job, the turn-around in Robert's treatment of Miss Mann marks the greatest change in how he treats women. Robert has earlier laughed at "her peculiarities" and mocked Miss Mann as being "Medusa" (177, 178). Robert's turnaround is so dramatic that his improved treatment of Miss Mann earns him praise in the form of Caroline's teasing that he is "flirting with Miss Mann" (608).

Throughout *Shirley*, Brontë uses narratives of illness both to promote the rights of middle-class women to lead fulfilled lives and to educate her male characters and readers to the importance of female health for the nation. Knowing female illness may represent a silent protest, one that is undecipherable to her male readers, Brontë includes a lesson in the feminization of men through illness.[19] Robert's time in the sickroom is politically more significant than Louis's since it leads Robert to a vision of his own contribution to female illness. Brontë feels that the "Men of England" first need to follow Robert's example and educate themselves about their own contributions to the current condition for women. Through Robert's example, social reform can happen. To help her male audience in this process, Brontë gives them *Shirley*, a book where women's bodies become the text to be read. Similarly, *Villette* too will be a book where one specific woman's body becomes a text for readers to interpret. However, by the time Brontë writes *Villette*, four years after writing *Shirley*, she will change her narrative strategy and no longer depend upon displacements to mask her core concern for middle-class women's plight. Equally important, she will no longer address her novel to a male audience. In *Villette*, there will be no appeals to the "Men of England" or to the "Men of Yorkshire," and the metaphors of plague and cholera will disappear. Brontë's intent that a male audience will provide the needed social reform in order for women's lives to improve is noticeably absent in *Villette*. Instead, *Villette* provides a blueprint aimed at teaching a female audience how to create a place for themselves within the given male power structure while honestly representing the bodily and psychic wounds that they, as women, will incur in the process.

Chapter 3

Hysteria, Female Desire, and Self-Control in *Villette*

Of the novels written by Charlotte Brontë, *Shirley* is most straightforward in its capturing of the idea that the body is the site of struggle where ideological battles are played out. In *Shirley*, the world is in flux, and the war abroad and the civil strife at home provide examples of how external circumstances affect the characters' lives. In *Villette*, however, the outer world is significantly more stable, and the wars are largely internal psychological tensions. In *Shirley*, Brontë highlights conflict and war, making war one of the novel's dominant metaphors. The war in France affects the English homefront. Ideologies are at war on both the national and international levels. *Shirley* explores the tensions at home in England between classes, between genders, between industry and nature, and between the Anglican church and the dissenters, all of which are heightened due to the war abroad. Caroline, Shirley, Robert, and Louis find their hopes and expectations in conflict with the reality that this war brings. Wherever there is conflict, there is a wounded body to signify this conflict. The bodies of the four leading characters can be seen as battlegrounds on which the ideological wars scar and deplete the wholeness of the individual.

The stable outer world found in *Villette* draws the readers' attention inward into the internal conflicts faced by Brontë's final heroine. Lucy Snowe leaves her Protestant England for Labassecour where she is confronted by that nation's Roman Catholic ideology as it is played out through its different concepts of education, religion, and love. Because Lucy must come to terms with her Protestant repression in a Catholic world where people's openness to emotion, excess, and the body simultaneously attracts and repels her, in *Villette*, the war of ideologies takes place primarily inside Lucy's own head.

In *Villette*, Protestantism and Catholicism are the primary ideological systems in conflict.[1] As a Protestant living in a Catholic country, Lucy must come to terms with both religions' scripts for her as a single woman. As Rosemary Clark-Beattie develops in "Fables of Rebellion: Anti-Catholicism and the Structure of *Villette*," "Lucy's exploration of powerlessness . . . takes place in the context of a clash between two different forms of social power" (823). Clark-Beattie acknowledges that placing Lucy within a foreign culture has value "both as a narrative structure and as a psychological strategy, in that it makes visible the selfhood that English society at once forces on her and obliterates from view" (825–26). In other words, in England, Lucy's very Englishness makes the values and beliefs that constitute her identity invisible. Once Lucy comes into contact with a second culture, these values and beliefs become much more apparent. Living abroad, Lucy must contend with both cultural systems' ideals of women, neither of which has developed meaningful options of existence for single women. The Protestants, as represented by Dr. John's understanding of Lucy's condition, assume a single woman should be an "inoffensive shadow" and as such be quietly resigned to her lot; the Catholics, as represented by Pére Silas's understanding of Lucy's condition, assume that a single woman should become a nun and dedicate her life to God (394). Neither ideology accounts for Lucy's desires to live actively in the world. The discrepancy between Lucy's inner and outer realities first manifests itself in Lucy's having the nervous condition of hysteria and ultimately in her having two episodes where hysteria results in actual illness.

In *Villette*, hysteria charts the conflicts between Lucy Snowe's image of herself and the concepts of womanhood of both the Protestant and Catholic patriarchal cultures. The language of nerves and hysteria is used throughout the text. Lucy Snowe admits she has a nervous condition, affirming, "I am constitutionally nervous" (460). Whereas in *Jane Eyre*, Bertha Mason's madness is explained by Rochester as a biological heredity condition—even though many contemporary feminists scholars starting with Gilbert and Gubar have argued with this explanation,—in *Villette*, Brontë is much more explicit that Lucy's nervous condition is brought about by the tenuous conditions of her life as a single woman alone, living abroad, a Protestant in a Roman Catholic country, without friends and family, forced to work for her livelihood. Here, through Lucy Snowe's conflicting needs of self-control and expression which result in hysterical episodes, Brontë chooses to look full face at the social forces behind mental illness. As Lucy herself states, " 'I really believe my nerves are getting over-stretched: my mind has suffered somewhat too much; a malady is growing upon it—what shall I do? How shall I keep well?' Indeed there was no way to keep well under the circumstances" (196–97). Brontë emphasizes the social context of Lucy's illness when writing to her publisher W.S. Williams on November 6, 1852, stating, "anybody living her life would necessarily become morbid" (Smith 3: 80).

While all of Charlotte Brontë's novels touch on the issue of mental illness, *Villette*'s exploration of psychological illness is much more sustained. In fact, here psychological illness is not just an incident that occurs as a one-time event, as in *The Professor* where Crimsworth suffers from an attack of hypochondria, which is of short duration and left largely unexplored.[2] Instead, in *Villette*, the illness functions as the narrative.[3] Outside of Lucy Snowe's rendering of her inner life, there is no story. As Athena Vrettos points out within the title of both her article and her chapter on *Villette*, "neurosis" becomes "narrative" (48).

Villette differs from *Jane Eyre*, where Brontë projects Jane's anger, female sexuality, and frustration onto Bertha Mason, creating a split psyche between the two female characters, with Jane representing the proper Victorian woman and thus "sane" and Bertha the "mad" woman who is the "dark double," the Other (Gilbert and Gubar 360). By the time Brontë wrote *Villette* six years later, her ability to create a more psychologically integrated character was more sophisticated, and consequently, Brontë no longer chose to displace her heroine's anger and sexuality onto a second female character. By using the nineteenth-century's concept of hysteria, Brontë can locate all of the heroine's inner turmoil within Lucy Snowe herself. While Vashti, the actress in *Villette* whose great passions metaphorically cause the theater to erupt in flames, is the character closest to Bertha, her existence does not need to end to ensure Lucy's inner stability.

Villette differs from *Shirley* in that Lucy experiences a more ongoing and pressing version of Caroline Helstone's mental stress and isolated circumstances. Caroline has a home; Lucy has not. Caroline can make her way on English soil; Lucy cannot. Caroline is surrounded by family and friends who love her and provide for her; Lucy is alone. Caroline will marry; Lucy will not. Lucy's reality is much harsher than Caroline's. Caroline's more privileged situation provides her the luxury, as it were, to nurse her illness and sink into an emotional paralysis, where she is unable to make and act on decisions that challenge other people's ideas of what she should do. Lucy, who must sustain herself through employment, must suppress her suffering and take action.

Similar to Caroline, Lucy as a good Protestant prides herself on her self-control and on her ability to repress her emotions. Lucy's greater self-control is perhaps a result of her lack of familial connections as a child, which may have reinforced this tendency as a method of survival in adverse circumstances. When we first meet Lucy as a child of fourteen, we see her condemning, even as she is fascinated by, the child Polly's emotional expression of her love and need for her father. For Lucy, lack of self-control is translated into being vulnerable to injury or loss. Because she has never known an outlet for her own emotions, Lucy takes her self-control and repression with her as part of what she defines as "England" when she sails for Labassecour.

Limiting our look at the Protestant ideology to its impact on emotions and sexuality, we can say the Protestant system is based on an internal control of both emotion and sexuality. Lucy's repressions show she has learned her home ideology well. She sees herself as "a mere looker-on at life" (174). In contrast, the Catholic system of Labassecour is based on external control of emotion and sexuality. Mme Beck's school is a perfect example of this. It is a school for girls, where men are forbidden entry except under special circumstances. The boys' school is separate, across what is appropriately named *l'allée defendue*, the forbidden alley.

Villette charts Lucy's inner development that grows out of the conflicts between these two ideologies. In simplistic terms, Lucy's growth moves from repression and self-control to a fuller, richer existence of emotional connection with others. However, this growth is not linear, nor is it immediate. In fact, when Lucy's Protestant internalized need for repression is first faced with the appeal of emotions, excess, and imagination, as they are presented to her by the Catholic culture of Labassecour, rather than respond at once to the appeal to be drawn outward toward others, she withdraws more into herself and depends on self-control as a defense against being hurt. When first in Labassecour, Lucy's need for self-control and her need to judge others on their self-control offer her a way to feel superior to the girls around her. She holds on to this sense of superiority as if it were a lifeline, particularly as potential friendships seem less and less likely when a wall of silence falls between her and her Catholic students at Mme Beck's command. The wall of silence is the consequence for Lucy's vocalizing a major difference in religious ideology. Lucy protests against the Catholic girls' tendency to lie, with their light-hearted confessions that "*J'ai menti plusieurs fois*" (101). Lucy expresses her Protestant ideas of "the evil and baseness of a lie" and explains that she "considered falsehood worse than an occasional lapse in church-attendance" (103). Once the girls have reported back to Mme Beck, "Something—an unseen, an indefinite, a nameless something—stole between myself and these my best pupils . . . conversation thenceforth became impracticable" due to the fact that either teachers or Mme Beck suddenly appear to ensure no discussion takes place (103). This wall of silence has been created between Lucy and her pupils both by Lucy's Protestant values which connect self-control, self-authority, and honesty and by the Catholic need to let outer authority, reinforced by surveillance, stand unchallenged by inner authority. Since the option no longer exists for her pupils to become her friends, this wall of silence, imposed from within and without, intensifies Lucy's growing sense of isolation within the Catholic community. Ultimately, this isolation leads to her breakdown and illness during the long vacation.

Lucy's first breakdown, due to a reactionary increase of repression and self-control, is instrumental in teaching Lucy the limitations of these emotional defenses, and she finally realizes she cannot be fully independent and autonomous. Because this breakdown is so dramatic, most scholarship focuses on it, without noticing that Lucy experiences a second breakdown, a second illness. Significantly, the plot does not end after the first illness, with Lucy simply coming to terms with her internal constraints. Once Lucy makes peace with her Protestant past and her internal repression lessens, then she must face the external control of Catholicism. The two Catholic authority figures in her life, Mme Beck and Pére Silas, representing education and religion respectively, work together in their efforts to exert greater external control over Lucy and, by extension, M. Paul. Like the first illness, the second illness results in Lucy's growing ability to come to terms with the cultural constraints that have power to shape her life.

At first, Lucy's own repression and self-control keep her in check. Consequently, earlier in the novel, the greatest hindrance to Lucy's connections with others is Lucy Snowe herself. Her repressed conduct fails her for she becomes more and more isolated from others, and the turning point comes with the loneliness of the long vacation. As she begins to take a more active role in life, it ends with her allowing herself to love M. Paul. Here, the dynamic of her place in the two ideological systems shift. Suddenly, the Catholic system which has originally designated that "*Les Anglais, . . . il n'est pas besoin de les surveiller*" (365–66) now must rally its force to keep the "raising character" Lucy Snowe in check (384). Because Lucy chooses to remain a Protestant, she is outside the faith and her love for M. Paul is seen to be a threat to the self-interest of the Catholic Church. Because self-control is valued differently by the two cultures and because, as Lucy's case will make clear, self-control is interconnected with hysteria, a full exploration of how self-control is presented in Brontë's novel is worthwhile. As readers, we need to understand the following: (1) the different perceptions of self-control held by the Catholics and Protestants, (2) the importance the British placed on self-control as an indicator of mental health, and (3) finally, the interconnection between self-control and hysteria.

Brontë explores how the Labassecourian Catholic system of external control is in direct conflict with Lucy's own Protestant understanding of the need for self-control. When Lucy first arrives, she has repressed her own desires, her emotional and sexual needs so well that there is no need for outside constraints. At first, the Catholics in positions of power observe and scrutinize Lucy, such as when Mme Beck and M. Paul concern themselves with watching her, looking for impropriety. Both are astonished to realize the lack of necessity for this surveillance. Mme Beck eases up once she realizes that the letters between Lucy and Dr. John do not demand her surveillance skills. Instead of giving Lucy gifts such as those received by the other teachers, Mme Beck selects to "leave you alone with your liberty" as a reward for her dedication to the school (372). M. Paul is shocked not only that Lucy can view the Cleopatra without being aware of the impropriety of her being a single woman gazing on such a sexualized painting but also that she is not being openly corrupted by viewing it. His comment, "*Singulières femmes que ces Anglaises!*" (252), echoes Mme Beck's insight "*Les Anglais, . . . il n'est pas besoin de les surveiller*" (365–66). Both realize in Lucy's case, surveillance is unnecessary, a chaperone is unneeded.

Brontë connects Catholicism's system of education with its theology, connecting Mme Beck's system of surveillance with the Roman Catholic church's "surveillance of a sleepless eye," as Brontë calls the confessional (513). Both Catholicism's systems of education and theology are concerned with external control and policing of female energy and sexuality. In Lucy's view, Mme Beck follows the Catholic ideology, which focuses on maintaining healthy bodies for the church while maintaining minds that are enslaved:

> Each mind was being reared in slavery; but, to prevent reflection from dwelling on this fact, every pretext for physical recreation was seized

and made the most of. There, as elsewhere, the CHURCH strove to bring up her children robust in body, feeble in soul, fat, ruddy, hale, joyous, ignorant, unthinking, unquestioning. "Eat, drink, and live!" she says. "Look after your bodies; leave your souls to me." (157)

The dance at the finale for Mme Beck's birthday *Fête* is a good example of the Catholic system where the body is celebrated yet simultaneously externally controlled. Although the day is given to sensuality, with the girls eating, fixing their hair, and getting dressed, and although the night is given to dancing, there is an external constraint on the night's festivities. A ribbon divides the young men from the young women, and Mme Beck acts as sentry. Only married men, with the exception of the trusted professor M. Paul, are allowed to dance. The *allée défendue* has been reduced to a ribbon for the night of festivities, but the line is still there.

Despite this militancy, the Catholic external focus on the body seems to be more liberating than the Protestant ideology that the body is shameful, since Mme Beck's school is highly successful and her young charges are happy and physically healthy. Yet, Lucy continues to point out the danger of the students not thinking twice about lies, deceptions, or manipulations. While physically robust, these young women of Labassecour are morally unhealthy by Lucy's Protestant standards. Lucy points out that they also lack in mental rigor, indicating that moral and mental discipline overlap. For Lucy, self-discipline is equated with health. She condemns the Catholic system because its dependence upon external constraints, such as institutional authority, does not help her students develop a sense of self-discipline, which will impart a sense of their own self-authority. Without it, the girls need continual chaperoning, a situation which means the school functions as a chaperone, serving as a waiting room for marriage.

Because the Protestants placed so much value on self-control and self-authority, they greatly feared any loss of agency, of self-control. Protestants feared the Catholic confessional in particular because of the symbolic giving over of power to another person implicit in the act of confessing. The potentially sexually charged intimacy involved when young girls confessed to male priests seemed problematic. When men confessed, Protestants feared for their loss of self-authority and self-constraint; however, when women confessed, Protestants feared this same loss might result either in their sexual fall or, perhaps equally horrifying, their being convinced to become nuns and giving their worldly goods to the church. The power of the priest was highly suspect.

As the primary representative of the Catholic Church in *Villette*, Pére Silas is the locus for many of the Catholic issues. When Lucy confides in him at the confessional, it is a sign of how desperate she is for human connection and how vulnerable she is. All defenses are gone; her self-control has almost fully crumbled. Sally Shuttleworth points out that in Victorian England, the concept of selfhood depended upon not allowing others to have full knowledge of the self (46). Because of this philosophy, the Roman Catholic confessional represented a loss of autonomy since it gave someone else access to the inner person. Thus, Lucy's confession signifies that the isolation and deprivation she has endured during the long vacation have broken her down, leaving her open to new influences. With Pére Silas's invitation to visit him at his home, Lucy realizes, "the probabilities are that had I visited Numéro 3, Rue des Mages, at the hour and day appointed, I might just now, instead of writing this heretic narrative, be counting my beads in the cell of a certain Carmelite convent . . ." (201). For Lucy, converting to Catholicism represents the greatest threat since at its most extreme, with the taking of vows as a nun, it would negate her freedom of movement and require her to negate her human need for sexuality. Where Jane Eyre had to refuse St. John's call to religion as being too constraining of her sexual nature, Lucy Snowe must refuse Pére Silas's call to religion for similar reasons.

Shuttleworth shows that British medical literature and self-improvement literature of the nineteenth-century stressed the importance of self-control for both men and women. Indeed, self-control was "prized by the Victorians as the index of sanity" (227). However, for women while there was an emphasis on mental self-control, the literature also indicated a fear that women were always at the mercy of their bodies; that is, their bodies controlled them (Shuttleworth 71). This paradox led to the greater cultural scrutiny of women, always motivated by an attempt to control female emotion, energy, and sexuality. Shuttleworth argues this fear of female lack of control is a displacement of male fear about their own paradoxical situation in the new industrial economy, which while emphasizing their self-control, treated them as cogs in a machine (85–87). For men to feel more securely in control of their own lives, men displaced their fears of lack of control onto the female body. In " 'Experiments Made by Nature': Mapping the Nineteenth-Century Hysterical Body," Diane Sadoff agrees that nineteenth-century "[f]ears about the fragility of middle-class economic arrangements" are "displaced and described as anxiety about female sexual morality . . ." (43). Both Shuttleworth and

Sadoff extend Foucault's idea of the historical shift from external to internal control over the body, set forth most clearly in *Discipline and Punish*, to include its ramifications for women, noting this shift led in Victorian times to greater external control and policing of women's bodies, which then became internalized as women's sense of the need for self-control increased.

Because of Lucy's own internalized ideas of the value of self-control and her corresponding fears that the lack of it will result in her being vulnerable to injury or loss, Lucy continues to judge the female characters she meets in Villette based on their level of self-control. As the only male character to lose self-control, M. Paul may flare up, but "it was only his nerves that were irritable, not his temper . . ." (479). While as a man M. Paul can be excused from expressing emotion, female emotion must be hidden or rewritten until it no longer is threatening to male reason, especially as it relates to female sexual desire. In Lucy's estimate, for the female characters, self-control is paramount. All of the schoolgirls, including Ginevra, are deemed lacking in self-control. Lucy associates their lack of repression with their being Labassecourians and Catholic. She feels justified in judging them harshly since by her standards they are acting with impropriety. Ginevra, who as a Briton should be different, has been corrupted by her continental education in Catholic schools.

Lucy's relationship with Ginevra is complex. On the one hand, Lucy is drawn to Ginevra and often gives her own share of food to Ginevra; on the other hand, she condemns Ginevra as being a "feather-brained school-girl" lacking in self-control and propriety (272). Lucy becomes incensed when Ginevra's "selfishness" (104) leads to her encouraging her suitor Isidore "*furieusement*" (105) and berates Ginevra often on her "coquetry" and "vanity" (337). Judging that the only way Ginevra will learn her lesson is through experience, Lucy tells Dr. John, "If her beauty or her brains will not serve her so far, she merits the sharp lesson of experience" (186). At Lucy's peak of frustration with Ginevra's improprieties, Lucy's words of condemnation are strongest. She writes Ginevra off by calling her "that unsubstantial feather, that mealy-winged moth," and worse yet, she is "Small-beer" (337–38).

Lucy applauds only Mme Beck and the adult Polly for their self-control. Mme Beck's institutional system of control extends to her own controlling of the self. Mme Beck is applauded by Lucy, "Brava!" for not allowing her unrequited love for Dr. John—if Mme Beck's motives of self-interest can be termed "love"—to become public knowledge (129). Polly is applauded for self-control when she writes an appropriate lady-like affirmation of her feelings for Dr. John: "Yet I almost trembled for fear of making the answer too cordial: Graham's tastes are so fastidious. I wrote it three times—chastening and subduing the phrases at every rescript . . . till it seemed to me to resemble a morsel of ice . . ." (471). As part of her own system of self-control, Lucy does not tell Polly that she too has redrafted letters to Dr. John: "I wrote to these letters two answers—one for my own relief, the other for Graham's perusal" (316–17). Lucy explains that "Feeling" prompted the first, and "Reason" would "leap in vigorous and revengeful, snatch the full sheets, read, sneer, erase, tear up, re-write, fold, seal, direct, and send a terse curt missive of a page. She did right" (317).

All three women, Lucy, Polly, and Mme Beck, no matter what the status of the love situation is, in order to maintain not only their self-respect but also the respect of others, must repress emotions through self-control. "Reason" must subdue "Feeling." Their status as "proper" women demands it. For as Polly tells Lucy on the topic of self-control:

> If . . . if I liked Dr. John till I was fit to die for liking him, that alone could not license me to be otherwise than dumb—dumb as the grave— dumb as you, Lucy Snowe—you know it—and you know you would despise me if I failed in self-control, and whined about some ricketty liking that was all on my side. (468)

Silence and repression of emotion are requirements of self-control. To represent this repression of emotions, Brontë often describes her female characters' responses using stone metaphors. Polly "grew like a bit of marble" (31); Mme Beck's "face of stone . . . betrayed no response" (85); Lucy assures Mme Beck of her own lack of "nervous excitability" by claiming, "I am no more excited than this stone" (96). Lucy responds to M. Paul's public emotional outburst at her negligence in presenting him with flowers by sitting "insensate as any stone" (427). Lucy fears by showing any emotion, she may be thought to be romantically interested in the professor. In Brontë's letter dated April 2, 1845, written to reassure her friend Ellen Nussey, we learn that this is not just a literary presentation but an actual day-to-day concern for unmarried Victorian women. Nussey had committed the major social *faux pas* of being polite to a single man whom she mistakenly thought was married. Brontë's reassurance affirms women's need to look stone-like: "I know that if women wish to escape the stigma of husband-seeking they must act & look like marble or clay—cold—expressionless, bloodless—for every appearance of feeling of joy—sorrow—friendliness, antipathy, admiration—disgust are alike construed by the world into an attempt to hook in a husband—" (Smith 1: 388–89).[4] Brontë is highly aware that for Victorian women even the possibility of seeming forward could be enough to ruin their reputation. Given the daily pressure on Victorian women to stifle their emotions, the results would be debilitating.

Once we look at hysteria, the connection between hysteria and self-control becomes clear. Since ancient times, hysteria was understood to be connected with female sexuality, specifically with the female reproductive system. Elaine Showalter's *The Female Malady* details that the word "hysteria" has served through the centuries as a catch-all term for female maladies, even for the "feminine" itself (129). George Drinka explains in *The Birth of Neurosis: Myth, Malady and the Victorians*, that Hippocrates understood hysteria as the result of the uterus "wandering," literally moving through the body (31). Later, Galen's theory clarified that the uterus did not wander. Galen also clarified that while all women were susceptible to hysteria, it was understood to affect young single women or widowed women most often, due to their celibacy. It could affect married women, but since the cure was seen as sex with a man, they could be more easily cured, that is, by having sex with their husbands.[5]

In *Villette*, Brontë makes the connection between hysteria and female sexuality when Lucy Snowe hallucinates repeatedly at moments of heightened sexuality. Three ghostly appearances of a nun overlap with Lucy's romantic interest in Dr. John. The nun first appears when Lucy is elated at receiving Dr. John's first letter (306). The nun's second sighting occurs when Lucy knows she will be going unchaperoned to the theater with Dr. John (320). The nun reappears a third time when Lucy is burying Dr. John's letters (370). Two final appearances mark the shift in Lucy's romantic interest to M. Paul. The nun's last "live" appearance correlates to when Lucy and M. Paul are alone together in the *allée defendue*, when he is confessing his timidity in the area of love (462). For the final appearance, Lucy finds the nun's costume arranged in her bed on the night of the Festival when she fears she has lost M. Paul's love to a newly discovered rival, Justine Marie (587). Symbolically, the nun's five appearances represent Lucy's sexual desire for these men, a desire she feels it necessary to repress.

While the plot ultimately gives us a real person, Alfred de Hamal, using the nun costume as a ploy for his own sexual exploits, Dr. John's reading of the nun as a "hallucination" based on Lucy's hysterical tendencies has validity once we connect the Victorian concept that the need for self-control, taken to its extreme, resulted in the manifestation of hysteric symptoms. Because Lucy knows she has seen a physical being, not just a hallucination, she tends to discount Dr. John's theories since they are not complex enough to capture reality as she has experienced it. However, as we become increasingly skilled at reading Lucy's narrative omissions and misrepresentations, we should not so easily discount his reading of her bodily symptoms of hysteria. Because Dr. John does not think easily in sexual terms himself and is not aware of Lucy's passionate nature, he does not know the source of her symptoms nor his own involvement therein. He is aware only of the external symptoms of heightened emotional excitement, that is, the hysteria that Lucy is portraying.

Brontë is writing pre-Freud, so her use and understanding of hysteria must be seen in pre-Freudian terms. Freudians understand hysteria as being a somatization of psychic trauma, with sexual crimes, sexual violations, or sexual assaults as typically being the origin of the hysteric symptoms. However, the Victorians, rather than seeing hysteria as the result of a sexual encounter, perceived hysteria as sexual deprivation, as unexpressed sexual desire that must be repressed rather than realized. For Freudians, hysteria happens after the fact; for Victorians, hysteria happens before. Hysteria can be a sign of any excessive emotion as well as being related more specifically to sexual passions. Understanding this, we can see how the Victorian demand for self-control would paradoxically play into the rise of hysteric symptoms.

Perhaps the Victorian fear of the display of emotion resulted from their awareness of how emotion was contagious. Hysteric symptoms in one person could lead to hysteric symptoms in another. Throughout *Villette*, Brontë emphasizes the impact that emotions have not only on the person feeling them but also on the observer, or, as Lucy phrases it, the "spectator" (16). Lucy describes the reunion between Polly and her father in terms of how it affects her. She notes excessive emotion is linked to hysteria, and as such, can easily be "disdain[ed]" or "ridicule[d]" by the spectator who needs "relief" from viewing the overly intense scene (16). Yet, Lucy understands that a release of emotion can bring relief to the observer as well, since in listening to Polly's silence of repressed emotion, Lucy notes, "I wished *she* would utter some hysterical cry, so that *I* might get relief and be at ease" (italics added, 16). However, Lucy alternately recognizes that another's outlet of emotions can be potentially threatening to the self-possession of the observer. For example, when M. Paul's pending departure is announced, a departure that deeply distresses Lucy, the students break into tears. Again emotion and hysteria are expressly linked. Lucy writes,

> I remember feeling a sentiment of impatience towards the pupils who
> sobbed. Indeed, their emotion was not of much value; it was only an
> hysteric agitation. I told them so unsparingly. I half ridiculed them.
> I was severe. The truth was, I could not do with their tears, or that
> gasping sound; I could not bear it. (550)

It is Lucy's fear of her own emotions that make her condemn others'
emotions as "hysterical agitation" (550).

Lucy's insight that it is one's own fear of emotions which causes the
desire to control others' emotions is central to the book. She may not
theoretically link it specifically to men's new place in the industrial
economy the way Shuttleworth and Sadoff do; however, the psychological insight that the displacement of fear leads to the need to
control helps to illuminate the gender relations in the novel. It
explains why "Reason" must suppress "Feeling," why female emotion
and female sexuality are under surveillance of religious, medical, and
educational systems. It explains why social control of female energy
becomes internalized as the female need for self-control. Lucy's belief
in the positive benefits of self-control takes a turn when she begins to
question the costs of such all-consuming self-control that is required
of Victorian women. In extreme conditions, healthy self-control
becomes unhealthy self-control, which ultimately leaves one vulnerable to psychological illness, which may manifest itself as hysteria,
hallucinations, or monomania.[6] For Lucy, the turning point is the
long vacation.

By the time Lucy has her breakdown and becomes ill, Brontë has
already introduced the issue of illness into the novel through two
other female characters: the young twelve-year old Desirée Beck and
the mature Miss Maria Marchmont. Mme Beck's own daughter,
Desirée is the only person who overtly rebels against Mme Beck's
system of surveillance, and significantly, illness is her chosen form of
rebellion. As Lucy notes, "Never once, I believe did she [Mme Beck]
tell her [Desirée] faithfully of her faults, explain the evil of such habits,
and show the results which must thence ensue. Surveillance must
work the whole cure. It failed of course" (114). Desirée remains out
of control, until, in an effort to gain attention, Desirée thinks to
manipulate the system by feigning an illness. Yet, ironically, once
Desirée pretends to be ill, Mme Beck can regain control of this
wayward child. For the dual purposes of regaining familial control and
of spending time with the young British doctor who interests her

romantically, Mme Beck pretends that Desirée's illness is indeed real
and calls for medical attention. Dr. John is brought into the farce,
prescribing "harmless prescriptions" (119). His reasons for playing
along show that he too is manipulating the system for his own desires.
He desires to be in closer proximity to his "angel," Ginevra, who is a
young *pensionnaire* at Mme Beck's school. Desirée's illness momentarily wins her some attention, but it does her no real good in
challenging the system. In fact, the two authority figures in her life,
her mother and her doctor have their own reasons for allowing her
pretense to continue, so rather than become empowered through her
feigning of illness, Desirée loses her sense of agency. Desirée is indeed
fortunate when her mother decides to end the farce.

In contrast to Desirée's feigned illness, Miss Marchmont's is real.
Although Miss Marchmont's story was deemed "unnecessary, having
no obvious connection with the plot or the characters . . ." by George
Henry Lewes in the *Westminster Review* of April 1853 (qtd. in Allott
211), Brontë's emphasis on the overlap between spinsterhood and
illness is important for two reasons. First, it gives a sense of how
limited the life of a Victorian invalid woman can become. As a result
of Miss Marchmont's being a rheumatic cripple, her world has
narrowed to "two hot, close rooms" (45). Significantly, Brontë's first
description of the invalid includes the key word "impotent" (43).
Miss Marchmont's description as "not potent" echoes Diane Price
Herndl's description of invalid women not only as sick but also as
"not valid" (3). In illness, women become even more removed from
the active world. Although not ill herself, simply by being Miss
Marchmont's caretaker, Lucy adopts the narrow life of the invalid.
She writes, "I forgot that there were fields, woods, rivers, seas, an
ever-changing sky outside the steam-dimmed lattice of this sick-
chamber; I was almost content to forget it. All within me became
narrowed to my lot" (45).

Second, Miss Marchmont's story is significant because it demonstrates how cultural conflict leads to illness. After the sudden,
unexpected death of her fiancé Frank, Miss Marchmont's illness originates in her inability to reconcile the new reality with her expectations
of her role as married woman. Since Miss Marchmont cannot reclaim
a new identity as a single woman, the internal conflict results in a
decline in her health. She suffers from rheumatism for twenty years.
The discrepancy between what Miss Marchmont had desired as a
married woman and what fate makes available to her as a spinster is
too great. Marriage and motherhood are no longer an option, yet neither can Miss Marchmont be returned to the status of the innocence

of unbetrothed girlhood, nor can she claim the status of widowhood. The contradictions inherent in her situation reduce her to the "invalid" woman whose life is wholly that of illness.

While Desirée's illness is feigned and Miss Marchmont's is real, the power structure's response to both is similar. Neither woman gains in agency by becoming ill. Illness signals loss of agency. Others step in to care for and make decisions for the patient, with the result that the patient is more and more removed from the world. Whether the impact of illness is a conscious ploy for control, as in Desirée's case, or a resultant condition of one's life, as in Miss Marchmont's case, illness can be a rejection of or an evasion from external societal control. Although neither woman gains self-control through illness, they no longer have to submit to many of the culture's expectations of them as women. For example, Miss Marchmont's illness makes it possible for her to remain true to her love for Frank without directly challenging cultural expectations for her to marry someone else. Unfortunately, when women choose illness as a subversive strategy, they potentially lose more than they gain. Herndl's point that illness as a form of resistance to cultural constraints is ineffective in achieving political or social change is worth reiterating. As Herndl points out, "When women are taught that illness and death offer them the best route to power, we all suffer the loss of possibilities. There is nothing empowering about victimage" (3).[7] If caught in the paralysis and powerlessness generated by illness, invalid women face Miss Marchmont's fate of being invalids for life.

Because spinsters lived a life dramatically at odds with culturally prescribed roles for women, that is, marriage and motherhood, Miss Marchmont's fate is highly believable. It parallels the lives of both of the old maids that Brontë presents in *Shirley*. Even though readers may be disappointed that Lucy does not have both a career and a romantic partner at the end of *Villette*, as a spinster, her fate should be compared to those of other Brontë spinsters. Lucy's fate is a dramatic improvement over that of either Miss Mann or Miss Ainley because as a spinster, Lucy succeeds in achieving an active life more on her own terms. Tracing this improvement back to Lucy's response to illness, which contrasts with Miss Marchmont's, we can see Lucy does not become paralyzed by her illness. Miss Marchmont's response leads to a life doomed to chronic illness; Lucy's response to illness represents a step toward greater health.

To understand how Lucy grows and benefits from her illness, it is crucial to be aware that in spite of the dangers offered by illness, the loss of self-control experienced during illness paradoxically can be seen as a necessary first step toward greater self-authority. Illness, by allowing time for reflection and analysis, can grant greater cultural and self-awareness. Even more important than time is the actual bodily experience of illness, which radically challenges accepted notions of the self in relation to culture. According to medical anthropologists, since birth, the body–self has been leading a dual existence. The body–self is simultaneously a physical body and a cultural body defined by the ideals, values, and roles of the culture in which it exists.[8] In illness, Lucy's concept of self collapses, and her experience of her physical body, a body in pain, supersedes any other awareness of the body. This return to the physical body gives Lucy the opportunity to analyze the cultural constraints—ideals, values, and roles—placed upon her and to reframe her self-identity more in keeping with her inner values rather than culturally imposed ones. She can let go of the values, ideals, and roles that seem inauthentic and constraining by consciously claiming her self-authority in determining future roles within the larger culture.

As a woman who is ill, Lucy's body is out-of-control, but she has also momentarily evaded social control. Illness has rendered her culturally invalid since she can no longer fulfill her womanly prescribed destiny as wife and mother. Paradoxically, while illness is rendering her invalid, for her, illness is rendering her culture invalid. Lucy realizes that none of the cultural institutions that have helped create her cultural identity can help her during her immediate experience of illness. Religion, science, art—none of these can help her because they are not primary to the bodily experience of being a body, ill and in pain. Previously, all of these institutions have had ramifications on her physical body by remaking it into a cultural body. However, once ill, the overwhelming need of Lucy's physical body overshadows the cultural body. Once returned to the physical body, an analysis of the cultural body is possible. Illness is the necessary clearing of the field, thanks to its ability to expose the limitations of Lucy's home culture's value system. Lucy must suffer illness and the loss of self-control it entails as a necessary first step toward claiming her own self-authority, imperative before Lucy can take on others' cultural authority.

During her convalescence at La Terrasse, Lucy's reflection and analysis leads to three major cultural insights as religion, science, and art are each re-examined as cultural institutions. Lucy's first cultural insight grows out of her new awareness of the limitations of her Protestant ideology. Even the most insightful contemporary review to touch on the religious issues in *Villette* did not fully appreciate Brontë's exploration of the limits of Protestantism, nor of the appeal of Catholicism.[9] In *The Daily News*, Harriet Martineau emphasizes

Lucy's condemnation of Catholicism without once remarking on Lucy's attraction to it. Moreover, while Martineau seems uneasy with Brontë's portrayal of Protestantism, she misses the point that Brontë is actually writing a critique of Protestantism. Martineau remarks, "A better advocacy of protestantism would have been to show that it can give rest to the weary and heavy laden; whereas it seems to yield no comfort in return for every variety of sorrowful invocation" (qtd. in Allott 174). Brontë's point is not to advocate Protestantism; it is that under extreme conditions, Protestant self-control is, in fact, unhealthy.

Brontë's critique of Protestantism goes beyond the realm of the self to analyze limitations in connections with others. Brontë portrays illness as a time when Lucy most needs friendship. Nevertheless, Lucy's illness increases her awareness that her Protestant friends do not want to know her intimately, that they do not want to hear her story. Their idea of health is to return Lucy to the silence of self-constraint. In the boat analogy about Mrs. Bretton, Lucy writes, "No, the 'Louisa Bretton' never was out of harbour on such a night, and in such a scene: her crew could not conceive it; so the half-drowned life-boat man keeps his own counsel, and spins no yarns" (226). Lucy cannot tell her story, not simply because of her own inability to express her sufferings to others in dissimilar situations but also due to the Brettons' inability to hear her. In equating her extreme isolation to "solitary confinement" (341), Lucy notes, "how very wise it is in people placed in an exceptional position to hold their tongues and not rashly declare how such position galls them!" and she ends by lamenting the impossibility to "Speak of it!" (341). In contrast to this Protestant desire for a silence of self-constraint, the Catholic priest Pére Silas allows Lucy to express her heartfelt pain, even though she is not of his faith. Both the expression of emotion and the intimacy involved in this confession are appealing to Lucy. Nevertheless, since the solution Pére Silas offers is at the price of conversion to Catholicism, Lucy feels it is not the appropriate choice for her. Even with her rejection of it, for the first time Lucy has turned toward Catholicism after experiencing the limitations of Protestantism to remedy her pain.

Lucy's second cultural insight during her convalescence shifts focus from religious to scientific ideology. Brontë complicates the basic conflict in *Villette* between the two religious ideologies by introducing the scientific ideology reflected in medicine and phrenology. Science had begun to question the prominence of religion by the mid-nineteenth century. *Villette*, while not fully engaging this larger cultural debate, does address some of the burgeoning issues as they relate to defining women's role in the culture. Dr. John Graham, a medical doctor,[10] and M. Paul Emanuel, an amateur phrenologist, both represent versions of this new authority of the scientific gaze. According to Shuttleworth, phrenology was the first step in Victorian psychology toward understanding the inner contradictions of the psyche. By establishing that different parts of the brain were concerned with different functions, different "faculties," Victorians could understand how one faculty could be at odds with another. The founder of phrenology, Frances Joseph Gall, writes in 1835 that the science of phrenology "will explain the double man within you, and the reason why your propensities and your intellect, or your propensities and your reason are so often opposed to each other" (qtd. in Shuttleworth 63). In the popular mind phrenology and physiognomy were often thought to be the same things. Brontë conflates the two in *Villette*.

Shuttleworth clarifies the distinction between physiognomy and phrenology since both include readings of the body's external features to reveal internal qualities. Physiognomy is a reading of the features; phrenology is a reading of the skull. Physiognomy was more of a moral reading, which assumed that inner characteristics and outer signs correlated, that there was a one-on-one relationship between inner and outer states. Phrenology was more scientific, using a scientific language that was not readily available to everyone, but had to be learned. Phrenology had no simple one-to-one correlation between inner and outer; rather, it looked at relationships between competing organs, and thus competing faculties. When Mme Beck first asks M. Paul to use his "skill in physiognomy" in reading Lucy (81), he emphasizes Lucy's contradictory nature, stating "If good predominates in that nature, the action will bring its own reward; if evil— eh bien!" (82). While Brontë's text uses the term "physiognomy" in the request, because M. Paul's response takes into account the contradictory elements of Lucy's nature and relies upon future experience to bring out the latent qualities within these elements, Shuttleworth clarifies his reading is, in fact, a "phrenological diagnosis" (223).

Similar to M. Paul, Lucy is well-versed in phrenology and uses it to her advantage in analyzing herself and others. Like Catholicism, phrenology appeals to Lucy since it captures more of the reality of her own conflicted double life. Phrenology also grants Lucy greater insights by giving her skills to read others' conflicting desires. Lucy's phrenological skill is applied to reading people from all ranks of life, ranging from her students to the King of Labassecour. In the concert scene where she reads the King's "Hypochondria" and "constitutional melancholy," Lucy tells us that her ability to read others is unique (267). No one else in the audience seems aware of the King's hypochondria, not even Dr. John, who is her escort for the evening and who, as a doctor, should be more in tune with health issues around him.

Lucy sees her phrenological skills as giving her a sense of control, and she uses them to assess and judge others. Prior to her illness, her judgments have been passed predominately upon the Labassecourians around her. For example, following George Combe's description of the "uses" and "abuses" of the faculty of "philoprogenitiveness" in *The Constitution of Man*[11] (25), Lucy feels the Labassecourians' "large organ of philoprogenitiveness" is excessive, showing their love of children has resulted in their being overly indulgent and spoiling their children (123). Or, she judges Rosine, "a young lady in whose skull the organs of reverence and reserve were not largely developed" (443). Lucy judges the Labassecourrians because of her own need to feel intellectually and morally superior to a people whom she sees as inferior since their cultural focus is more on the physical and the emotional existence of the self. Phrenology gives Lucy scientific backing for her prejudice since phrenology's emphasis on "moral sentiments" and "intellect" as more valuable to man's progress reduces man's "animal faculties" to something that must be controlled. In *The Constitution of Man*, the most influential text which made phrenology a commonly accepted idea within Britain, Combe explains "the moral sentiments and intellect are higher instincts than the animal propensities" (28), and he dedicates an entire section "to consider[ing] the Moral Law, which is proclaimed by the higher sentiments and intellect acting harmoniously, and holding the animal propensities in subjection" (141).

Lucy's phrenological assessments prior to her illness have been limited to the Labassecourriens. As a fellow Briton, Dr. John has evaded Lucy's critical assessment. Perhaps more important than his nationality, Lucy's attraction to Dr. John has gotten in the way of her reading him. When Lucy first re-encounters Graham Bretton, now a grown man, her inability to look past the overall positive physical impression he makes is telling. In self-defense Lucy purposefully makes herself blind to his male beauty because it is so powerful a force for her both sexually and emotionally. At one point, she even tells Paulina that "*I never see him.* I looked at him twice or thrice about a year ago, before he recognized me, and then I shut my eyes. . . . I value vision, and dread being struck stone blind" (italics in original, 532). In

"The Clinical Novel: Phrenology and *Villette*," Nicholas Dames asserts,

> Graham is the object of beauty that evades the phrenological grasp. Lucy is reduced to the most standard novelistic terms [instead of her scientific categorizing], to what we might call the traditional dyad of tall and handsome, and the effect on her is not salutary—she must look away. (373)

Her emotional response to his beauty cannot be contained by her use of science as a method of controlling emotion. Her only option to stay in control is to look away.

During her convalescence, for the first time Lucy is able to apply her phrenological skills to reading Dr. John. Ironically, Dr. John's own inability to see the true Ginevra is the catalyst that sparks Lucy's indignation, consequently liberating her to read him more accurately. Lucy does not acknowledge her anger in her description of this turning point. Rather, illness is her excuse for this new self-assertion. She writes, "My patience really gave way . . . I suppose illness and weakness had worn it and made it brittle" (237). Illness gives her new power to confront Dr. John and to speak the truth. Once Lucy asserts "Dr. Breton . . . there is no delusion like your own" (237), she can read the true character of her idealized Dr. John, finally seeing his limitations. For the first time in the text, Lucy notes a phrenological flaw in Dr. John, stating, "the sympathetic faculty was not prominent in him" (237).

Not wanting the reader, and perhaps herself, to be too judgmental of this newfound flaw, Lucy qualifies her assertion, giving a mini-lesson in phrenology:

> to feel, and to seize quickly another's feelings, are separate properties; a few constructions possess both, some neither. Dr. John had the one gift in exquisite perfection; and because I have admitted that he was not endowed with the other in equal degree, the reader will considerately refrain from passing to an extreme, and pronouncing him *un*sympathizing, unfeeling: on the contrary, he was a kind, generous man. Make your need known, his hand was open. Put your grief into words, he turned no deaf ear. Expect refinements of perception, miracles of intuition, and realize disappointment. (italics in original, 237)

Within Lucy's attempt to minimize the impact of Dr. John's phrenological lack of the "sympathetic faculty," she gives a clear reading of why Dr. John will never be a gifted phrenologist. Due to his lack of "perception," his lack of "intuition," he will never excel at reading character but will always be dependent upon being told what is happening.

Thus, Lucy learns to read Dr. John, but Dr. John never learns to read Lucy. Ironically, because Dr. John believes in the authority of medicine, he is always certain of his ability to look at Lucy and to read her. He assures her of his ability to read her, saying "I look on you now from a professional point of view, and I read, perhaps, all you would conceal—in your eye, which is curiously vivid and restless; in your cheek, which the blood has forsaken; in your hand, which you cannot steady" (310). Yet, he ends this arrogant assurance with an appeal, "Come, Lucy, speak and tell me" (310). While he does see perhaps more than Lucy would like him to see, his claims to read Lucy fall short. He can only see the symptoms without having insight as to their origins. He must depend on Lucy's telling him what should be readily available for him to know if he were truly skilled in phrenology. Dr. John claims, "We each have an observant faculty. You, perhaps, don't give me credit for the possession; yet I have it" (393). Yet, time and time again, Lucy makes us aware of the inadequacy of Dr. John's gaze, which will have ramifications leading to both the inadequacy of his explanations for her condition and the inadequacy of his recommendations for cure. Lucy writes of his limited knowledge of her, "He wanted always to give me a rôle not mine. Nature and I opposed him . . . he did not read my eyes, or face, or gestures; though I, doubt not, all spoke" (395).

One reason Dr. John seems unable to move toward a phrenological reading of Lucy is that he equates the outer and inner person in the one-to-one correspondence involved in physiognomy. He sees Lucy as an "inoffensive shadow" without ever realizing the passionate nature that is at odds with her cold exterior (394), just as he sees Ginevra's beauty and mistakenly assumes she is an "angel" (272). As a Protestant, Dr. John should be more in touch with the value of phrenology since it had become assimilated into the Protestant culture of self-advancement when Combe built upon Gall's work.[12] Gall had claimed the "faculties" were static. Combe felt that once the "faculties" were analyzed, people could then use this analysis to develop those faculties which they deemed important and to downplay those faculties which needed to be subjected and controlled (*Constitution of Man* 141). However, in *Villette*, it is not the Protestant Dr. John but the Catholic M. Paul who sees the value of phrenology.

Because the Catholicism presented in *Villette* more willingly grants that people have conflicting desires—thus the need for external societal controls to keep these desires in check,—it makes sense that the

Catholic M. Paul is more drawn to phrenology than the Protestant Dr. John. In contrast to Dr. John's superficial reading of Lucy, M. Paul tells Lucy "I know you! I know you! Other people in this house see you pass, and think that a colourless shadow has gone by. As for me, I scrutinized your face once, and it sufficed" (191). M. Paul can read the conflict between Lucy's outward, seemingly stoic, acceptance of her role and of the inner passions of Lucy's nature since he is skilled in phrenology.

Similar to Lucy's difficulties in reading Dr. John, Lucy also wrestles with difficulties in reading M. Paul. Lucy claims her difficulty in reading M. Paul is because of his *lunettes*, his glasses. As readers, we understand more clearly than she does how her emotional response to M. Paul, as to Dr. John, makes it difficult for her to be scientifically objective about him. Her sexual attraction to both men renders her intellectual system of analysis inadequate.

Mirroring her increased skill in reading Dr. John, Lucy's skill in reading M. Paul also begins during her convalescence. At the concert, in addition to reading the King, she reads M. Paul. While most phrenological readings depend upon proximity to grant a closer reading of the skull, Brontë makes the physical distance between Lucy and M. Paul at the concert act in Lucy's favor since it allows her to see more than his glasses. Lucy declares,

> nor could I be blind to certain vigorous characteristics of his physiog-
> nomy, rendered conspicuous now by the contrast with a throng of
> tamer faces: the deep, intent keenness of his eye, the power of his
> forehead—pale, broad, and full—the mobility of his most flexile
> mouth. He lacked the calm of force, but its movement and its fire he
> signally possessed. (275)

Lucy's inclusion of the reading of M. Paul's forehead is important. The forehead is the one overlapping area analyzed by both phys-iognomists and phrenologists. Both readings stressed, as Jeanne Fahnestock notes, "the higher and broader the forehead, the more intelligent the owner" (345). Fahnestock connects this interpretation with a gender bias which makes literary descriptions of heroes, not heroines, depend upon the lofty forehead, stating, "The physiogno-mists' theories and the novelists' descriptions tell us some of the current notions about women's intellect, or rather lack of it, for one and all the physiognomists prefer low foreheads and little intellect in women" (345). In *Villette*, we find one of the literary exceptions to this trend.[13] Lucy's prominent forehead clearly asserts her status as the heroine. Even Mme Beck's forehead is described as "high but narrow" (88), yet she is an unworthy candidate for being the heroine of a Victorian novel because, as Fahnestock reports, "A forehead which is high without being broad indicates a quick, sharp mind, but one without the nobler quality of wisdom" (347). Mme Beck's forehead foretells her shrewdness; she is intelligent without being moral.

With their destiny written on their foreheads, M. Paul and Lucy are the novel's true hero and heroine, fated to fall in love. During their first intimate conversation together in the *allée defendue*, a romantic *tête-à-tête* which results in the appearance of the nun, M. Paul confronts Lucy about their physical—and thus psychological—affinities, asking, "Do you see it, mademoiselle, when you look in the glass? Do you observe that your forehead is shaped like mine—that your eyes are cut like mine?" (460).[14] Not only do M. Paul and Lucy share physical affinities, they share the same scientific language to understand them. His ability to see her, to talk with her about these findings, to push her capabilities based on this knowledge, all bring them closer together. Lucy's own ability to read M. Paul makes the relationship mutual. In addressing Dr. John's and M. Paul's differing abilities to see Lucy, Nicholas Dames writes,

> This is perhaps the novel's central paradox: only through the most brutally scientific of gazes will desire be fulfilled . . . For Graham, who cannot truly see Lucy, she is nothing; for Paul Emanuel, who can see through her, she will become a force to reckon with. (374)

Intriguingly, the ideological conflict between the two branches of science—phrenology or medicine—like the ideological conflict between the two religions—Catholicism or Protestantism—has been intimately woven into the novel's love story, with its two potential, yet dramatically different, suitors.

Lucy's third cultural insight connects the materialism of science with the materialism of art, neither of which she feels adequately capture complex realities in their representation of women. Through her outings with Dr. John to the theater and the art museum, Lucy becomes aware that male artistic representations of women are as problematically materialistic as Dr. John's scientific understanding of women. First, Lucy takes issue with Dr. John's materialist reading of her encounters with the nun, a reading which reduces her experience to being simply a result of her nervous system. She writes, "it was all optical illusion—nervous malady, and so on. Not one bit did I believe him; but I dared not contradict: doctors are so self-opinionated, so immovable in their dry, materialist views" (321). Then, once Lucy sees Vashti's theatrical performance and experiences her artistic mastery, with Vashti's ability to "immediately embod[y]" whatever abstraction she is representing, no matter how painful, Lucy fully realizes the inadequacy of the male artist of the Cleopatra (322). Lucy issues a challenge: "Where was the artist of the Cleopatra? Let him come and sit down and study this different vision . . . let all materialists draw nigh and look on" (322). As Shuttleworth rightly claims, Lucy's

> rejection of medical and artistic materialism stems rather from the rigid and incomplete nature of their conception; she objects less to the idea of an interrelationship between body and mind, than to their rather partial vision of this union. Under the medical and artistic gaze, woman is *reduced* to flesh and the material function of nerves. (italics in original, 239)

In addition, Lucy condemns a set of four paintings, "*La vie d'une femme*," which M. Paul deems more appropriate for her viewing than the Cleopatra. Lucy condemns not the materialism of these paintings, with the reduction of women to their physical bodies, but rather their artistic rendering of a womanly ideal, which denies women their bodies. The Cleopatra was all body; these paintings are of idealized women, angelic in their perfection, each of whom represent a prescripted idealized stage in woman's life as defined by the patriarchal ideology of the domestic ideal. Lucy's condemnation of M. Paul's painted *anges* parallels her earlier condemnation of Dr. John's idealized view of Ginevra as an angel. Lucy declares, "All these four '*Anges*' were grim and gray as burglars, and cold and vapid as ghosts. What women to live with! insincere, ill-humoured, bloodless, brainless nonentities!" (253). Bloodless and brainless, these artistic representations as well as other *chef d'oeuvres* viewed by Lucy are condemned for being "not a whit like nature" (249). As "non-entities," these female images do not represent women's reality, but rather some male artist's idealized vision of what women should be.

Lucy's awareness of what this idealization of womanhood means in denying women their complex realities is echoed in Ginevra's analysis of Dr. John. Even Ginevra realizes Dr. John's limited ability to see her is due to his idealization of her as the "perfect" woman (111).[15] Ginevra complains, "the man is too romantic and devoted, and he expects something more of me than I find it convenient to be. He thinks I am perfect: furnished with all sorts of sterling qualities and solid virtues, such as I never had, nor intend to have" (111). Ginevra admits trying to live up to his ideas when she is in his presence, but she admits the effort—and presumably the self-control—required makes it quite tiring to do so. She prefers being with Lucy who can see her as she really is, or as she phrases it, for "tak[ing] me at my lowest, and know[ing] me to be coquettish, and ignorant, and flirting, and fickle, and silly, and selfish, and all the other sweet things you and I have agreed to be a part of my character" (111). Considering Ginevra is often written off by Lucy Snowe and critics alike as being a silly character, Ginevra shows much wisdom not only in her honest self-appraisal but also in her desire to be seen for one's self, with all of one's flaws, rather than capitulating to the need to live up to someone else's ideal, a process which renders her invisible. The cost of women being idealized is apparent even to Ginevra.

Once Lucy reexamines religion, science, and art as cultural institutions, she begins to reclaim her identity in new ways, including her choice to let go of her need for repressing her emotions. Consequently, as a result of her illness, Lucy's emotional growth is significant. For the first time, she comprehends the importance of intimacy and begins to make personal strides toward achieving meaningful intimacy. Even though her connection to Dr. John deepens, ultimately her love for him is unrequited. In spite of Dr. John's loving someone else, Lucy has grown herself in loving him. Regarding Lucy's ritual burial of Dr. John's letters, John Maynard notes, "Yet Lucy is a very different person for having opened her heart, even if only to be hurt in consequence. In the long vacation she had been unable to admit, far less express, her feelings. Now when she goes to bury her letters she performs a conscious and deliberate ritual of expressing her feelings and her loss" (193). The result of the ritualized expression is Lucy's sense of feeling "not happy, far otherwise, but strong with reinforced strength" (370). Although the burial represents lost potential for a greater development of emotional life through mutual love, Lucy is claiming her emotions and through them, she gains in inner strength. Immediately after this burial, when Lucy is again confronted with the nun, she faces it and drives it away. Maynard asserts, "the symbol begins to turn into one real prankster to be confronted and exposed as Lucy feels confident in her feelings" (193).

Lucy's greater emotional health is tried by events in the latter half of *Villette*. During the period of time when M. Paul is making ready for his departure for the West Indies, Lucy experiences a second breakdown, when Mme Beck's and Pére Silas's interfering influence isolates her from M. Paul. Earlier during the long vacation, the isolation and the resulting illness had not been specifically anyone's fault. Lucy explains to Dr. John when he tries to blame Mme Beck, "It was not Madame Beck's fault . . . it is no living being's fault, and I won't hear any one blamed" (232), rather it was the fault of "me and Fate" (232).

Now, Lucy blames Mme Beck since she is actively interfering in Lucy's life and using her knowledge of Lucy's character to do so. Writing in phrenological terms, Lucy laments her characteristic inability to seek out M. Paul: "To follow, to seek out, to remind, to recall—for these things I had no faculty. M. Emanuel might have passed within reach of my arm: had he passed silent and unnoticing . . . should I have suffered him to go by" (554). Lucy's desire to connect with M. Paul before he sails and her passivity of action leads to an internal conflict that renders her "quite sick" (554). When M. Paul comes to the school, she goes to him, hoping that simply being in his presence will be enough to give him the opportunity of speaking to her for she finds herself unable to take any initiative in speaking to him. Unfortunately, Lucy is blocked by the machinations of Mme Beck, who uses her larger form and drapery to hide Lucy from M. Paul's sight. Lucy laments, "she eclipsed me; I was hid. She knew my weakness and deficiency; she could calculate the degree of moral paralysis—the total default of self-assertion—with which, in a crisis, I could be struck" (556). Lucy describes the crisis that ensues as "a grief inexpressible over a loss unendurable" (556), noting its interiority by indicating "the raging yet silent centre of that inward conflict" (556).

Whereas in the first breakdown, Lucy turns to Catholicism, in the second breakdown, she must challenge Catholicism's external control of her world. The confession to Pére Silas is replaced with her confrontation with Mme Beck. Both the confession and the confrontation are moments of truth-telling achieved through illness. When Lucy stands up to Mme Beck, her choice of language is not strictly phrenological, yet it uses phrenological assumptions. In her outrage at Mme Beck's interference, Lucy condemns her for being a "sensualist" (559). This put down reinforces Lucy's sense of superiority over Mme Beck. In Lucy's eyes, Mme Beck's focus is on the gratification of the physical body, the lower, animal faculties, whereas Lucy herself takes into account the moral sentiments, the more advanced, higher faculties. When Mme Beck declares that Lucy needs someone to watch over her, Lucy's anger is strong enough for her to forbid this surveillance. She writes, "I forbid it . . . Keep your hand off me, and my life, and my troubles. Oh, Madame! In *your* hand there is both chill and

poison. You envenom and you paralyze" (italics in original, 559).
Here, Lucy shifts the focus from her own internal paralysis, the result
of her adherence to Protestant ideology, to Mme Beck's ability to
paralyze her, the result of Lucy's passive acquiescence to Mme Beck's
adherence to the Catholic ideology. Both forms of paralysis must be
challenged. Lucy can see Mme Beck fully, "her habitual disguise, her
mask and her domino, were to me a mere network reticulated with
holes; and I saw underneath a being heartless, self-indulgent, and
ignoble" (560).

During Lucy's second bout with illness, in addition to breaking
through external constraints, such as those imposed by Mme Beck,
Lucy also makes headway breaking through her internal constraints in
order to vocalize her emotional needs. The first breakthrough comes
when she can openly declare to M. Paul: "My heart will break!"
(600). A second breakthrough occurs with Lucy's open acknowledgment, first to herself and later to M. Paul, of the jealousy she felt
during the night of the *fête* toward Justine Marie. In *Charlotte Brontë
and Sexuality*, Maynard contends that Lucy's "jealousy, as always in
Brontë, is a sign of mature sexual engagement" (206). Both of these
emotional avowals indicate how far Lucy has moved from suppressing
her feelings for M. Paul. These breakthroughs allow Lucy to begin
fully experiencing her passionate sexual nature.

Lucy's jealousy is also instrumental in her exposure and destruction
of the nun, another sign of her increased health. On Lucy's return
from the *fête*, she confronts the nun for the final time. She writes,
"Tempered by late incidents, my nerves disdained hysteria. . . . I defied
spectra" (587). Having openly acknowledged her jealousy, Lucy no
longer feels the need for emotional repression. The imposed need for
self-control has been successfully challenged. Consequently, hysteria
can now be "disdained" for it is no longer needed as an outlet for
repressed emotion and sexuality. No longer afraid of claiming her
emotions, Lucy can destroy the nun. Lucy describes the event:

> I had rushed on the haunted couch; nothing leaped out, or sprang, or
> stirred; all the movement was mine, so was all the life, the reality, the
> substance, the force; as my instinct felt. I tore her up—the incubus!
> I held her on high—the goblin! I shook her loose—the mystery! And
> down she fell—down all round me—down in shreds and fragments—
> and I trode upon her. (587)

The tearing up of the nun—the incubus, the goblin, the mystery—
signals that Lucy can no longer be held back by cultural constraints for

single women as symbolized by the nun. Because it was Lucy who gave "the life, the reality, the substance" to these cultural constraints, she can also deny them life, reality, and substance. Once the "mystery" of ideology is understood, its power is limited and it can be "trode upon" (587).[16] Insights gained through illness help Lucy to see that the cultural constraints symbolized by the nun are not inherent to the body. Once Lucy sees them as the cultural cobwebs they are, the mythical nun becomes a tangible entity—a real person—that then can be disregarded. Brontë's choice of Alfred de Hamal to play the role of the exposed Oz once the curtain is pulled aside is telling. The aristocratic de Hamal is the male character of the least weight in *Villette*. While Lucy had immediately realized not to take de Hamal too seriously, now she realizes the importance of not taking the cultural symbolism of the nun seriously either. If she denies her passionate nature and leads the life prescribed by the nun, it will limit her options and negate the complexity of her experience as a single woman.

The culmination of Lucy's emotional fulfillment with M. Paul occurs in the sensually described mythical Eden as represented by the new school in the Faubourg Clotide, which M. Paul has found and fitted for Lucy's use. Brontë's sensual descriptions are paralleled by the two characters' sensual actions. For the first time in the novel, Lucy and M. Paul are openly showing each other physical affection: Lucy strokes M. Paul's hand; he strokes her hair; she kisses his hand; they share a meal that they have made together. By creating a new reality, a new school, outside of the surveillance of Mme Beck and Pére Silas, Lucy and M. Paul can step free from the destructive myths that have been binding them. M. Paul explains that using the new school's address means there will be no surveillance of his correspondence with Lucy. Lucy's indignation shows she no longer perceives herself at the mercy of Mme Beck's control. She declares emphatically, "But if you write . . . I *must* have your letters; and I *will* have them: ten directors, twenty directresses, shall not keep them from me. I am a Protestant: I will not bear that kind of discipline: monsieur, I *will not*" (italics in original, 604). Lucy's new ability to express her emotional needs, gives her strength to openly disclaim the Catholic need for surveillance.

Counterbalancing the joy of the Faubourg Clotide union, M. Paul is absent for three years. Literal food is replaced by the symbolic nourishment of letters. Lucy is sustained on letter writing since M. Paul's "letters were real food that nourished, living water that refreshed" (616). Because Lucy's and M. Paul's union is a communion of letters rather than a communion of bodies, the lack of a sexual fulfillment is disappointing to many modern readers. Yet, even though Lucy and M. Paul never marry and consummate their passion, it would be wrong to negate that such a passion exists. The reality of loss does not diminish the maturity Lucy has achieved in feeling such love. Because writing and reading of letters is equated with nourishment, an important part of health, Lucy's writing of the book can also be seen in terms of health. Told from the point of view of age, with Lucy's hair "white under a white cap, like snow beneath snow" (55), *Villette*'s narrative style documents the growth between what the young Lucy Snowe experienced and how the mature Lucy Snowe interprets it. Imbedded within Lucy's story is Miss Marchmont's story, a signpost of how much Lucy grows in comparison. Unlike Miss Marchmont who retreats from the world, Lucy realizes that the end of love does not need to be equated with the end of life.

Lucy's economic freedom and independence with the opening of her own school is celebrated as a sign of her health by many scholars. Lucy's decision to leave Mme Beck's school to establish her own school should be seen as a large step in personal growth. It may be true, as Gilbert and Gubar point out, "only in his [M. Paul's] absence that she can exert herself fully to exercise her own powers"; however, it seems more important to celebrate Lucy's achievements as given in the text rather than question what they would have been had the reality been otherwise (438).[17]

Vrettos argues that at the end of *Villette*, Lucy is still suffering from neurosis and that no cure has been achieved. Writing of the need for narrative closure, Vrettos comments,

> One must, it appears, cure the heroine in order to end the text. As in a medical case history, the state of wellness collapses the need for narrative. Yet most readings of *Villette* . . . fail to account for lingering evidence of neurosis and fail to recognize that Lucy's . . . attempts to achieve self-control continue to receive authorial skepticism amidst formal gestures of closure. (77)

Vrettos sees *Villette* as resisting closure in two ways. First, the ambiguous ending of M. Paul's return or death at sea leaves Lucy's fate uncharted and her life in emotional turmoil. Second, the storm imagery at the end of the novel, which recalls how earlier storms have affected Lucy's nerves, indicates Lucy's neurosis continues, extending the "disruptive energy of nervous illness beyond the space of the text" (79). Both of Vrettos's points about the disruption of the novel's formal closure are appropriate. However, because Lucy Snowe writes her narrative years after the storm, the completion of the text itself should be read as an indication of the state of her psychological health. Due to the continued contrast between the life Lucy may have desired being married to M. Paul and the reality of her life as a spinster who runs a girls' school, some level of internal conflict must be present. As such, Lucy may never achieve perfect health. Yet, as the Victorians were becoming aware, sanity and insanity, health and illness, were no longer polar opposites but rather degrees on a continuum.

CHAPTER 4

VAMPIRES, GHOSTS, AND
THE DISEASE OF DIS/POSSESSION
IN *WUTHERING HEIGHTS*

Perhaps of all of the Brontë novels, Emily Brontë's *Wuthering Heights* is the one novel most obsessed with illness. In 1963, Charles Lemon provided the first scholarly look at Emily Brontë's obsessive use of illness in "Sickness and Health in *Wuthering Heights*." Lemon's early essay chronicles when Brontë's characters become ill within the plot, summarizes what illnesses they suffer, and where possible, gives the ages of the characters' deaths. More recent critics, including Graeme Tytler and Susan Rubinow Gorsky, are beginning to look at Brontë's use of specific illnesses, such as monomania and "anorexia."[1]

Because Brontë's novel resonates with a variety of illnesses as well as debilities, such as gunshot wounds, knifecuts, and dogbites, which require care and time for convalescence, it is time to take another look at the role illness plays in *Wuthering Heights*. Once we realize that *all* of Brontë's characters in *Wuthering Heights* become sick within the novel, we must ask ourselves why. Even our two narrators, Nelly Dean and Lockwood, become ill at crucial points. Nelly Dean prides herself on her good health, yet she catches a cold and is incapacitated for three weeks. Lockwood's illness provides the premise for the story-telling in *Wuthering Heights* since Lockwood has caught a cold that lasts for the majority of the winter, and Nelly, "the housekeeper, a matronly lady taken as a fixture along with the house," amuses him during his convalescence with stories (7). Lockwood himself equates listening to Nelly's stories as part of his cure, reflecting that though her stories are "not exactly of the kind which I should have chosen to amuse me . . . . I'll extract wholesome medicines from Mrs. Dean's bitter herbs" (121). When Lockwood first states his goal of "extract[ing] wholesome medicines from Mrs. Dean's bitter herbs," as readers we expect that he will succeed in this endeavor during the course of the novel. If this were a novel by Charlotte Brontë, Lockwood would indeed grow through his illness and the resulting insights it would give him. For Charlotte Brontë, the use of illness signals moral growth or psychological transformation within a character. Charlotte Brontë's characters are different people before and after their illness. In their growth, Charlotte Brontë explores the transformative properties of illness.

Emily Brontë's use of illness differs radically from Charlotte Brontë's. While both Charlotte and Emily Brontë are concerned with a critique of the constraints of patriarchal culture, Charlotte Brontë stresses the internal psychological changes as individual characters, such as Jane Eyre, Caroline Helstone, or Lucy Snowe, pit themselves against a system which denies their personal value. Through her focus on one character's internal psychological changes, Charlotte Brontë is basically critiquing the system from a position *inside* the system, asking for a little breathing room. Because Emily Brontë denies the transformative power of illness while analyzing the impact of the cultural system on *all* of her characters, she places herself much farther *outside* the system and consequently critiques the patriarchal system as a whole.

Thus, even though Lockwood's first experience of illness at the Heights allows him to enter Cathy's oak-paneled bed, the innermost sanctuary of the Heights, and his second illness offers the repetition of this privileged position when he convalesces in Cathy's sickroom at the Grange, Lockwood does not use illness to his own advantage for psychological growth. Lockwood learns nothing in the course of his own illness nor in hearing the stories of others' illnesses and deaths which are given him as "bitter herbs" to cure him. Lockwood is still the same Lockwood at the end of the story as he was at the beginning.[2]

In fact, all of Emily Brontë's characters remain psychologically unchanged, not just Lockwood. The psychological essence of each is static in this highly tumultuous novel.[3] By bombarding her readers with the multitude of non-transformative illnesses which make up *Wuthering Heights*, Emily Brontë's readers are better positioned to analyze "Civilization," which Brontë presents as the common source of all of the illnesses. By creating a theoretical paradigm which equates civilization with illness, Brontë emphasizes that the various representations of illness within the novel are simply symptoms of an unnatural, man-made cultural system.

Thanks to Sue Lonoff's scholarship, which has made nine essays written by Emily Brontë under Monsieur Heger's direction during her schooldays in Brussels available to scholars, the theoretical ideas found in Brontë's essays can be applied toward a fuller understanding of *Wuthering Heights*. This theoretical background deepens our understanding of Brontë's analysis of her patriarchal culture, which she refers to as "Civilization" (228) or "society" (56), and ultimately confirms she is much less optimistic than her sister Charlotte about individual people addressing the wrongs of the system. Indeed, Emily Brontë stresses not only that no single individual's inner change, gained through illness, will be enough to challenge the rigidity of the system, but also that all variations of characters' new alliances gained through illness which could potentially challenge the system will, in fact, fail to do so. Consequently, in *Wuthering Heights*, Brontë stresses the external structure of the patriarchal system with its primary dependence upon the possession of land. In such a system, power perpetuates itself no matter what, preying upon the life-energies of those caught within it.

In Brontë's Belgian essays, she develops her philosophical stance concerning Nature and Civilization. Brontë first theorizes that nature is based upon a natural process of destruction. In her essay entitled "The Butterfly," Brontë writes, "Nature is an inexplicable problem; it exists on a principle of destruction. Every being must be the tireless instrument of death to others, or itself must cease to live . . ." (176). In *Wuthering Heights*, Brontë uses cat and mouse imagery to capture the difference between nature's "natural" principle of destruction and culture's "unnatural," that is "man-made," principle of destruction. Cathy and Edgar are compared to a cat and a mouse during the scene where Edgar proposes marriage. The scene begins when Cathy slaps Edgar in one of her tantrums and he responds first by claiming he is "afraid" and "ashamed" of her (56). He leaves, only to return and to propose marriage to her. Nelly's commentary of the scene reads, "he possessed the power to depart, as much as a cat possesses the power to leave a mouse half killed, or a bird half eaten" (57). She continues, "Ah, I thought, there will be no saving him—He's doomed, and flies to his fate!" (57). The passage originally reads as if Edgar were the cat, but it shifts to Edgar as mouse or bird. However, events show that Cathy, not Edgar, is the one who is "doomed" by his return and consequent proposal of marriage since it will lead to her psychological self-division and ultimately to her death.

Brontë's cat and mouse metaphor points out the distortion of nature's principle of destruction under patriarchy. Whereas in nature one species lives off another species by destroying it, it is rare that members of the same species destroy each other. Whether one believes that Cathy's feminine wiles "doom" Edgar or that Edgar's position of power within the patriarchy "dooms" Cathy, either way, members of the same species are forced by the man-made system in which they live to "consume" the other in order to survive. Civilization and consumption are aligned again in *Wuthering Heights* in the character of Frances Earnshaw, Hindley's young wife. Brontë overlaps Frances's death in childbirth with her illness of consumption. This overlap links the consumption of the woman's body as necessary for the perpetuation of the patriarchal line. Frances's sole function in the novel is to provide a male heir to facilitate the transmission of land and then to disappear, exiting through death.

While in "The Butterfly" Brontë focuses only on the principle of destruction found in nature, in *Wuthering Heights*, Brontë develops the interplay between culture and nature, showing not only that mankind destroys his own species to survive but that culture itself is based on the death of natural beings. The clearest example of this occurs during Cathy's delirium from brain fever when she rips apart her pillow and looks for blood on the lapwing feathers. Like Ophelia's "mad scene" in *Hamlet*, Cathy's offers a critique of patriarchal culture; however, Cathy focuses on dead birds rather than cut flowers. As Stevie Davies declares in *Emily Brontë: Heretic*, "the undone pillow of civilization . . . is decomposed to reveal the dead lives upon which it depends but denies. Human life rests its head on their death" (135). Natural resources must be killed and appropriated for cultural purposes.

Brontë points out culture's distortion of nature's principle of destruction again in the essays when she condemns men for hunting simply for sport. She implies that hunting and living off the land are "natural," but when men become disconnected to the natural process of food gathering for bodily sustenance, the system is out of whack. In her Belgian essay "The Cat," which compares acculturated men and the domestic cat, Brontë emphasizes men who hunt for sport routinely torture their victims before killing them. Brontë writes,

> Your husband, for, example, likes hunting very much, but foxes being rare on his land, he would not have the means to pursue this amusement often, if he did not manage his supplies thus: once he has run an animal to its last breath, he snatches it from the jaws of the hounds and saves it to suffer the same infliction two or three more times, ending finally in death. (58)

Both men and cats once relied on the hunt for survival, but now both hunt for sport and play with their prey.

In *Wuthering Heights*, Brontë designates Lockwood, in opposition to the men at the Heights, as the one man who hunts simply for sport. Lockwood's choice of words, "I was invited to devastate the moors," not only informs readers of the hunting expedition which accounts for his final return to the neighborhood of the Heights, but it also gives Brontë's ironic commentary on Lockwood's lack of a "natural" connection to the land (232). The novel begins and ends stressing Lockwood's alienation from understanding the people, the land, and life itself at Wuthering Heights. As an acculturated man from the city, Lockwood is presented by Brontë as foolish. In "Violence in the Sitting Room: *Wuthering Heights* and the Woman's Novel," Patricia Yaeger develops the idea that "Brontë has as much fun as the inhabitants of the Heights poking fun at him [Lockwood]" (204). In Charlotte Brontë's letter of February 15, 1848, to William Smith Williams, she explains why her sister Emily refuses to visit the "great world" of London (Smith 2: 28). Charlotte fears that "Ellis, I imagine, would soon turn aside from the spectacle in disgust" and asserts that Ellis was not interested in studying the "artificial man of cities" (Smith 2: 28). Lockwood is clearly an "artificial man of cities" that Emily Brontë denigrates.

Brontë again emphasizes the destructiveness of the "unnatural" man-made system of a patriarchal culture in her allegorical essay "The Palace of Death." Lonoff notes that Monsieur Heger's assignment was to create an allegorical story in which Death is searching for a prime minister to assist him (233). After interviewing several possibilities, such as Fever, Gout, War, and Plague, Death chooses Intemperance. Since this essay was an assignment given to both Emily and Charlotte Brontë by Monsieur Heger, the difference between the sisters' essays is telling. Both sisters follow the basic story outline given to them; however, Emily's version differs from Charlotte's in that Emily subsumes "Intemperance" under the dominion of "Civilization." Emily's revision highlights that it is *Civilization* who will help Death in his destruction of the human race. Her logic declares that Intemperance is just a symptom of Civilization.

In Emily Brontë's version of "The Palace of Death," Intemperance proclaims the power of Civilization, saying,

> I have a friend before whom this whole assembly will be forced to succumb. Her name is Civilization: in a few years she will come to dwell on this earth with us, and each century will amplify her power . . . I alone

will grow and flourish under her reign; the power of all the others will
expire with their partisans; mine will exist even when I am dead. If once
I make acquaintance with the father, my influence will extend to the
son, and before men unite to banish me from their society, I will have
changed their entire nature and made the whole species an easier prey
for your Majesty [Death], so effectively, in fact, that Old Age will have
almost a sinecure and your palace will be gorged with victims. (228–30)

Because "each century will amplify her [Civilization's] power,"
Brontë implies that this man-made solipsistic system has the ongoing
and ever-increasing potential to destroy those caught up in it.

Brontë's essays serve to highlight her fundamental points about
Civilization. First, Civilization is an unnatural, man-made construction. Second, Civilization depends upon members of the human
species "consuming" each other for survival. In the essays, Brontë
equates civilization with an unnatural distortion of nature. To capture
the essence of this distortion, Brontë distorts metaphors of the natural
activities of eating and drinking into metaphors of illness, such as
when eating becomes "consumption" and drinking becomes "intemperance." The rejection of culture present in Brontë's Belgian essays
exists throughout her poetry, such as her poem to Imagination,
"Plead for Me," where Imagination must "speak and say / Why I did
cast the world away," (9–10) and in her novel *Wuthering Heights*.[4]
Consequently, a theoretical reading of the illnesses within the novel
will serve to highlight Brontë's radical critique and rejection of
Civilization, that is, of Victorian patriarchal culture.

In *Wuthering Heights*, illness becomes a dominant metaphor for
the flaws within a land-based patriarchy since Brontë views the patriarchy as a system where power perpetuates itself no matter what, preying upon the life-energies of those caught within the system. To
highlight the unnaturalness of a cultural system which ultimately
drains individuals' life blood, resulting in illness, Brontë metaphorically creates two supernatural creatures—the vampire and the ghost.
Brontë's representations of vampires and ghosts provide her readers a
clearer view of her rejection of culture, especially given that her alignment of the supernatural and the natural together point toward the
unnaturalness of culture.[5] Developing how male vampires and female
ghosts are two sides of the same coin, Brontë explores how women
become ghosts through the life-denying and blood-draining qualities
inherent in such a self-alienating cultural system, vampiric in its very
nature. Consequently, throughout *Wuthering Heights*, images of vampires and ghosts are interwoven with illness—with "consumption"
and "intemperance" being two of Brontë's most symbolic illnesses.

Brontë's images of vampires underscore patriarchy's emphasis on "possession" while images of ghosts render visible "dispossession" and the powerlessness of the dispossessed. Together these three inter-related metaphors—illness, vampires, and ghosts—signal Brontë's critique of her culture's disease of dis/possession.

Through Brontë's focus on two generations of two specific families to capture the essence of Victorian civilization, we can see that such a patriarchal system attempts to destroy first those whom the power system excludes—women, such as Cathy, and outsiders, such as Heathcliff. *Wuthering Heights* connects the patriarchy's focus on land, power, greed, money, and self-interest with cultural conflicts which result in self-alienation,—an alienation from nature that occurs as an acculturated "self" becomes increasingly alienated from the "body" and from the "land" which nourishes and sustains it, an alienation that is faced by all members of a patriarchal system, the haves and have nots alike. However, Brontë places the greater emphasis on how those outside the system are condemned by the rigidity of the system to lives of dis/possession, self-alienation, conflict, and illness. Since Cathy and Heathcliff's status as outsiders develops into the novel's two most dramatic stories of illness, their respective illnesses together provide a paradigm of the effects of a patriarchal culture on its victims as they move from childhood to adulthood. The other illnesses exist within the paradigm presented by Cathy and Heathcliff's fall into culture.

As children, Cathy and Heathcliff are intimately linked to nature, with them often escaping to the moors. The moors are crucial to understanding Emily Brontë's novel. Whereas in *Villette*, Charlotte Brontë uses illness as a means of returning to the natural body and stepping momentarily outside of cultural constraints, Emily Brontë uses the escape into the moors as the return to the natural body outside of cultural constraints. Strongly contrasting with her sister Charlotte's hopeful reading of illness, Emily Brontë uses illness to signify the power of culture to create such extreme self-alienation that once illness is present, it—often literally, always figuratively—means the kiss of death. Illness and culture are aligned; health and nature are aligned. For Brontë, the only escape from culture is an escape into nature or a return to nature through death.

Thus, because the moors are outside of culture, outside of the land inheritance system, they offer sustenance to the young rebellious outsiders, Cathy and Heathcliff. Yet as adults, because Cathy and Heathcliff cannot live on the moors, the moors come to represent the freedom from the acculturated body found only in death. When Cathy is dying, she says, "I'm sure I should be myself were I once more among the heather on those hills" (98). Cathy's awareness that she will not be able to return to the moors until she is freed from "this shattered prison" of her body grows out of Brontë's idea of the moors as natural body (125). Because Brontë's understanding of nature emphasizes the interrelationship of all beings, Cathy's leaving behind the "shattered prison" of her mortal body will allow her to merge with the greater body of nature.

Hindley's attempts at restricting and acculturating Cathy and Heathcliff can be laughed at, for, with the moors to sustain them, they see themselves as beyond human laws. It is not until their encounter with Thrushcross Grange where the patriarchal bulldog that guards property attacks and bites Cathy, that they—first Cathy, and then Heathcliff—learn to live by man's laws and social norms. Cathy's dog-bite and convalescence for five weeks at Thrushcross Grange result in self-alienating transformations for both Cathy and Heathcliff. Cathy's external transformation into a "lady" is directly presented as the result of her illness when Hindley declares to Cathy upon her return home from her convalescence at Thrushcross Grange, "you look like a lady now" (41). Yet, Cathy's dogbite and convalescence are equally responsible for Heathcliff's later external transformation into a "gentleman" since it is, simultaneously, Cathy's sense of ladylike propriety that prompts her to admit marriage to Heathcliff would "degrade" her and Heathcliff's need to please her that culminates in his becoming a gentleman (63). As Heathcliff tells Cathy upon his return, "I've fought through a bitter life since I last heard your voice, and you must forgive me, for I struggled only for you" (76).

To point out the destructive nature of a cultural system based on dis/possession, Brontë carries these external transformations to their logical ends. At its most extreme, the system requires ladies to become ghosts and gentlemen to become vampires. Cathy loses her vibrant health and is reduced to the wailing girl-ghost Lockwood encounters at the beginning of the novel. Since, according to Heathcliff, Cathy represents the physical manifestation of his "soul" (130), the loss of his "soul" reduces him to being represented as a "vampire" by the conclusion of the novel (252).

While she is dying, Heathcliff laments that his physical strength means that he will outlive Cathy, saying, " 'Do I want to live? What kind of living will it be when you—oh, God! would *you* like to live with your soul in the grave?' " (italics in original, 126). After her death, he despairs, " 'only *do* not leave me in this abyss, where I cannot find you! Oh, God! It is unutterable! I *cannot* live without my life! I *cannot* live without my soul!' " (italics in original, 130). Through the choice of having a second person be equated with an abstract concept like the soul, Brontë can more tangibly show the consequences of the extreme self-alienation induced by cultural constraints. Heathcliff's use of the word "abyss" describes the crisis of his extreme self-alienation because in losing Cathy, he feels he has lost his soul. Cathy chooses the same word, "abyss," to describe her own crisis of self-alienation (98). Cathy tells Nelly,

> But, supposing at twelve years old, I had been wrenched from the Heights, and every early association, and my all in all, as Heathcliff was at that time, and been converted at a stroke into Mrs. Linton, the Lady of Thrushcross Grange, and the wife of a stranger; an exile, and outcast, thenceforth, from what had been my world. You may fancy a glimpse of the abyss where I grovelled! (98)

The external transformations as Heathcliff and Cathy become acculturated into their roles as "gentleman" and "lady" result in an "abyss" of self-alienation because the distance between who they are psychologically and who they are culturally is too great.

Ironically, rather than risk a "glimpse of the abyss" faced by both Cathy and Heathcliff, many readings of *Wuthering Heights* romanticize the love between Cathy and Heathcliff by placing it outside of cultural constraints. For example, in *A Chainless Soul*, Katherine Frank writes, "Catherine and Heathcliff are chainless souls: no social or religious or moral laws constrain them" (220). Frank may be correct that their "souls" are "chainless"; however, Brontë's point is to demonstrate how immoveable are the cultural constraints, the cultural "chains" if you will, that determine how Cathy and Heathcliff live out their lives. Each one's "soul" and "body" are at odds when the cultural forces that demand Cathy marry Edgar rather than Heathcliff condemn them both to lives of self-alienation and illness.[6]

Brontë's representations of such extreme cultural self-alienation, with Cathy as ghost and Heathcliff as vampire, are so intimately interwoven as to be inseparable within her critique of the patriarchy. Because the *two* metaphors work together to represent *one* cultural process, it is difficult to separate them and address each metaphor individually. However, in the cause-and-effect world of logic, because vampires represent the draining of the life blood and ghosts the resultant lack of life, I will begin with the pivotal change in Heathcliff which transforms him from someone whose values are most openly aligned with sharing into someone who is described as a "vampire" (252). Because Brontë's use of vampire imagery extends in application from

Heathcliff to the entire cultural system, which ultimately reduces its victims to becoming ghostlike versions of themselves, an understanding of Heathcliff's transformation is crucial to seeing Brontë's larger cultural paradigm.

Heathcliff's first words in the novel are an assertion of his status as a property owner. He tells the newly arrived Lockwood, " 'Thrushcross Grange is my own, sir' " (3). Lockwood's assessment of his landlord indicates that the cultural contradiction of Heathcliff's position is apparent even to Lockwood's limited perception. Lockwood describes the contradiction in Heathcliff's appearance, writing "He is a dark-skinned gypsy in aspect, in dress and manners a gentleman . . ." (5). Heathcliff's history explains how he can be simultaneously and paradoxically both a "gypsy" and a "gentleman." By being the cultural exception, Heathcliff allows us to see the rules. His status as outsider-turned-insider tears off the veil from the entire cultural system and opens it up for viewing.

From the moment of Heathcliff's introduction into the Earnshaw family, he has had the status of being an outsider, of being a "gipsy brat" with no name (29). Even if we were to follow Q.D. Leavis's reading of Heathcliff as the illegitimate son of Mr. Earnshaw (308), Heathcliff would still be an outsider to the power system. With primogeniture being the law of the land, only the oldest legitimate son will inherit land—and the power and status that land brings. In Earnshaw's ironic choice of giving Heathcliff the name belonging to his oldest son who had died, Brontë emphasizes the artificial nature of such a system of power transmission. Although named for the dead son, Heathcliff cannot be the legal heir who replaces the dead son. Culturally designated the legitimate heir, Hindley perceives the threat of usurpation implicit in Heathcliff's admittance to the family. Hindley's need to emphasize Heathcliff's outsider status results in his calling Heathcliff a " 'vagabond' " (18), in his threatening Cathy and Heathcliff that he would " 'turn him out of the house if we break his orders' " (18), and in his swearing " 'he will reduce him to his right place—' " (18).

Hindley's attempts to "reduce him to his right place" are not successful because the young Heathcliff is healthy and happy without status and luxury as long as he is able to share his life with Cathy and both are aligned with nature. In contrast, from the moment of his childhood request for a violin from Liverpool, Hindley has been aligned with culture.[7] Hindley's inability to connect emotionally with his sister Cathy contrasts sharply with Heathcliff's relationship with her, which emphasizes togetherness and sharing. Even in light of the two men's rivalry, Heathcliff is aligned more with sharing, whereas Hindley is aligned with individual self-interest.[8]

Brontë repeatedly emphasizes the value Heathcliff places on sharing with Cathy. For example, after Cathy and Heathcliff's first encounter with Thrushcross Grange, in which he has seen the Linton children's petty fighting over a pet dog, Heathcliff tells Nelly,

> "When would you catch me wishing to have what Catherine wanted? . . . I'd not exchange, for a thousand lives, my condition here, for Edgar Linton's at Thrushcross Grange—not if I might have the privilege of flinging Joseph off the highest gable, and painting the house-front with Hindley's blood!" (38).

This is a powerful statement of the value Heathcliff places on his emotional life with Catherine over material possessions. Even given the opportunity of revenging Hindley's or Joseph's cruelty toward him, Heathcliff would turn the opportunity down.

Brontë connects Heathcliff's ability to share with his inability to understand the concept of envy. Once Cathy has been transformed into a lady, Nelly reprimands Heathcliff, " 'It looks as if you envied her, because she is more thought of than you,' " but his response makes Nelly admit, "The notion of *envying* Catherine was incomprehensible to him . . ." (italics in original, 44). Throughout the novel, Nelly contrasts with Heathcliff, with her motto of self-interest: "Well, we *must* be for ourselves in the long run" (italics in original, 72). Whereas Heathcliff's loyalty is always constant to Cathy, Nelly constantly shifts her allegiance since Nelly's own self-interest is dictated by her need to please her current employer.

In Cathy's decision that Edgar is an appropriate marriage partner, she feels she has not only her own self-interest but also Heathcliff's best interests at heart. Her logic, " 'if I marry Linton, I can aid Heathcliff to rise, and place him out of my brother's power'," faulty as it is, indicates that she also hopes to promote Heathcliff's interests (64). The reality of Cathy's marriage means, however, she becomes more enmeshed in the system that values land, status, and power, and consequently, she becomes more likely to think in terms of protecting her position. Cathy chastises Heathcliff, " 'You are too prone to covet your neighbour's goods: remember *this* neighbor's goods are mine' " (italics in original, 84). In response, Heathcliff tells Cathy, " 'If they were *mine*, they would be none the less that' " (italics in original, 84). The difference in Cathy and Heathcliff's values become obvious, with Cathy's verbal reminder to Heathcliff, " 'remember *this* neighbor's goods are mine,' " underscoring her new awareness of her dependence upon Edgar's property for her status and her consequent unwillingness to share that property. Heathcliff, in contrast, still thinks in terms of sharing with her and sees no discrepancy between their mutual interests.

Heathcliff is not only willing to share with Cathy, he is willing to share Cathy with Edgar Linton—if that is what Cathy desires. Heathcliff distinguishes between his ability to tolerate Edgar for Cathy's sake and Edgar's inability to tolerate Heathcliff for Cathy's sake. Yet, significantly, Heathcliff's admission of how much this sharing of the woman he loves is costing him includes Brontë's first use of the rhetoric of vampirism. Heathcliff tells Nelly,

> I never would have banished him from her society, as long as she desired his. The moment her regard ceased, *I would have torn his heart out, and drank his blood!* But till then—if you don't believe me, you don't know me—till then, I would have died by inches before I touched a single hair of his head! (italics added, 116)

Heathcliff's sharing of Cathy with Edgar, even if it means a slow painful death to him, shows his continuing ability to put Cathy's interests above his own. Heathcliff's words also indicate his awareness that it is only Cathy's presence that is protecting Edgar from harm. Once she no longer loves Edgar or once she dies, Heathcliff's desire for blood will grow in magnitude.

After Cathy's death and thus the death of his soul, Heathcliff's self-alienation increases. Heathcliff's words upon learning of Cathy's death indicate his inability to envision a way to remedy the self-alienation that he and Cathy have experienced at the hands of culture. His words represent a "curse" rather than a "cure" of their mutual malady. Instead of allowing Cathy's death to heal them both, Heathcliff curses Cathy and himself by saying,

> Catherine Earnshaw, may you not rest, as long as I am living! You said I killed you—haunt me, then! The murdered *do* haunt their murderers, I believe. I know that ghosts *have* wandered on earth. Be with me always—take any form—drive me mad! (italics in original, 130)

Heathcliff's curse becomes fully realized with the dead Cathy having a ghost-like presence in the novel and with Heathcliff being driven "mad" by her loss as represented by his "monomania on the subject of his departed idol" (248).

To understand how Brontë connects Heathcliff's "monomania" with the idea of Heathcliff as a vampire and to Brontë's larger cultural critique, we must first understand this specific Victorian category of mental illness. According to Tytler in "Heathcliff's Monomania: An Anachronism in *Wuthering Heights*," the term "monomania" was first coined around 1810 by Jean-Etienne-Dominique Esquirol, one of the founders of modern psychiatry (331). Monomania, meaning literally "one madness," was to be "distinguished from 'mania' as a form of partial insanity, whereby the understanding is diseased in some respects, and healthy and well-ordered in others" (332). Significantly, Esquirol regarded monomania, as Tytler notes, "first and foremost as 'the disease of advancing civilization,' or more specifically, the disease of the rising bourgeoisie, with its determined quest for self-fulfilment . . ." (334). Historically, as a class, the "rising bourgeoisie" understands "self-fulfillment" in terms of acquiring money, possessions, and land. Esquirol theorizes that monomania, "the disease of going to extremes, of singularization, of one-sidedness" is caused "by thwarted love, by fear, vanity, wounded self-love, or disappointed ambition" (qtd. in Tytler 335). These causal emotions all relate to psychic loss.[9] In Esquirol's theory, psychic loss and the "disease of advancing civilization" are related. In *Wuthering Heights*, Brontë's representation of Heathcliff's monomania also equates psychic loss with the advance of civilization and with the rise of the bourgeoisie, as developed through Heathcliff's rise to power.

Monomania is important to an understanding of Heathcliff's psychology—and by extension to all of the patriarchs—because it provides Brontë's theory on the psychologic need to accumulate material possessions and land. Tytler reads Heathcliff's monomania solely in terms of "his determination to remain in some sort of relationship with Cathy after her death" (335). I agree that this motivation is behind the monomania, but I would extend Tytler's reading of Heathcliff's monomania to include its ability to illuminate what is driving Heathcliff's need to own possessions. In a culture that fosters self-alienation, once culture negates Heathcliff's desire to stay emotionally united with Cathy, psychologically, he is doomed to try and capture what he has lost through material objects which work as representations of her. With Cathy's death, Heathcliff's psychological need becomes even greater, and thus he is even more compelled to accumulate representations of her. For example, in his monomania, Heathcliff collects Wuthering Heights, the Grange, the portrait of Cathy, and other material objects which remind him of Cathy. Wuthering Heights reminds him of Cathy's and his youth together.

Heathcliff himself expresses his "attachment to the house where we lived together," a statement which Cathy repeats to Nelly (78). As the site symbolic of Heathcliff's having lost her, the Grange is important to gain in Heathcliff's attempt to heal an inner psychic wound externally through material objects. Not only does Heathcliff collect Cathy's portrait, but also he keeps her room at the Heights as a shrine to her memory with her books intact. Heathcliff even collects people who remind him of Cathy through the similarity in their eyes.[10] Hindley, Hareton, and Catherine all have Cathy's eyes.

Following Esquirol's connection of loss with the advance of civilization and the rise of the bourgeoisie, Heathcliff's monomania intimately connects with his rise to power. Brontë presents Heathcliff's rise to power as a parody of patriarchal capitalism.[11] As an outsider who becomes a "self-made man"—that glory of Victorian capitalist ideology,—Heathcliff uses the patriarchal laws to promote his own self-interest. Such laws automatically negate the possibility of "self-made women" existing in Victorian England due to the fact that men, not women, have access to economic power.[12] What Heathcliff accomplishes is denied Cathy, since as a Victorian woman, Cathy's only power is sexual. Marriage is Cathy's sole option for ameliorating her status. Heathcliff's outsider status makes his manipulation of the system more clearly visible than the use of it by "legitimate" insiders, such as Mr. Linton who uses bulldogs to protect his property and his rent-day collections of money, or Edgar Linton and Hindley Earnshaw whose propertied status gives them the "right" of refusal in acknowledging Heathcliff's own "right" to be treated with respect regardless of his lack of surname, property, and light skin. As an outsider, Heathcliff's monomania and vampirism are more visibly apparent, yet the patriarchs inside the system are driven by the same psychological needs. Heathcliff's is the psychology of patriarchy. Heathcliff's vampirism mirrors that of Mr. Linton, Edgar, and Hindley. While at the heights of their powers, patriarchs are doomed by the very nature of the system to be metaphorical vampires.

Brontë uses Heathcliff's ascent to power to critique the very worst aspects of patriarchy. Heathcliff manipulates the inheritance and property laws to gain illegal access to lands. In addition to gaining control over land and property, Heathcliff uses his knowledge of the law to gain control over people. Ironically, Heathcliff's monomaniacal madness gives him insight in how to manipulate situations concerning others' states of mental health. Not coincidently, Hindley and Isabella, two of the people dis-possessed through Heathcliff's rise to power, are the ones vulnerable to Heathcliff's control. Heathcliff threatens Hindley by implying to Joseph that he will use his authority to have Hindley locked away. Heathcliff tells Joseph, " 'your master's mad; and should he last another month, I'll have him to an asylum' " (138). Hindley's alleged madness grants Heathcliff the right to remove Hindley to an asylum. But when Heathcliff threatens to confine Isabella for her alleged madness, he plans to confine her at home. Heathcliff tells Nelly, " 'If you are called upon in a court of law, you'll remember her language, Nelly! And take a good look at that countenance—she's near the point that would suit me. No, you're not fit to be your own guardian, Isabella, now: and I, being your legal protector, must retain you in my custody, however distasteful the obligation may be' " (119). By his choice of the words "near the point *that would suit me*," Heathcliff implies he knows he is using his power to drive Isabella to the point of insanity while simultaneously using his legal power as her husband to declare that he alone is responsible for Isabella, even if it means imprisoning her (italics added, 119). The impossible nature of Isabella's predicament is already present in Heathcliff's claiming of *his* right to protect *his* reputation by saying, " 'I'll take care she does not disgrace me by rambling abroad' " (117). Yet Isabella's freedom of movement is not a question of disgrace, it is a question of power. Until her escape, Isabella is a virtual prisoner in her husband's house.[13]

Brontë's critique of patriarchy shows Heathcliff changing from someone willing to share to someone whose psychic loss is so great that paradoxically he is driven to accumulate and possess material wealth, dispossessing others in the process. Not understanding the extreme nature of Heathcliff's inner self-alienation, Nelly and other characters read his actions as being driven by greed and power. However, the imagery Brontë uses to describe Heathcliff's increasing self-alienation presents itself in physiological descriptions where Heathcliff becomes more and more wolf-like, more and more of a "vampire" (252). Giles Mitchell notes in "Incest, Demonism, and Death in *Wuthering Heights*," that Heathcliff is "compared to Satan, devils, demons, fiends, spectres, ghouls, goblins, ghosts, and vampires, as well as to demonically related animals such as wolves" (30). Of these descriptors, Heathcliff is most often described with wolf-like characteristics. In vampire folklore, wolves and vampires are closely related, sometimes considered to be first cousins. According to Brian J. Frost, in *The Monster with a Thousand Faces: Guises of the Vampire in Myth and Literature*, vampires can direct wolves to "do their bidding" and "when it suits their purpose can assume lupine form themselves" (19).

In the first vampire story to be written in English, John Polidori romanticizes the vampire legend of east European folklore by making his vampire an aristocrat. Frost notes that up until the publication of Polidori's *The Vampyre* in 1819, a vampire was portrayed in folklore as an "uncouth disease-ridden peasant" (38). Polidori's vampire Ruthvan is the first aristocrat, as are all of the literary vampires who follow him. While Heathcliff may not truly qualify as aristocracy, it is not until he is in possession of *both* estates—Wuthering Heights and Thrushcross Grange—that Mr. Heathcliff is overtly called a "vampire." Earlier when Heathcliff is in possession of only the Heights, Isabella questions " 'Is Mr. Heathcliff a man? . . . is he a devil?' " (106). Once he owns both estates Nelly questions, " 'Is he a ghoul, or a vampire?' " (252). Through this change in terms, Brontë connects Heathcliff's vampirism to his accumulation of land and power.

Brontë's descriptions of Heathcliff as a "vampire" are echoed by Karl Marx's use of vampire imagery for his critique of capitalism in *Das Kapital*. Writing at approximately the same time and critiquing the same culture, both Brontë and Marx are interested in the de-mystification of a cultural system based on exploitation and both turn to vampire imagery to portray that exploitation.[14] However, Marx's focus is specifically on the effects of industrial capitalism, whereas Brontë's focus is on the effects of patriarchal possession of land, equating possession with dispossession and disease. Both Brontë and Marx try to capture the grotesqueness of the system, by focusing on how the system becomes destructive to its human counterparts and on how the system becomes metaphorically vampiric, based on human blood. Marx writes of the "vampire thirst for the living blood of labour" (282). Marx asserts, "Capital is dead labour, that vampire-like, only lives by sucking live labour, and lives the more, the more labour it sucks" (257).[15] Fittingly, once Heathcliff connects with the vampiric energies of accumulating land and capital, he lives longer than the other characters of his generation. Only two servants, Nelly and Joseph, live as long as he does.[16] Hindley, Cathy, Edgar, and Isabella all precede him in death.

In the days before his death, Heathcliff refuses to eat and his mortal body begins to wither away. Nelly's concern about Heathcliff's physical change prompts her to note, "the same unnatural—it was unnatural—appearance of joy under his black brows; the same blood-less hue, and his teeth visible, now and then, in a kind of smile . . ." (250). Nelly's description of Heathcliff after his death focuses on his vampire-like teeth. Nelly declares, "his parted lips and sharp, white teeth sneered too!" (256). This description recalls Isabella's earlier description of how Heathcliff's " 'sharp cannibal teeth, revealed by cold and wrath, gleamed through the dark' " (137). Whereas Nelly emphasizes Heathcliff's vampiric nature and Isabella emphasizes Heathcliff's cannibal nature, the two terms are related. One term, "cannibal," indicates a man who survives by eating the flesh of other men, a state seen as unnatural because, as already developed, nature's principle of destruction is based on one species feeding off another rather than its own species. The other term, "vampire," indicates another unnatural state because something higher than man exists on the hierarchical food chain and survives by drinking the blood of men. Whether Heathcliff is seen metaphorically as a "cannibal" or a "vampire," Brontë is reinforcing the unnaturalness of the patriarchal cultural system.

In *Wuthering Heights*, it first appears that Emily Brontë is more willing than Charlotte Brontë is in *Shirley* to follow through on her vision of an outsider's ability to challenge the patriarchy. Purportedly, Heathcliff's extended "revenge" on the patriarchal system, which would exclude him, succeeds in doing what Michael Hartley's gun only envisions. Yet, Heathcliff's "revenge" fails because it never actually challenges the system, it only perpetuates it, while making openly visible the violence inherent in the system. It is a misreading to see Emily Brontë's hero as challenging the system. The adult Heathcliff does not challenge the system; he *represents* it. Heathcliff is only a stand-in for a vampiric culture. Consequently, while Heathcliff's actions do not challenge the patriarchal system, Brontë's novel as a whole must be understood as working toward this purpose. Unable to challenge the system which has not only divided him from Cathy but has destroyed her, Heathcliff's death through self-starvation signals that he is no longer self-divided. Because death provides a release from the acculturated self, death represents a return to nature. Heathcliff feels he will be at peace after eighteen years, for in death he feels he will be reunited with Cathy.

Heathcliff's representation as a vampire mirrors Cathy's representation as ghost. Both supernatural creations are Brontë's means of moving outside her readers' frame of reference to point out the destructive nature of a cultural system based on dis/possession which leads to self-alienation. Under such a system, where at its most extreme "possession" requires gentlemen to become vampires, "dis/possession" requires ladies to become ghosts. During her own process of self-alienation, Cathy loses her vibrant health and is reduced to the wailing girl-ghost of Lockwood's dream. Because Cathy's ghost appears in Lockwood's second dream, the dream is best understood in the context of Lockwood's first dream. Both dreams are about the violence of the patriarchy. The first dream, even with its shift in focus, stresses male violence against other men.[17] At first, the dream focuses on the connection between violence and property as represented by Lockwood's need for a "weapon to gain admittance into my own residence" (18). Then it refocuses on religion's way of turning men against each other through the excessive categorizing of sin which ends by making everyone sinners. In this dreamworld where men are judging, condemning, and turning on each other, "having no weapon to raise in self-defence" Lockwood turns on Joseph to take his weapon (20). Soon, "Every man's hand was against his neighbour" (20). If the first dream represents the male violence inherent in a patriarchal culture, the second dream looks more closely at the cost of the violence to the women in such cultures.

In the second dream, this citified self-proclaimed dandy is brought face to face with the price of civilization—woman reduced to ghost. Lockwood's second dream makes visible how the patriarchal fear of women begets cruelty in its need to negate woman's bodily presence. In explaining his violence against Cathy's ghost, whose wrists he rubs over the windowpane until he draws blood, Lockwood admits that "Terror made me cruel" (20). Brontë repeats this image of a victimized and bleeding woman with its underlying message of male fear of women when Linton Heathcliff admits his fear of his cousin Catherine. When Catherine's mouth fills with blood following a blow to her face, Linton announces, " 'I'm afraid of her!' " and retreats physically and emotionally from her (215). Yet, because it is Heathcliff, not Linton, who violently strikes Catherine, Linton could choose to empathize with her as the victim of another's abuse. In both instances, men inflict violence on women, but unable to face their own fear, men distance themselves from women's experience of pain and blood.

As characters, Lockwood and Linton are thematically linked in the novel even though they never meet within the time frame of the novel. Both men are afraid of women. Both men treat women cruelly. Both characters are portrayed as acculturated men, completely unable to adapt to the life at Wuthering Heights. Neither man is ever at home on the moors. Instead, both men are mocked by Brontë as being "civilized" men. It is easier to gain a sense of Brontë's contempt in Linton's case because we see him through others' eyes. Heathcliff continually exudes contempt and disgust with his son; Nelly calls Linton a " 'little perishing monkey' " (208); and Catherine commands him " 'Rise, and don't degrade yourself into an abject reptile—*don't*' " (italics in original, 203). Because Lockwood is one of our narrators, we see him through his own eyes and his own words. Yet, Brontë's narrative technique succeeds in making him appear a self-important fool. Like Linton, he is worthless, that is, without value according to Brontë's own value system, which is significantly at odds with the value system of her culture.[18] As such, Lockwood and Linton offer some of Brontë's most easily recognizable cultural critiques. If we juxtapose Lockwood's dream that "every man's hand was against his neighbor," Brontë's cannibal/vampire metaphor, Linton's selfishness and lust for property, and women's dis/possession, all aspects of Brontë's cultural critique come together in the following scene with Linton at its center.

Linton is self-congratulatory when he tells Nelly about Heathcliff's discussion with Doctor Kenneth, reporting,

> Doctor Kenneth . . . says uncle is dying, truly, at last. I'm glad, for I shall be master of the Grange after him—and Catherine always spoke of it as *her* house. It isn't hers! It's mine—papa says everything she has is mine . . . . She offered to give me them . . . but I told her she had nothing to give, they were all, all mine. And then she cried . . . (italics in original, 214)

When he desires his uncle's death, Linton Heathcliff becomes the mouthpiece for the cannibalistic system which depends upon the deaths of members of the same species. Linton is so consumed with his self-importance that he is not bothered that his right of possession depends upon the death of his uncle and upon the denial of his cousin's right of possession. Moreover, Linton's lust for land makes him completely oblivious to the emotional component of what he sees simply as a land transaction. He is not aware of his cousin's feelings about her father's approaching death or her own approaching dispossession. Linton, like Lockwood, represents acculturated man at his worst.

Lockwood and Linton are not Brontë's only representations of men who fear women or the bodily and emotional intimacy women represent. Male fear of women in Brontë's novel ranges from Joseph's misogyny to Edgar's attempts to placate Cathy's temper. As our male narrator, Lockwood's purpose is to put this experience into words. His admission that the sight of a female ghost was "almost maddening me with fear" and that "Terror made me cruel" is significant because it directly links fear and violence (20). While *both* of Lockwood's dreams allow us a peek into the violence of the male psyche, the second dream specifically shows the cost of male violence to women. In exploring one woman's dispossession of her body, through the representation of Cathy as a ghost of her former self, trying to reclaim her home, the dream speaks to all women's dispossession. Lockwood recounts how Cathy-as-ghost declares, " 'I'm come home, I'd lost my way on the moor!' " (20). From his secure position of male privilege, Lockwood condemns her walking the earth for twenty years, judging her ghostly exile as a "just punishment for her mortal transgressions" (22). However, Brontë's reading of Cathy's exile is more compassionate in its presentation of the plight of the girl-ghost. Instead of blaming the victim as Lockwood does, Brontë has Cathy directly confront Heathcliff for his role and Edgar's in her death, saying, " 'You and Edgar have broken my heart, Heathcliff! . . . You have killed me—and thriven on it, I think' " (124). And Cathy foresees that after her death, " 'I shall not be at peace' " (124). Since ghosts are thought to haunt to have specific wrongs addressed, Cathy's ghost haunts to have wrongs done to her addressed.

Cathy's ghost metaphorically represents the situation of all acculturated women under a patriarchal system which denies them bodily presence through the process of dis/possession. The self-alienation inherent in becoming a proper lady is disease-producing. As Gilbert and Gubar proclaim, "to be a lady is to be diseased" (268). Cathy's ghostly reappearance after death simply represents the most extreme case because Brontë represents the other female characters' fading away in life. I concur with Gilbert and Gubar's reading that Frances is "already half a ghost" (268) and that "As a metaphor, Frances's tuberculosis means that she is in an advanced state of just that *social* 'consumption' which will eventually kill Catherine, too" (italics in original, 268–69). Isabella also begins her descent into a ghostlike presence when she pleads "ill health" (79) and Nelly comments, "she was dwindling and fading before our eyes" (79). In addition, Isabella's move to the south, near London, effectively makes her a ghost-like presence in the text long before her death finalizes this point. In fact, *all* of the married women within the novel can be seen to cast their ghostly presence over the book because they all, save one, become ill and die years before their husbands. Mrs. Earnshaw dies four years before Mr. Earnshaw.[19] Frances's death following the birth of Hareton occurs four-and-a-half years before Hindley's death.[20] Cathy's death in childbirth occurs eighteen years before Edgar's death. Isabella's escape from Heathcliff probably adds years to her life, yet she still dies five years before Heathcliff.[21] The first Mrs. Linton is the sole exception since her illness and death from fever occur simultaneously with her husband's. Brontë's decision to ghost-out

her female characters serves to highlight a patriarchal culture's
dis/possession of women and its dependence upon the denial and
death of women's bodies, which culturally mirrors its dependence
upon the death and denial of nature.[22]

Brontë's critique of patriarchy's dis/possession of women emphasizes that women are not allowed to own land. The dis/possession of
land is shown to be intimately connected with questions of possession
of the women's bodies and identities. Since the patriarchal system of
power is aligned to land-ownership—with land passed down through
the male line—issues concerning inheritance of land are prominent
throughout the novel. This self-enclosed power system is problematic
for all of the outsiders in the novel, whether it be for outsiders based
on gender, such as Cathy, Isabella, Catherine, and Nelly, or for outsiders based on ethnicity or race, such as Heathcliff. Nonetheless,
because male gender grants status, Heathcliff can work to manipulate
the system and gain land, prestige, and power. As women, Cathy,
Isabella, Catherine, and Nelly are closed off from the possibility of
owning land. As a servant, Nelly is removed even more completely
from the option of owning land.[23] Cathy, Isabella, and Catherine all
must face the event of being dispossessed of the land which they grew
up knowing as "home." Since a sense of identity is connected with
"home" and thus with a sense of geography and landscape, the
dispossession of land begets one level of the dispossession of identity.

In terms of inheritance, there is no question that Cathy's brother
Hindley and Isabella's brother Edgar will inherit their families' respective estates. By focusing on issues of inheritance, Brontë's novel
emphasizes that the system perpetuates itself through the generations,
so that the vulnerability of girls at the hands of their fathers continues
with women remaining vulnerable to the whims of their brothers who
inherit the land. Brontë twice addresses women's vulnerability at the
hands of their more powerful brothers, first by Cathy and later by
Isabella. Cathy writes in her journal of her early realization that with
her father's death, Hindley now has power over her, power enough to
make her cry. Cathy writes, " 'How little did I dream that Hindley
would ever make me cry so! . . . My head aches, till I cannot keep it
on the pillow' " (18). His power over her is directly related to her
headaches, her first symptom of dis-ease with the culture. Brontë
stresses that Cathy's dilemma is not a singular event, dependent upon
one man's individual personality and caprice, but an integral part of
the power structure that will play itself out generation after generation, through Cathy's insight that young Hareton, presently just a
baby, will grow up to be similar to Hindley. Cathy's insight that

Hareton will follow Hindley implies that his gender alone is enough to distance him from the women around him as he grows up to replace the males before him in the power structure. Cathy rewords Nelly's "How sweetly he [Hareton] smiles in his sleep!" (62) and rephrases it, "Yes; and how sweetly his father curses in his solitude!" (62). This triangle of Cathy, Nelly, and a baby, which leads to Cathy's acknowledgment of her brother's power, is reproduced with a modified triangle, having Isabella, Nelly, and a baby, when Isabella, after her escape from Heathcliff, also acknowledges her brother's power over her. In this scene, Isabella's bleeding head wound replaces Cathy's headache, magnifying the symptoms of cultural disease.

Isabella's escape from her husband's house foregrounds her lack of a home since she is unwelcome in her brother's house. Isabella's dilemma manifestly expresses her powerlessness at the hands of her husband, yet implicit in her dilemma is her vulnerability at the hands of her brother. Isabella's awareness that both Heathcliff and Edgar are to blame for her homelessness is voiced when she tells Nelly, " 'And besides, Edgar has not been kind, has he?' " (133). Given that Edgar disowned her once she formed her alliance with Heathcliff and disclaimed any connection with her, his lack of concern for her has placed her in an extremely vulnerable position where not only does her husband have all of the legal rights within their union, but she has no male figure with any semblance of power to offset her own lack of power within the marriage—within the culture—and to look out for her best interests. Isabella's understanding that Edgar is "not nice" echoes Cathy's insight that Hindley can make her cry.

Because of the patriarchal nature of the culture, not only can women not own land, they are themselves seen as possessions. When Lockwood arrives at the Heights, he questions to whom Catherine belongs. First, Lockwood uses the possessive pronoun when in talking with Heathcliff, he assumes that Catherine is "*your* amiable lady," "*your* wife" (italics added, 10). Once Heathcliff declares his wife to no longer be living, Lockwood turns to Hareton and declares him "the favoured *possessor* of the beneficent fairy" (italics added, 11). Heathcliff corrects him, saying "we neither of us have the privilege of *owning* your good fairy; her mate is dead" (italics added, 11). Within approximately one page of text, Brontë has attached Catherine to three different men—Heathcliff, Hareton, the dead mate—who could be her potential "owner" or "possessor." She is not currently "owned," only because the man who "owns" her through marriage is dead.

Under patriarchy, women's names change as they change their status from single women to married women. Cathy's early deliberations over her name "Cathy Earnshaw," "Cathy Heathcliff," "Cathy Linton" set up the dilemma of women not having one constant name from which to claim a steadfast source of identity (15–16). Legally, as married women, under Victorian laws of *couverture*, they become one person in the eyes of the law and that one is the husband. Not being separate legal entities, women have no rights to deny their husbands access to their bodies nor do they have rights over the children given birth from their bodies. Consequently, they are not allowed to own their own bodies nor their own children.[24] Because Victorian children were legally the property of their fathers, Linton is Heathcliff's property. It does not matter that Isabella "desired him to remain under my [Edgar's] guardianship" to protect her son and keep him from his father; her wishes are null and void in the eyes of the law (157). As a magistrate, Edgar Linton knows the law negates Isabella's concerns, no matter how legitimate and justifiable these concerns are, and he concedes Linton must go to his father once Heathcliff has demanded "*his* lad" (italics added, 157). Heathcliff's own certainty of his legal right to his child is first asserted when he claims, " 'But I'll have it . . . when I want it' " (142). After Isabella's death, Heathcliff tells Nelly when she brings Linton to him, "I feared I should have to come down and fetch *my property* myself" (italics added, 160). In *Ecofeminism as Politics*, Ariel Salleh explains the logic behind the patriarchal legal system which claims children as men's property. Salleh theorizes, "At childbirth, it is the man who 'lacks.'. . . Nevertheless, paternity, basically a property relation, soon reinstates the correct 1/0 order of things. Once Named, the baby becomes 'his' child and the woman is incidental again" (39).[25]

Within a system where women have only sexual power, Cathy has no choice but to marry. Culturally denied any form of independent power on her own terms, she covets the power that Edgar's money, land, and status offers. In marrying Edgar, Cathy hopes to outwit the system, simultaneously promoting her own and Heathcliff's interests. Because of her naiveté about her own powerlessness once married, she does not understand that marriage will ensure a separation between her and her childhood friend. Cathy tells Nelly, " 'I shouldn't be Mrs. Linton were such a price demanded!' " (64). Cathy assumes she can have both men in her life without consequences. Cathy's disclosures to Nelly show Cathy's greater loyalty to Heathcliff and her sense that marriage to Edgar Linton is her only option, especially given that Cathy does not want the two childhood friends to be separated. Until Heathcliff actually leaves, Cathy seems not to have considered, even remotely, the option of him leaving. Yet, as a man, Heathcliff does have the option to leave and make his fortune elsewhere, an option denied Cathy. Cathy sees only that she must marry and that Hindley's degradation of Heathcliff rules him out as a possible marriage partner. When Cathy tells Nelly, " 'if Heathcliff and I married, we should be beggars," she does not exaggerate the case (64).

Because Cathy does not fully understand the patriarchal system, she does not appreciate until it is too late that once she has legally aligned herself with Edgar, she is *more* constrained by the system than before. She no longer has any legal power over her own destiny since she is no longer considered her own person in the eyes of the law. A married woman, she no longer can choose whether or not to stay connected to Heathcliff. She can petition, coax, entreat, and cajole her husband to tolerate Heathcliff's presence in their life, but the ultimate power of decision lies with her husband. Edgar's self-interest will be more of a determining factor than his wife's affections. Cathy's marriage to Edgar effectively divides her sense of self. Once she sacrifices herself in an effort to manipulate the system and help Heathcliff, she becomes self-divided, with the conflicts inherent in her divided loyalty pulling her into illness.

Ultimately, Cathy's self-division leads to her death. In " 'I'll Cry Myself Sick': Illness in *Wuthering Heights*," Gorsky develops Cathy's internal conflicts, asserting,

> Acknowledging the power of society, Brontë shows how Catherine reacts internally to the external division between a natural free spirit and a trammeled nineteenth-century lady. Suffering from not being allowed to be herself, from conflict with society, and from thwarted love, divided from her soul and her soul-mate, she both acts out and falls ill. (178)

Gorsky is correct that Cathy does become ill when Heathcliff leaves. This illness lasts three years, postponing her marriage to Edgar. Yet, this should not be seen as Cathy's first illness but as a continuation of the illness which signified her fall into culture—the dogbite of Skulker. From that point on, the text makes clear that Cathy fades by degrees. Once in the jaws of culture, Cathy never fully rallies from her first illness, nor from any of the consequent illnesses.

On Heathcliff's return, Cathy symbolically tries to force the two men together when "she seized Linton's reluctant fingers and crushed them into his [Heathcliff's]" (75). Cathy realizes her health and happiness depends upon the two men tolerating each other because then she would no longer feel self-divided. Her solution is to try to force an external joining of their bodies, as represented by their hands, rather than resolve her internal conflict. Cathy's external solution fails when the conflicts between the two men escalate, and Cathy finally forces a confrontation between the two men by locking the kitchen door so that Edgar cannot call his servants to act his part in the confrontation. Cathy's explanation of her actions here is significant. She declares, " 'Edgar, I was defending you and yours: and I wish Heathcliff may flog you sick, for daring to think an evil thought of me!' " (90). The scene ends with Edgar not being "sick" from flogging but from his realization of his momentary predicament of vulnerability. Nelly tells us that "Mr. Edgar was taken with a nervous trembling, and his countenance grew deadly pale" (90); however, his secure position within the patriarchy insures that this momentary lapse into illness is just that—momentary. In this confrontation scene, Brontë points out that the patriarchy is not based on physical strength, for Edgar has more power than Heathcliff, just as later the "perishing monkey" Linton Heathcliff will have more power than the stronger, more physically healthy Hareton (208).

Heathcliff's greater physical strength is negated in his inability to compete with Edgar, for as Heathcliff tells Nelly, " 'But, Nelly, if I knocked him down twenty times, that wouldn't make him less handsome, or me more so. I wish I had light hair and a fair skin, and was dressed and behaved as well, and had a chance of being as rich as he will be!' " (45). Edgar's light skin is an important signifier of Edgar's greater cultural power. The power signified by light skin seems a fitting topic in a discussion of vampirism and of a patriarchal culture's simultaneous dependence on and fear of nature, especially because light skin, symbolic of a lack of blood, is aligned with cultural power throughout the novel. In *Wuthering Heights*, light skin equates with cultural power because light skin is a sign not only of being English, rather than of another ethnic or racial origin, but also a sign of being financially well off enough to forego doing labor outdoors, such as when Cathy's lightened hands after her five weeks at the Grange signal her ascent to becoming a "lady" (41). Not only does Heathcliff witness Cathy's transformation into a lady with her whitened hands, but he also witnesses Hindley's cultural transformation into a gentleman who has "lost his colour" after his return from school (36). Brontë juxtaposes Hindley's newly whitened skin, Hindley's new rise in power within the family following his father's death, and Hindley's removing himself from manual labor by degrading Heathcliff's status to that of farmhand. Because of the male-bias within the cultural system, as men become acculturated, their light skin symbolizes greater cultural power, such as when Hindley's lightened skin indicates a move up the power system. However, women's lightened skin, while representing that they are "ladies" and hence have more status than working-class men and women, does not represent an equivalent degree of cultural power within their own class. This acculturated power is shown to be at the expense of the women's natural power and the lightened skin becomes a symptom of their sickening and fading away into ghosts.

Brontë also points out that emotional power, like physical power, is not sufficient to outmaneuver the patriarchy. Cathy assumes she can outsmart Edgar emotionally since he bends his will to hers to keep her happy; however, he holds the land and the legal power. Her insight that "I have such faith in Linton's love that I believe I might kill him, and he wouldn't wish to retaliate" is inaccurate. Because of the power difference, he can only love her until he kills her (77). The scene developed earlier where Edgar, not Cathy, is the cat in the cat and mouse analogy demonstrates this point.

Brontë indicates that Cathy's illness-as-strategy is yet another insufficient attempt at outmaneuvering the patriarchy. Gorsky contends that Cathy understands illness as a form of power over others, writing, "She [Cathy] tries to use her illness to order the world, but finally her illness and her world destroy her" (177). After the row with Edgar that ultimately results in their engagement, Cathy threatens him by saying, " 'And now I'll cry—I'll cry myself sick' " (56). Later after the row with Edgar where he demands that she choose between him and Heathcliff, Cathy tells Nelly to tell Edgar " 'I'm in danger of being seriously ill' " (91). Cathy even projects on Edgar her own ability to be ill at will when she grumbles, " 'he affirmed I was cruel and selfish for wishing to talk when he was so sick and sleepy. He always contrives to be sick at the least cross!' " (77). Whether Edgar is truly ill, he is successful at sidelining the discussion whereas Cathy's attempts are much less successful. Even within illness, the male's position of power remains.[26]

Cathy's illness is a distorted strategy of power, for it is based on the illusion that through illness, she can control others through controlling herself. Cathy tells Nelly of her plan of action, " 'Well, if I cannot keep Heathcliff for my friend, if Edgar will be mean and jealous, I'll try to break their hearts by breaking my own' " (92). Her strategic use of illness is aimed at affecting both men, but her words indicate her sense that the source of her powerlessness is at the hands of her husband. She realizes the self-destructive nature of her attempt. Her illness may affect the men in her life, but only at the cost of her own health and life because she will not succeed except through death.

Cathy's death mirrors Frances's death before her with both women's deaths following childbirth. In giving birth to the next generation, both Cathy and Frances lose their own lives. Unable to describe overtly the loss of blood and the loss of life involved in these childbirths, Brontë uses metaphors which will not shock the sensibilities of her Victorian audience.[27] Taking into account Brontë's metaphorical language, both women's deaths can be seen as represented in the text as directly related to their loss of blood. Frances's illness of consumption serves this purpose because consumption and loss of blood would be linked in the minds of Brontë's contemporary readers. Cathy's loss of blood is also described indirectly through metaphor, but here the description is once removed. It is not represented through an illness that Cathy herself has, as with Frances's consumption, but rather it is represented, twice, through another's loss of blood. First, Cathy's loss of blood is metaphorically represented by the blood on the lapwing feathers, an image given during her delirium. The birds' deaths foretells Cathy's own imminent death. In a second metaphorical representation of Cathy's loss of blood during labor and delivery, Brontë describes Heathcliff's loss of blood as he waits outside. Given the metaphorical connection Brontë has created between Cathy and Heathcliff, Heathcliff's loss of blood must be a part of our reading of why Cathy's giving birth can simultaneously become Cathy's death: she has lost too much blood.

Cathy's death, in addition to having a dramatic impact on Heathcliff, also affects Edgar and Hindley. Edgar removes himself from his magistrate position, stops his socializing with the community, becomes a ghost of his former self, and ultimately dies of a slow fever. Until Cathy's death, her sisterly affection has protected Hindley from "bodily harm" at the hands of Heathcliff (78). Both she and Isabella make this point (140). However, once Cathy's death removes her emotional presence from the lives of these two antagonistic men, murder and suicide become new possibilities. Heathcliff's desire for revenge almost results in his murdering Hindley, as when Heathcliff "kicked and trampled on him" in one of his drunken stupors (138). Hindley's own self-destructiveness accelerates, too, and he chooses suicide from alcohol by drinking himself to death. Similar to Cathy and Isabella, Nelly is also aware that women serve emotional roles in the lives of men by preventing their destroying themselves or others. Nelly argues with Hindley's demand of "no women in the house" because she does not want to leave him alone at the Heights after Hindley's wife's death and Cathy's removal to the Grange through marriage (70). Equating the removal of the women from the Heights with Hindley's self-destruction, Nelly tells Hindley that "he got rid of all decent people only to run to ruin a little faster" (70).

Cathy's death, like Frances's death before her, shows that in all cases, the deaths of women are destructive to the men who loved them. Hindley becomes a broken man at Frances's death, and Heathcliff and Edgar follow his lead at Cathy's death. The women's deaths are pivotal in accelerating the men's self-destruction by intensifying their self-alienation because the women represented their connection to nature, to the body, to the emotions. Yet none of these men use their power to take steps toward creating a world which would be more healthy to the women they love, and by extension, more healthy to themselves. Instead, their need to focus on their own self-interest makes them "consume" their women, not realizing by doing so they move closer to their own self-destruction.

Thus, even though the women are much more immediately affected by the cultural disease of dis/possession, Brontë's critique ultimately demonstrates that patriarchy results not only in women-as-ghosts of their former selves but also in men-as-ghosts. Heathcliff is aligned with vampire imagery because his gender grants him power denied women, yet even Heathcliff's self-alienation ends with him as a ghost, who according to "the country folks, if you asked them, would swear on their Bible that he *walks*" (italics in original, 257). Since all of the men under patriarchy depend metaphorically upon the blood and bodies of the women, all of the novel's men are more aligned with vampirism until they fall into dis-empowerment through old age, illness, or alcoholism. With their women already dead, and past their own days of vampiric power, Heathcliff, Hindley, and Edgar end as ghost-like versions of their younger selves.

Turning to the second generation, Brontë creates a new heroine and a new hero to test the same old patriarchal power system. Catherine, unlike her mother Cathy, is an acculturated lady from birth, with her acculturation manifested in her fair skin. While Catherine's higher social position should grant her greater power, Brontë repeatedly links Catherine's paleness with powerlessness, such as when, after she has lost the battle to keep Linton's letters, Nelly describes Catherine as "pale and red about the eyes, and marvelously subdued in outward aspect" (176). Compared with her mother's early healthy exuberance and rebelliousness, Catherine is already ghostlike. Nelly's telling Catherine "your cheeks are bloodless" (177), Nelly's describing that Catherine's "countenance grew wan" (202), and Zillah's reporting to Nelly of Catherine's "white face and heavy eyes" (223), all reinforce that Catherine's acculturated paleness is related to her lack of power. Catherine's transformation from "lady" to "ghost" is already in process.

For Catherine, as for her mother before her, critical moments of powerlessness are accentuated in the novel with explicit references to illness. Catherine twice strategically uses illness to manipulate Nelly during her courtship with Linton Heathcliff. First, Catherine feigns illness, crying " 'Ellen! Ellen! come upstairs—I'm sick!' " in her efforts to speak alone with Nelly after her discovery of the theft of Linton's love letters (174). The second time occurs when Nelly's restored health following her three-week cold ends Catherine's freedom to ride over to the Heights in the evenings to visit Linton. Not wanting her clandestine visits to end, Catherine uses illness as a strategy. At first, Catherine worries that Nelly will relapse and make herself sick by pushing herself too hard. When this strategy fails because Nelly herself does not fear a relapse, Catherine finally pleads a "head-ache" herself (188). She feigns illness in order to break from Nelly's presence. In both cases, Catherine's use of a feigned illness shows her limited power.[28]

Nevertheless, Catherine's familial position grounds her in ways unavailable to any other woman in the novel. Unlike her mother Cathy or her aunt Isabella, Catherine is an only child. As an only child, without a brother to usurp her rights as heir, Catherine is not immediately aware of her own position of vulnerability. This unique familial position accounts for Catherine's ability to express directly her disapproval over her dispossession—even though it has not been enough to prevent her dispossession in the first place. Catherine's exchange with Heathcliff is the most overt expression in the novel of all of the women's dispossession of land:

> "You shouldn't grudge a few yards of earth for me to ornament, when you have taken all my land!"
> "Your land, insolent slut? you never had any!" said Heathcliff.
> "And my money." (244)

Catherine is determined to have the last word in this exchange. However, legally, Heathcliff is right. Cathy "never had any" land because as a woman, she is not part of the male line who will inherit (244). Heathcliff's chosen insult of "slut" is significant in this context, for it highlights the gendered division of power under a patriarchal culture where women have only sexual power in contrast to men's economic and legal power. Heathcliff's insult points to the limitations of sexual power because men can use it against women by implying that sexual power is appropriate only in the reproduction of children. If a woman is not a mother, then, by default, she must be a whore. Because the term "slut" indicates a lack of any real power, Heathcliff's put-down of Catherine as an "insolent slut" reinforces Catherine's inability to address her dis/possession (244).

Because of her status as only child, Catherine proves an exception to the rule of inheritance when she momentarily repossesses her familial estates. The land becomes hers by a twist of fate which leads to the death of the entire male line, including Heathcliff who has married into the family. As Charles Percy Sanger delineates in "The Structure of *Wuthering Heights*," old Mr. Linton's will originally left the Grange to Catherine's father Edgar; however, since Edgar had no sons, it by-passes Edgar's daughter to start down the male line of Isabella's descendants. Thus, Linton Heathcliff is to inherit the Grange. Once Linton's death follows Edgar's, because Heathcliff is still alive, his claims to the Grange are "in his wife's right" (her property would be his through marriage) and in his son's name (225). However, Nelly clarifies that Linton's status as a "minor" means Heathcliff's claiming the land through his son is problematic (225). Yet, Nelly concedes that Catherine "destitute of cash and friends, cannot disturb his possession" (225). Heathcliff is quick to contradict Nelly's assertion that if Linton died, "Catherine would be the heir" by replying, "There is no clause in the will to secure it so; his property would go to me; but to prevent disputes, I desire their union . . ." (166).[29] Although Catherine does reclaim her familial land after Heathcliff's death, the land is to be hers only momentarily, for as soon as she marries Hareton, legal ownership will again pass out of her hands.

By the novel's ending, Catherine's only personal experience of illness is brought about as a result of her powerlessness in the struggle between Heathcliff and Edgar over land. However, before Catherine's position as pawn in the fighting between men over land is shown through her own illness, Brontë develops the theme of illness by having Edgar and Linton both ill and in a race toward death. Nelly tells us that Edgar "divined that one of his enemy's purposes was to secure the personal property, as well as the estate, to his son, or rather himself; yet why he did not wait till his decease, was a puzzle to my master, because ignorant how nearly he and his nephew would quit the world together" (215). Heathcliff's machinations to force Catherine to marry Linton before Edgar's death are to insure his own access to the land. Significantly, this patriarchal power struggle over land with Catherine as pawn not only is itself explicitly represented through illness; it results in Catherine's illness.

Thus, Catherine's first authentic illness occurs after both the death of her father and of her husband. After Linton Heathcliff's death, she tells Heathcliff, " 'you have left me so long to struggle against death, alone, that I feel and see only death! I feel like death!' " (224). Zillah, Heathcliff's housekeeper, tells Nelly, " 'And she looked like it too!' " (224). Catherine's looking as pale as "death" parallels with her first experience of dispossession: Catherine has lost her father, husband, land, property, and name. Catherine's convalescence, reported by Zillah, is for "a fortnight" (224). Upon leaving her sickroom, Catherine comments, " 'I've been starved a month and more' " (226).

Numerous feminist scholars, such as Gilbert and Gubar, Gorsky, Frank, and Guiliana Giobbi, have focused on the theme of hunger in *Wuthering Heights*, showing how women's hunger relates to powerlessness. Here, Catherine's feeling of being "starved" relates to her current situation of being dispossessed of her property and unable to disturb Heathcliff's possession of it. Brontë emphasizes the magnitude of her powerlessness by having two female servants, Zillah and Nelly, discuss Catherine's plight. Zillah informs Nelly: " 'She's as poor as you or I—poorer, I'll be bound; you're saving, and I'm doing my little all, that road' " (225). Zillah's words capture the economic devastation of Catherine's dispossession. Brontë further develops Catherine's plight with Zillah's question to Nelly, " 'And what will all her learning and her daintiness do for her, now?' " (225). From a servant's perspective, middle-class learning and culture is meaningless when not aligned with land and money. Zillah's solution for Catherine is marriage to Hareton, which Zillah foresees will " 'bring her pride a peg lower' " (225).

The alliance between Catherine and Hareton, which will lead to their marriage and their move to the Grange, originates during Hareton's convalescing from a gun accident in which "His gun burst . . . a splinter cut his arm, and he lost a good deal of blood . . ." (238). Within Brontë's metaphorical realm, Hareton's loss of blood symbolizes his movement toward becoming an acculturated man. Originally aligned with Nature and the moors, once indoors, Hareton's affections are realigned, shifting from Heathcliff to Catherine, from outdoor labor to book reading, from nature to culture.

For Hareton's illness to succeed in creating an alliance between Catherine and him, it must follow Catherine's own illness. Prior to her forced marriage, Catherine thought her social position mirrored that of her father. As the only child of a landed esquire and local magistrate, Catherine assumed she too had social power. Her dispossession of land and money which follows her marriage to Linton and his subsequent death gives Catherine a new awareness of her vulnerability within the patriarchal cultural system. This new awareness of her vulnerability accounts for her new openness toward the idea of allying herself with Hareton. Prior to her dispossession, Catherine felt she was socially above him.[30] Now, both are dealing with their respective dispossession at the hands of Heathcliff.

The cousins' alliance which seems to offer so much promise at the end of the novel must be seen both in terms of how it fits in with Brontë's larger framework where acculturation results in ladies becoming ghosts through dispossession and gentlemen becoming vampires through possession and in terms of how it mirrors other alliances gained through illness that occur throughout the novel. An analysis of the plot structure of *Wuthering Heights* reveals that illness is central in structuring all of the main events in the novel. Brontë's novel reads as if it were a play and as if Brontë were a dramaturge using illnesses to decide who was on-stage or off-stage at certain points to develop what new possibilities each grouping of characters provide in her effort to test the limits of the power inherent in the patriarchal system. Seen in this light, Brontë's strategic use of illnesses functions to create new alliances to shift the power relationships. For example, Cathy's alliance with the higher-classed Linton first starts during Cathy's convalescence from the dogbite. Cathy's new friendship with the Lintons, specifically with Edgar Linton, shifts her allegiance to Heathcliff. Following Heathcliff's measles, Nelly becomes Heathcliff's ally which results in the fact that "Hindley lost his last ally" (31). Isabella's illness, which takes Edgar Linton away from home, triggers the first meeting between Catherine and Hareton when Catherine makes use of her father's absence to escape the confines of the Park for the first time. Similarly, Edgar's and Nelly's colds, which conveniently overlap in time, make possible Catherine's growing friendship with Linton Heathcliff. Linton Heathcliff's own ill-health plays a role in his pleading with Catherine to marry him because he believes that her presence will protect him from Heathcliff. Even such unlikely characters as Isabella and Hindley are brought together as allies through Brontë's careful structuring of the novel's use of illnesses if we consider that, when his alcoholism is at its height, Hindley asks Isabella to become his ally against Heathcliff. Nevertheless, whatever new alliances are formed through illness in efforts to challenge the patriarchy, Brontë presents them as faltering under the rigidity of the system. Knowing readers will hope that Catherine and Hareton will prove the exception, Brontë has both narrators, Lockwood and Nelly, anticipate such optimistic readings of their alliance.

Nelly tells Lockwood, " 'I shall envy no one on their wedding-day—there won't be a happier woman than myself in England' " (241). Lockwood romanticizes the alliance between Catherine and Hareton when he gives his parting commentary on the new lovers, saying " '*They* are afraid of nothing . . . Together they would brave Satan and all his legions' " (italics in original, 258). Both Nelly's and Lockwood's words promise a happy conclusion. Through Lockwood and Nelly, we see Catherine and Hareton's alliance as promising and the closing of the Heights and the remove to the Grange as a progressive step. Yet, neither Lockwood's values nor Nelly's values are those of Emily Brontë's. This happy ending must be read as suspect. Nevertheless, even critics who focus on the "unreliability" of either one, or both, of these narrators, tend to follow the typical optimistic view of the ending.[31] Perhaps finding relief in the knowledge that the violence of the first generation is muted in the lives of the second, critics, almost unilaterally, interpret the ending of *Wuthering Heights* as an affirmative step toward resolution and harmony, often focusing on the peaceful coexistence of nature and culture that Catherine's milder nature will make possible. For example, Gorsky's optimistic reading of the ending asserts, "Her [Cathy's] daughter moves from Grange to Heights and back, but because she differs in nature and nurture, this Catherine is only injured emotionally. Once healed, she can unite the two worlds in herself and for the future" (179). Or, as Beth Newman affirms that the novel "revises domestic relations to suggest mutuality, not the unequal power relations of male dominance" (1036). Or, as Terry Eagleton asserts, "the antimonies of passion and civility will be harmonized by the genetic fusion of both strains in the offspring of Catherine and Hareton, effecting an equable interchange of Nature and culture, biology and education" (119).

Even with his emphasis on the "equable interchange of Nature and culture," Eagleton is the rare critic in his willingness to look beneath the surface happiness of the ending when he continues, "But those possibilities of growth are exploratory and underdeveloped, darkened by the shadow of the tragic action" (119). To give Brontë's novel its full due, we must look beyond Lockwood's and Nelly's happy endings to grasp Brontë's dark vision. Eagleton's reading takes a step into the darkness in its ability to see that "The world of the Heights is over" (119) and that the marriage of Hareton to Catherine symbolizes the "grafting of the values of a dying class on to a thriving progressive one" (119).[32] Eagleton explores the class implications of Hareton's new position as squire with dual ownership of the Heights and Thrushcross Grange, writing, "As a survivor of yeoman stock," Hareton's

> social class is effectively swallowed up into the hegemony of the
> Grange . . . since the basis of that fusion is the absorption and effective
> disappearance of a class on which the novel places considerable value,
> Emily's conclusion is a good deal more subtly shaded than anything in
> her sister's work. (119–20)

Yet even Eagleton's brilliant analysis, with its appreciation for the
disappearance of life at the Heights, stops short. While focusing on
Hareton's rise to power and possession, Eagleton's more literal reading does not pull into play Brontë's metaphors associated with such a
self-alienating cultural transformation. With Hareton's acculturation
into a "gentleman," the process of his transformation into a "vampire" has been set in motion.[33] In Brontë's metaphorical realm, land-
possessing patriarchs are vampires since their possession will be based
on someone else's dispossession. Like Heathcliff, who is overtly called
a "vampire" once he owns two estates, Hareton, soon to be the owner
of two estates, will become one of Brontë's metaphorical vampires.

In addition, Eagleton's class-based reading neglects to take into
account issues of gender. Consequently, Eagleton completely omits
mentioning Catherine's dispossession, the attendant consequence of
Hareton's rise. At first it appears Catherine's position of pawn
between men fighting for power and land concludes with Heathcliff's
death. Yet, through Brontë's strategic choice to end the novel with
Catherine as a young widow, before her second marriage is finalized,
the novel closes prior to Catherine's second experience of being
dispossessed of her land, her name, her legal rights, her power. Hareton,
not Catherine, will own the land where Catherine was born. Once
married, Catherine will follow her mother and her aunt before her and
will be once more legally dispossessed of her birth home.

Perhaps Brontë's ending is optimistic in that it represents the best
possible solution within a diseased cultural system. Catherine is
restored to her homeland and is married to a man whose own past
experience allows him to appreciate the feminized position of powerlessness based on dispossession, given that Hareton's position was
similar to women's position in the patriarchy prior to Heathcliff's
death, which reinstates Hareton's status as land-holder. Similar to the
novel's married middle-class women, Hareton has been dispossessed
of his land and his name has been stripped of power. During his dispossession, while owning nothing, Hareton, like the young Heathcliff
before him, is willing to share. On Hareton's first meeting with

Catherine, he gives her "a fine crooked-legged terrier whelp from the kennel," which, significantly, she rejects (152). Hareton is willing to share, the acculturated Catherine is not. By emphasizing the young Hareton's ability to share prior to his reinstatement of status and property, Brontë's novel raises the following questions: Since patriarchs, while at the heights of their powers, are doomed by the very nature of the system to become metaphorical vampires, will Hareton be able to maintain his personal value system based on sharing once he is reinstated as the owner of the Heights and once his marriage to Catherine raises him to the status of the new squire of Thrushcross Grange? Will Hareton's legal "ownership" of Catherine and of her land through marriage warp his sensibilities as it has the other men encountered in the novel before him? Given Catherine's acculturation in a value system which stresses self-interest and given Catherine's protests that " 'he has no right to appropriate what is mine' " (230) when Hareton attempted to share books that were originally hers, how will she feel when Hareton attempts to share, or claim as his own, land and property that were originally hers?

Brontë's novel ends during the transitional twilight time before marriage where Catherine and Hareton's courtship is taking place largely on the moors during their evening walks. As always, Brontë sees the moors and nature being equated with health. Because the moors are outside of culture, outside of the land inheritance system, they can offer sustenance to Catherine and Hareton, just as they had to Cathy and Heathcliff, the generation before. Yet as adults, neither pair of lovers can live on the moors. With the moors to sustain them, just as Cathy and Heathcliff laughed at Hindley's attempts at acculturating them, Catherine and Hareton also envision their love as placing them beyond human laws.

During this transitional period before marriage, both Catherine's economic and sexual powers are at their heights. In terms of her economic power, Catherine is momentarily the sole proprietor of the Grange, with Lockwood paying rent to her and Nelly taking care of accounts. In terms of her sexual power, Catherine is free to chastise Hareton physically with the slap of her hand, just as her mother physically chastised her father prior to their marriage. Replaying the cat and mouse analogy, Brontë asks her readers to recall that even if Catherine sees herself as the cat toying with Hareton as mouse, Catherine will learn, similar to her mother, how her position of dispossession within marriage dooms her to the position of mouse and Hareton's position of possession within marriage relegates him to the position of cat.

If we are willing to project past this transitional period of pre-marital promise, Brontë's ending foretells trouble. Earlier, it was not until Cathy and Heathcliff's encounter with Thrushcross Grange where the patriarchal bulldog that guards property attacks and bites Cathy, that they—first Cathy, and then Heathcliff—learn to live by man's laws and social norms. Now the new move to Thrushcross Grange also indicates un-health because Thrushcross Grange represents civilization, with Catherine and Hareton being more and more removed from Nature and more and more alienated from the natural body. Hareton's change in status foretells trouble because Hareton will become a landed esquire who will collect rent from others who work the land in his stead. Once the dispossessed farmhand who did not receive compensation for his production, Hareton will become the landed proprietor who lives off the production of others' laboring bodies.

Even with the veneer of civilization in place once more, because Heathcliff's takeover of the system has shown it in its truest light, Brontë's choice of vampiric imagery in describing Heathcliff during his ascent to power also applies to Hareton's ascent. The system has not changed, only the visibility of its violence is again hidden from view. With the novel ending on Hareton's ascendency to the squireship at Thrushcross Grange, Brontë hints that this is not a correction of the system but a continuation of the system. Nothing has necessarily changed, even if new people are in place of the old. Brontë's critique of the system implies that the system is larger than anyone within it, that ultimately the system will decide the future because it shapes people's bodies and psychologies. The novel ends with apparent health, but only if we deny all of what has happened before. If we apply Brontë's critique of patriarchy to this new pair of lovers, the sight it provides should be unsettling. Catherine will once again be dispossessed of her land, her name, her legal rights. She will once again be enclosed by the limited role that marriage will allow her. Catherine's being caught in the patriarchy's lack of place for her makes her potentially vulnerable to illness and early death as it did for her mother Cathy, her aunt Frances, and her aunt Isabella.

While Heathcliff was still alive, Hareton appears to provide Catherine with the ability to challenge Heathcliff as patriarch as when Catherine announces, " 'Hareton and I are friends now' " after Hareton has taken action on Catherine's behalf by making her a garden (244). Once Hareton replaces Heathcliff as patriarch, when Catherine needs to claim her interest is not always the same as that of the system that denies her, will Hareton still be able to take her side?

A closer look at how successfully their alliance challenges the patriarchy when Heathcliff is still alive enables us to predict how successful their alliance through marriage will be. In Lockwood's romantic appraisal of the alliance between Catherine and Hareton, he claims, " 'Together, they would brave Satan and all his legions' " (258). However, the reality of Brontë's text has already proven that Catherine and Hareton together have been unsuccessful even in the much more mundane task of moving Joseph's garden. Joseph's complaints to Heathcliff have resulted in the reinstatement of Joseph's garden of currant and gooseberry bushes, with Catherine's flower garden being relegated to the corner of the garden where there is a fir tree—not the most promising growing site for a garden of primroses. This failure indicates that Catherine and Hareton's alliance is just one more of the alliances created through illness, which will ultimately fall short in its potential to challenge the power system.

Moreover, the reinstatement and prime location of Joseph's gooseberry and currant bushes is also symbolic in understanding the implications of the ending of Brontë's novel. In addition to being used for desserts, gooseberries and currants are used for making wine. According to George William Johnson's *The Cucumber and the Gooseberry; Their Culture, Uses and History*, published in 1847, "The gooseberry . . . is in particular well known as an ingredient in brisk wines . . ." (178).[34] In her essay "The Palace of Death," Brontë equates "Civilization" with "Intemperance," showing how it is the right hand of "Death" (228–30). If Intemperance is a symptom of Civilization, alcohol, wine, ale, brandy, all function as symbols of Civilization. Throughout *Wuthering Heights*, alcohol is offered during social visits and, ironically if seen through Brontë's values, for medicinal purposes.[35] During Lockwood's first visit to the Heights, he drinks wine offered him by Heathcliff, just as during his final visit to the Heights, Lockwood drinks ale offered him by Nelly. When Lockwood gets a bloody nose during his second visit, he is "sick exceedingly, and dizzy and faint" (15) and is given a glass of brandy for medicinal purposes, "whereby I was somewhat revived" (15).[36]

Joseph brings Heathcliff and Lockwood wine during their first encounter. Joseph himself drinks ale, sometimes evidently to such a degree that Heathcliff can question, " 'Is the fool drunk?' " (244). Joseph's gooseberry bushes, wine, ale, and brandy together work in the novel to signal another dimension of man's division from man and self-alienation under the patriarchy. Brontë does not follow the standard Victorian view of alcohol as "Liquid Food," as given in Thomas

Graham's chapter title on alcohol in his medical treatise entitled *Sure Methods of Improving Health or Prolonging Life*. For Brontë, wine and other alcohols are no longer seen positively as medicinal but are viewed negatively as the curses of Civilization. Instead of alcohol bringing men together and being medicinal, Brontë implies that alcohol is one of civilization's greatest weapons in turning men against each other. Fittingly, Lockwood's dream of "every man's hand was against his neighbour" is a brandy-induced nightmare (20, 15). Fittingly, Heathcliff and Hindley's greatest physical conflict occurs during one of Hindley's drinking sprees. Given Brontë's stance on Intemperance, Heathcliff's toast to Lockwood: " 'Your health, sir!' " can be seen as ironic (7). Even if Heathcliff himself is not being ironic, Brontë is.

Although Lockwood accepts Heathcliff's medicinal brandy, Lockwood never uses "Mrs. Dean's bitter herbs," as he calls her narrative, to cure himself (121). In addition, Lockwood never makes peace with the moors, instead choosing to make an early return to London. Nelly herself simply follows another master and mistress back to the Grange. Neither of Brontë's narrators undergoes the inner psychological changes denied the characters. In a novel obsessed with illness, where neither the characters nor the narrators grow from their exposure to illness, perhaps Brontë is more optimistic that her readers will benefit from her metaphorical exploration of cultural sickness inherent within a land-based patriarchy. Reading beyond Lockwood and Nelly's happy ending, such readers can "extract wholesome medicines" from Brontë's own "bitter herbs" given metaphorically throughout *Wuthering Heights* in the guise of vampires, ghosts, and illness.

Through these interrelated metaphors, Brontë portrays her dark vision of Civilization's distortion of Nature. In Brontë's world, culture suffers from the dis-ease of dis/possession, causing gentlemen to become vampires and ladies to become ghosts. It is a world where self-interest results in men being disconnected from each other and alienated from themselves. It is a world where the natural processes of eating and drinking become distorted into metaphors of illness, with eating becoming "consumption" and drinking becoming "intemperance." Together, these metaphors are Brontë's own "bitter herbs" (121).

Not all readers will be Lockwoods, leaving Wuthering Heights the same as they came to it. Some readers will benefit from Brontë's "bitter herbs," even if a complete cure is not possible while a cultural system continues to dispossess women of their names, rights, and property.[37] Brontë's hope of readers who can use her "bitter herbs" in their own cure provides the most optimistic spin possible on Brontë's dark view of her culture's disease of dis/possession. Yet, if we fully grant her dark vision, Brontë's "bitter herbs" may not even provide even this degree of optimism. For, as Brontë attests in "There was a time when my cheek burned," a poem that predates her novel, "Only I know, however I frown, / The same world will go rolling on" (17–18).

CONCLUSION

In bringing medical anthropology and the history of medicine together as a new lens through which to look at the Brontë novels, this study is multifaceted in what it offers. First, it offers a greater appreciation of the lives of the Brontës within their historical and cultural context. An awareness of how disease, illness, and death were prominent parts of Victorian life heightens our appreciation of the role disease and death played within the Brontës' lives. Moving beyond a general knowledge of this fact to a greater understanding of how specific diseases were culturally understood enhances our ability to understand individual illness experiences within this particular culture. Such an appreciation enables us to see how specific Victorian diseases, such as cholera, rabies, consumption, or hypochondria had an impact upon the Brontë family as either family members or friends experienced these diseases. We can also gain appreciation of how the Victorian cultural understanding of intemperance, a condition, which had not yet achieved the status of being considered a disease, would shape the experience of those, such as the Brontë family, who were living with it.

Second, such an appreciation enables us to see how these experiences with illness inform their work. While any scholarly attempt at analysis based on the connection between biography and literature is suspect because we cannot know authorial intentions, the connections between life and literature are clearly present in terms of which illnesses the Brontës chose to develop within their fiction. For example, consumption is the disease that had the greatest impact on the Brontës' lives because it killed five of the six siblings. Therefore, it should not be too surprising that two out of the three sisters employ representations of consumption within their novels. Given the fact that Anne Brontë was less than two years old at the time of Maria's and Elizabeth's deaths from consumption, her young age may explain why representations of consumption do not appear within her novels while they appear in novels written by both Charlotte and Emily. For example, Helen Burns's death in *Jane Eyre* is a result of consumption. Likewise, in *Wuthering Heights*, the death of Frances, Hindley's wife, is a result of consumption, although pregnancy and childbirth are also factors in her death. Within the highly metaphorical world of *Wuthering Heights*, Emily Brontë uses a multitude of interrelated metaphors for eating and drinking, including the contrast between the body's consumption of food and consumption's consuming of the body. Charlotte Brontë returns to the use of consumption in *Shirley*, interweaving the metaphors of consumption and decline in her novel after her experience watching consumption destroy Branwell, Emily, and Anne within a nine-month period.

Other familial illnesses appear in the literature as well, including hypochondria, rabies, blindness, and what we now know as alcoholism. If the sheer number of literary allusions to alcoholism is any indication, Branwell Brontë's alcoholism deeply affected his family. Anne, Charlotte, and Emily Brontë all explore issues relating to intemperance within their novels. Even though Anne Brontë's *The Tenant of Wildfell Hall* is the novel best known for its sustained realistic portrayal of Victorian alcoholism, representations of intemperate, alcoholic characters find their way into novels written by the other sisters as well. Charlotte Brontë uses her own experience of hypochondria to create both Crimsworth's experience of hypochondria in *The Professor* and Lucy Snowe's experience of hysteria in *Villette*. Emily Brontë's encounter with a dog thought to be rabid appears in Shirley's encounter with Phoebe in *Shirley*. Charlotte Brontë's insights into Rochester's blindness in *Jane Eyre* may have found their source in her experience with her father's growing blindness due to problems with cataracts. In fact, Charlotte Brontë began writing *Jane Eyre* while in Manchester attending her father for a month after the eye surgery which restored his sight.

Third, a medical anthropological study of the representations of disease and illness in the Brontë novels offers insight in how such representations fundamentally inform the novels. By analyzing Anne Brontë's use of Victorian concepts of alcoholism in *Agnes Grey* as well as in *The Tenant of Wildfell Hall*, this study breaks new ground in two ways. First, her literary treatment of intemperance differs from that of her contemporaries in its focus on middle- and upper-class drinking, and second, her exploration of the psychology of alcoholism underscores the pathology of the Victorian gender ideals which, when taken to their extremes, makes men self-centered and women self-effacing, thereby perpetuating an unhealthy social structure. By analyzing

Charlotte Brontë's use of cholera in *Shirley*, this study develops another level of displacement in Brontë's historical novel, which allows us to see how a new paradigm for understanding disease as a call for social reform informs Brontë's use of the other illnesses within the novel. By analyzing Charlotte Brontë's representations of hysteria in *Villette*, this study includes both of Lucy Snowe's breakdowns rather than following the tradition of looking only at her first experience with illness. Once the second episode of illness is taken into consideration, a new appreciation can be gained of how both illnesses are central to Lucy's rethinking of her two cultures' ideologies, a process which results in her claiming a new self-identity more in keeping with her own inner values. By analyzing Emily Brontë's obsessive use of illness in *Wuthering Heights*, this study explores the interconnections between all of the illnesses rather than just focusing on specific illnesses, such as Cathy's "anorexia" or Heathcliff's monomania. In taking into account the multitude of illnesses represented in the novel, we can see how together they create a larger metaphorical disease, the disease of dis/possession, which Brontë uses to critique her culture's disease-producing values of possession and dispossession. All four of these analyses bring to light aspects of the Brontë novels which have been overlooked, thereby adding to our appreciation and knowledge of their works.

The application of ideas from medical anthropology indicates that all three Brontës use representations of disease and illness to explore the cultural constraints faced by their characters, especially their heroines, within a patriarchal culture. Not only does each sister's use of illness change from novel to novel as her understanding of life increases and her writing abilities develop, but each sister's individual beliefs also help shape her use of illness as cultural critique in her novels. Anne Brontë's critique of alcoholism in *The Tenant of Wildfell Hall* is more sophisticated than her earlier critique in *Agnes Grey*, but the core ideas correlating intemperance, abuse, and illness are already present in the earlier text.

For Charlotte Brontë, the difference between *Shirley* and *Villette* in the use of representations of illness manifests a dramatic shift in authorial purpose and in an understanding of her audience. In *Shirley*, Brontë's projected audience is a male audience as her authorial addresses to the "Men of England" and "Men of Yorkshire" indicate. In *Shirley*, issues of female health for individual women, while seen to have a national impact on the health of the nation, are to be remedied specifically by men who have the social and cultural power to address such problems. In *Villette*, not only do these authorial addresses to a male audience disappear, the idea that men can be called upon to remedy problems concerning women's health has also disappeared. In addition, not a single male character in *Villette* undergoes a transformative illness on par with those experienced by either Robert or Louis Moore in *Shirley*, or that experienced by Rochester in *Jane Eyre*. Given the fact that in her early novels, Charlotte Brontë uses illness and a sojourn in the sickroom to feminize her male characters, offering them a new and deeper appreciation of the life of the body and of the emotions, which not only helps to heal them but which sustains them once they leave the sickroom, the lack of such a technique for developing her male characters' psychological growth in her final novel is significant. Because *Villette* by-passes the earlier focus both on male characters' growth through illness and on a male audience taking the lead in health reform, Brontë's exclusive focus on Lucy Snowe's progression through two bouts of illness should be seen to signify a major shift. Not only is the implied audience now female, but also the purpose in writing is rethought to help a specifically female audience understand how to arrive at a new vision of female health even if no social reforms are initiated. Charlotte Brontë's literary representation of illness provides her readers new ways to analyze the ideologies of patriarchal cultures, which inform religion, science, and art, leading to a vision of female health that female readers can enact internally within themselves, whether or not social changes come from outside of themselves. Because Brontë uses illness to demonstrate issues of conflict between two different cultures, England and Labassecour, she interweaves illness with her exploration of the cultural dimensions of self-identity to arrive at her vision of female health.

Because we only have one novel by Emily Brontë, it is impossible to know what she would have been able to do in her next novel with representations of disease and what type of cultural critique such representations would encompass. Yet, even in the move from the use of intemperance in her Belgium essay "The Palace of Death" to the multitude of illnesses, including intemperance and monomania, in *Wuthering Heights*, the power of her social critique is visibly increasing.

In terms of how individual value systems determine how the use of representations of disease informs each Brontë sister's cultural critique of the patriarchy, it is easier to understand the differences by looking at some of the similarities. For example, both Anne and Charlotte Brontë differ from Emily Brontë in that their characters challenge the early nineteenth-century concept of the ego as stable. Both Anne and Charlotte Brontë's novels point toward the psychological growth that illness makes possible. Nonetheless, their novels differ in how illness disrupts this stable self to provide for new possibilities for future growth. Anne Brontë's heroines grow in response to an illness experienced by important men in their lives. In Agnes Grey's case, her new identity as governess occurs in response to her father's illness; in Helen Huntingdon's case, her new growth occurs in response to her husband's alcoholism. In contrast, Charlotte Brontë's heroes and heroines grow through their own experience of illness. All four of the main characters in *Shirley* rethink themselves through their personal experience of illness. Of the four, Caroline Helstone's illness provides the most in-depth development of this process. Nevertheless, *Villette*'s exclusive focus on Lucy Snowe's growth through illness proves Brontë's most insightful exploration in how illness breaks down and reconfigures the self.

Charlotte Brontë's novels stress the internal psychological changes as individual characters, such as Jane Eyre or Lucy Snowe, pit themselves against a system that denies their personal value. Through her focus on one character's internal psychological changes, Charlotte Brontë is basically critiquing the system from a position inside the system, asking for a little breathing room for her middle-class heroines. At first glance, Anne Brontë's novels appear to follow a similar pattern. However, Anne Brontë's values are at odds with Charlotte Brontë's values because the latter's primary concern is to show that her middle-class heroines deserve to enjoy the privileges currently reserved for middle- and upper-class males. In contrast, Anne Brontë writes out of a strong base of spiritual values at odds with the Victorian culture's more worldly values that promote wealth, fame, power, and status. Unlike Charlotte Brontë's heroines who question only hierarchies of power which directly affect them, Anne Brontë's heroines question all hierarchies of power, ideally placing everyone on an equal level: men, women, children, and animals. Because of this strong spiritual dimension on the part of the youngest Brontë sister, the idealized healthy society that Anne Brontë promotes differs greatly from that envisioned by her sister Charlotte.

Emily Brontë sides with Anne Brontë in their mutual critiques of the worldly values still desired by Charlotte Brontë for her heroines. However, Emily Brontë differs from both sisters' portrayal of illness as *not* resulting in psychological growth for her characters. As a result of this difference, Emily Brontë's vision is much darker, much more pessimistic than that of either of her sisters whose optimism is apparent in their visions that people can be educated and can grow through an experience with illness. By denying the psychologically transformative power of illness while analyzing the impact of the cultural system on all of her characters, Emily Brontë places herself outside the system and, consequently, critiques the patriarchal system as a whole. Some critics might argue that by choosing this philosophical technique of placing herself outside of civilization in her efforts to analyze it, Brontë is forced into living in a romantic fantasy. Yet, by being bombarded by the multitude of non-transformative illnesses which make up *Wuthering Heights*, Emily Brontë's readers are better positioned to analyze "Civilization," which Brontë presents as the common source of all of the illnesses. By creating metaphors which equate civilization with illness, Brontë emphasizes that the various representations of illness within the novel are simply symptoms of an unnatural, man-made patriarchal cultural system. Emily Brontë stresses not only that no single individual's inner change, gained through illness, will be enough to challenge the rigidity of the patriarchal system, but also that all variations of characters' new alliances gained through illness, which could potentially challenge the system, will, in fact, fail to do so. Perhaps through her critique, Brontë is challenging her readers to make the transformations which her characters fail to make. However, in not providing readers with any character in transition to health with whom to identify, Brontë's novel does not point the direction toward change as does Helen Huntingdon in *The Tenant of Wildfell Hall* or as does Lucy Snowe in *Villette*. Neither Cathy nor Heathcliff provides such direction in the first generation. Neither Catherine nor Hareton provides it in the second. Neither Lockwood nor Nelly provides it as narrators. Yet, to use Mikhail Bakhtin's term, in the *heteroglossia* that these voices of unhealth provide, perhaps in its larger picture, Emily Brontë's novel does point the way to health.

In terms of the radical nature of their cultural critiques, Emily Brontë's cultural critique is the darkest and most radical, whereas Charlotte Brontë's is the most conservative since it demands the smallest degree of social reform. Yet, in her final novel, Charlotte Brontë implicitly acknowledges the improbability that her male characters and male audience will make the desired social changes for the greater health of British women, and she shifts her focus from outer social change to inner psychological change. Consequently, in terms of offering her female readers a vivid and convincing portrait of inner change, Charlotte Brontë's heroine Lucy Snowe offers more than any other Brontë character for she provides a psychological blueprint for individual change. Even though Anne Brontë's Helen Huntingdon does not undergo the inner transformation which Lucy Snowe experiences, she still has much to offer readers in terms of providing a step-by-step process of working with illness to arrive at a new position of authority. In dealing with her husband's intemperance, Helen has proven herself, to herself and to others. Because Anne Brontë's cultural critiques are based on spiritual values, her ideas are often dismissed or overlooked, because as a secular culture we no longer place the same value upon religion as did the Victorians. Yet Anne Brontë's spiritual values offered her the ability to critique her culture to the extent that she could even critique religion and its beliefs concerning the salvation of sinners, such as the drunken Arthur Huntingdon.

Fourth, this study participates in the larger theoretical conversation concerning the interplay between body and culture. The significance of a greater awareness of the interplay between body and culture across time and across cultures is becoming apparent as more scholars in a variety of fields are beginning to share their knowledge. By working with the interrelated fields of medical anthropology and the history of medicine, this study contributes to a deeper understanding of the ways in which Victorian concepts of the body, including ideas concerning health, illness, disease, and medicine, inform texts of the time, including literary texts. In addition, this study indicates that Victorian ideas of the body were in flux, often shifting as new information about the body and about disease required the rethinking of older constructs. Consequently, the chapter on Anne Brontë's representation of Victorian alcoholism works with the historical shift from thinking about "intemperance" as a moral crime to reconceptualizing "alcoholism" as a disease. The chapter on Charlotte Brontë's use of cholera works with the historical shift from thinking about diseases as a divine punishment from God to reconceptualizing disease as having its source in social conditions, thus making social reform more central to concepts of public health. The chapter on Charlotte Brontë's use of hysteria works with the historical shift that leads to the understanding of hysteria and hypochondria as psychological illnesses rather than as illnesses that are both physical and psychological in origin. Taken together, these historical shifts indicate that ideas of the Victorian body were dynamic and ever-changing, responding to the larger changes occurring within the culture.

The related concepts from medical anthropology that ideologies need the body to be inscribed and made real and that the body thereby becomes the site for all ideological conflicts provides powerful tools for a cultural analysis of literary texts. By applying these concepts in a focused analysis of the Brontës' use of representations of illness and disease within their novels, I hope to have illuminated each of the sisters' individual cultural critiques, as well as provide theoretical and historical backgrounds to suggest possible application of these concepts to other Victorian writings.

Fifth, in addition to providing a methodology for an analysis of literary texts, medical anthropology also provides a methodology to renegotiate the gap between the Victorian understanding of the body and our own. In understanding how even as late as the early Victorian period diseases were still classified by symptoms, we can gain a greater appreciation of the modern biomedical concept of disease which helps us classify diseases by whatever virus or bacterium causes them. In understanding how the biomedical concept of disease means we now focus on smaller and smaller units of the body, we can gain a greater appreciation of how the Victorian concept of disease as affecting the constitution as a whole allowed them to treat the patient more holistically, without having to separate the mind/body connection. The modern definition of hysteria and hypochondria as psychological illnesses is again important here. An appreciation of the gap between Victorian thought and modern thought is crucial in the shift from the pre-Freudian understanding of hysteria to our post-Freudian under-standing of it as well as in the loss in concepts from Victorian psy-chology, such as phrenology and monomania, as new understandings of modern psychology have evolved.

It is my hope that a cultural appreciation of Victorian medicine and the Victorian body will provide insight into our own culture. As always, an anthropological study of another culture offers a mirror in which to see our own customs and values more clearly. In terms of the Brontës' own use of anthropology, Charlotte Brontë is the only one who uses the study of another culture as a mirror for her English readers to see themselves. Both *The Professor* and *Villette* develop around the main characters' growth occurring in response to their time living abroad. The power of *Villette* comes from Brontë's full realization of what such an experience offers in terms of re-creating identity. In my offering of an anthropological study, such a perspective of Victorian culture enables us to reassess not only the Victorians' relationship with the body and how that relationship is presented in texts but also our own culture's relationship with the body.

Finally, I would like to propose that not only can medical anthro-pology benefit literary studies but also that our own skills as literary critics and as rhetoricians aware of the nuances of language can benefit the work of medical anthropologists. In their work with illness, many of these scholars have explored the interrelationships between illness, silence, lack of voice, loss of agency, and loss of health. Elaine Scarry's *The Body in Pain: The Making and Unmaking of the World* has already made connections between pain and language, how pain itself results in a loss of language and how a movement away from pain is signified by a movement into voice. Similarly, Arthur Frank in *The Wounded Storyteller* indicates that illness is a call to story, that illness by its nature demands a narrative. Within this study, I have tentatively found myself grappling with questions of silence and voice, pain and language, illness and narrative as I have attempted to unravel the ways in which the Brontës play out these questions in descriptions of their characters' experiences of illness. Because of the narrative techniques in *Villette* that attempt to recapture Lucy Snowe's pain and lack of voice, my exploration of Charlotte Brontë's use of hysteria provides the best example of how literary critics could offer insights into the use of language within the illness experience, even if that experience is fictional rather than autobiographical. Here as elsewhere, the cultural and historical interplay between "body as text" and "text as body" can offer all of us insights that have the potential to enrich our lives.

NOTES

INTRODUCTION

1. Medicine's ability to cure smallpox as the only exception is found in Roy Porter's three-century overview of medicine, *Disease, Medicine, and Society in England, 1550–1860*. Porter asserts, "Medicine succeeded in making only marginal inroads into serious diseases. It scored one notable triumph. Between them, small pox inoculation . . . and vaccination . . . diminished the terrors of a once-prevalent and commonly fatal disease . . ." (61).

2. In "A Medical Appraisal of the Brontës," Philip Rhodes, professor of obstetrics and gynecology, specifies that a combination of "chronic pelvic sepsis" and "increasing anaemia" was the "probable cause" of Maria Branwell Brontë's death (131).

3. It is commonly accepted that Branwell's death was caused by consumption; however, in a recent article, W.H. Helm questions this reading of his death. Helm also argues that Charlotte should be seen as suffering from chronic pulmonary tuberculosis even though it was not the principal cause of her death. See Helm's "Tuberculosis and the Brontë Family."

   Brontë scholars often mention Branwell Brontë's use of opium and his possible addiction to it; however, no one has made the connection that opium was becoming known in the 1840s as a possible medical cure for the "insanity" brought on by excessive alcohol consumption. As early as 1836, Robert Macnish writes in *The Anatomy of Drunkenness*, "In attempting to cure the habit of drunkenness, opium may sometimes be used with advantage" (214). Although Patrick Brontë was relying upon his own copy of the first edition of Thomas John Graham's *Modern Domestic Medicine* (1826) in his treatment of Branwell's *delirium tremens*, in which "no opium" is recommended for this condition (395), because Patrick was constantly trying to keep up on the latest developments in medicine, he may well have been aware of Macnish's medical advice or that the celebrated Graham would revise his medical treatise from the eighth edition (1840) to the eleventh edition (1853) to recommend the use of opium, if specifically given in the "form of muriate of morphia" (563). If Patrick had acted upon these recommendations, or others like them, he may have unwittingly compounded his only son's sufferings as he lay dying in the fall of 1848. To understand how the reliance on opium was growing stronger as a possible treatment throughout the 1840s and 1850s, it is helpful to know that by 1858, Graham's medical treatise is revised again, this time to record the use of opium as crucial to recovery from *delirium tremens*. Graham now writes, "In many cases, the patient *must sleep or die*. Give two grains of opium every two hours, to be continued until sleep ensues" (italics in original, 394). If the Brontës did turn to opium as a recommended cure for Branwell's alcoholism, it adds a certain poignancy to assumptions that he was using opium simply for pleasure and for its easy availability.

4. Of Foucault's books, the two most pertinent to this study are *The Birth of the Clinic* and *Madness and Civilization* since together they provide an overview of the development of Western medicine, both in the hospital and the asylum, with its historical shift in the nineteenth century wherein "normality" replaced earlier concepts of health (*Birth of the Clinic* 35). Foucault's work always centers on the idea that the body is not just cultural, it is political. Butler never directly addresses issues of medicine or of illness; however, her overall idea of the plasticity of identity is helpful to anyone working with concepts of the body, particularly the postmodern body. Perhaps most helpful for scholars working with historically earlier constructs of the body is Butler's "theory of performativity," a theory which she develops in *Gender Trouble* and refines in *Bodies that Matter*. This theory, especially in its refined version, addresses with sophistication the actual ongoing, never-ending process by which, at the most basic levels of identity formation, bodies do in fact become cultural bodies.

5. In *The Greatest Benefit to Mankind*, Roy Porter documents the significance of each man's contributions to medical science. Giovanni Battista Morgagni's *De sedibus et causis morborum* [*On the Sites and Causes of Disease*], published in 1761, was the first work to draw on "the findings of some 700 autopsies to show how bodily organs revealed the footprints of disease" (263). It was translated into English in 1769. Marie François Xavier Bichat's *Traité des membranes* (1799) and *Anatomie générale* (1801) documented the "doctrine of tissues," showing how different types of tissue were "distinguished by appearance and vital qualities" (265). Rudolf Virchow was the first to develop the medical implications of cell theory. His book *Die Cellularpathologie* (1858) [*Cell Pathology*] explained that diseases "came from abnormal changes within cells, and abnormal cells in turn multiplied through division—diseases were thus the result of disturbances in the body's cellular structures" (331).

6. As Porter explains in *The Greatest Benefit to Mankind*, Robert Koch was responsible for bacteriology becoming a scientific discipline since he and his followers "established the germ concept of disease and systematically developed its potential" (436). His paper on the etiology of infectious diseases came out in 1879.

7. Thomas John Graham is thought to have written another popular medical treatise, *Sure Methods of Improving Health, and Prolonging*

Life; or, A Treatise on the Art of Living Long and Comfortably, by Regulating the Diet and Regimen, anonymously given as "Written by a Physician," published in 1828. Within the text, the "physician" uses references to various other physicians to set up his own authority on the subject of health. Since the physician he quotes most often and gives the greatest accolades to is Thomas John Graham, current scholars assume that the anonymous physician is none other than Graham himself. Published only two years following his *Modern Domestic Medicine* in 1826, this text could have been an attempt to boost the prestige—and sales—of the earlier text.

8. Patrick Brontë's marginalia shows his familiarity with other medical texts of the period, including his knowledge of William Buchan's *Domestic Medicine*. It is possible that he owned Buchan's text as well as Graham's *Modern Domestic Medicine*; however, because the sales catalogue from the sale of 1861 lists the number of books sold rather than the names of the specific books, we are unable to know this for sure.

9. See Foucault's *The Birth of the Clinic* for a fascinating overview of the discovery of pathological anatomy and its impact on the medical field in post-revolutionary France, and by extension, on all of Western medicine. His chapter, "Open Up a Few Corpses" is particularly helpful.

   In the nineteenth-century the scientific and medical community which exchanged ideas consisted primarily of France, Germany, Great Britain—Edinburgh's contributions are definitely more cutting-edge throughout the century than London's—and America. Lieden, the Netherlands and Vienna, Austria make the occasional contribution. Italy, which played such a dominant role in earlier centuries, had taken more of a backseat.

10. The role female modesty plays in the invention of the stethoscope is interesting. During a consultation with a female patient who complained of symptoms indicating possible heart disease, Laennec recorded that "the patient's age and sex did not permit me to resort to [direct application of ear to chest]. I recalled a well-known acoustic phenomenon . . . Taking a sheet of paper I rolled it into a very tight roll . . . I was both surprised and gratified at being able to hear the beating of the heart with much greater clearness and distinctness than I had ever before by direct application of my ear" (qtd. in Porter 308–09).

11. Of the two extremes, the Victorians seemed much more concerned with controlling excessive emotions through their ideal of self-control.

12. Because Emily Brontë's novel includes monomania, a Victorian concept of mental illness now long abandoned, an exploration of it is included within the chapter. However, monomania is not strong enough to bear the weight of an analysis of Brontë's philosophical novel since it is only one of the many diseases developed in the novel.

Chapter 1 "Sick of Mankind and Their Disgusting Ways": Victorian Alcoholism, Social Reform, and Anne Brontë's Narratives of Illness

1. Elizabeth Langland's *Anne Brontë: The Other One* records this and other marginalia scribbled in Brontë's books (17). The quotation "Sick of mankind and their disgusting ways" is to be found penciled on the back flyleaf of Anne Brontë's *Book of Common Prayer*, a gift from her godmother in February 1827, located in the Brontë Parsonage Museum. When I first saw the original, what struck me was that, this quotation was the only annotation made by Brontë in her entire prayer book. It makes one wonder, when and under what circumstances would she have written such a telling comment?

2. Terms concerning Victorian concepts of alcoholism are not as clearly defined as modern terms. In *Drink and the Victorians*, Brian Harrison explains how Victorian terms often overlapped. Harrison asserts,

> The Victorians often failed to distinguish between alcoholism, drinking and drunkenness. Temperance reformers argued that drinking inevitably led to drunkenness, and society at large failed to distinguish between drunkenness and alcoholism. The word drunkenness—"the state of being drunk"—has been regularly used by Englishmen at least since A.D. 893, whereas the word alcoholism—"the diseased condition produced by alcohol"— appeared only about 1860. Thomas Trotter, in his *Essay on Drunkenness* published in 1804, was among the earliest to describe habitual drunkenness as a disease: but he was unable to describe the condition in terms which were free from moral overtones. (21–22)

According to Roy Porter in "The Drinking Man's Disease: The 'Pre-History' of Alcoholism in Georgian Britain," the term "alcoholism" was coined as early as 1852 (390). Just as the term "alcoholism" began replacing "intemperance," the term "alcoholic" replaced "drunkard" and the term "recovery" replaced "reform." Such changes in the terminology became possible once alcoholism became seen as a disease rather than as a moral crime. Even today, the debate about alcoholism continues, with a moral stigma frequently assigned to the alcoholic.

Even with Brontë's modern psychological insights into the addiction of alcoholism, because Brontë's terminology and belief system indicate her understanding of Arthur's drunkenness within the traditional moral framework where drinking is still seen as a moral crime, I use the Victorian terms within my text to place Brontë's understanding of "alcoholism" within the larger Victorian culture's understanding of intemperance, while using the modern terms for my analysis of these Victorian texts.

3. Scholars have developed the idea that Branwell's drinking may have been a large influence on Anne Brontë's choice of topics in *The Tenant of Wildfell Hall*. Three Brontë scholars have specifically written articles on the issue of alcoholism in *The Tenant of Wildfell Hall*; however, no Brontë scholar has looked at the issue of alcoholism within *Agnes Grey* or at other issues of illness. Annette Federico's " 'I must have drink': Addiction, Angst, and Victorian Realism" places *The Tenant of Wildfell Hall* in a larger Victorian literary tradition which uses both alcoholism and opium addiction to explore modern angst. Catherine MacGregor's " 'I Cannot Trust Your Oaths and Promises: I Must Have a Written Agreement': Talk and Text in *The Tenant of Wildfell Hall*" argues for the text's privileging of the written word over the oral word, relating it back to how alcoholism creates a world where the oral word is unreliable since broken promises, mis-communications, and lies are rife within it. Marianne Thormählen's "The Villain of *Wildfell Hall*: Aspects and Prospects of Arthur Huntingdon" uses early nineteenth-century theology, science, medicine, and social developments to place Arthur Huntingdon in his historical context.

4. See Nicholas Mason's " 'The Sovereign People are in a Beastly State': The Beer Act of 1830 and Victorian Discourse on Working-Class Drunkenness" as well as Harrison's *Drink and the Victorians* for their analyses of the historical impact of the Beer Act of 1830.

5. French reports that it was not until 1839 that legislature made it a crime for "*selling spirits to young persons under sixteen years of age*" (italics in original, 359). French also records the 1879 recommendations of the "Lord's Committee on Intemperance" which enlarged the scope of this legislation. Article 19 reads "That in Ireland and Scotland, as in England, no spirits should be sold to children under sixteen" (370).

6. Following Gaskell's example, in the 1850s both Charles Dickens and George Eliot create female working-class drunkards. According to the Victorian temperance reformers, female alcoholics almost always found it impossible to reform. Dickens's Mrs. Stephen Blackpool appears in *Hard Times* (1854), where her inability to stop drinking has ramifications for the novel's plot. Eliot's "Janet's Repentance" (1857) is significant in literary history since its narrative concerns a female alcoholic who successfully recovers.

7. George Gissing's *The Odd Women* (1893) and many of Thomas Hardy's novels, such as *The Mayor of Casterbridge* (1886), *Tess of the D'Urbervilles* (1891), and *Jude the Obscure* (1896), all focus on working-class drinking.

8. Specific information about the Haworth Temperance Society and Patrick Brontë's role in it is hard to piece together. Shiman's *Crusade Against Drink in Victorian England* records that the first meeting to form the Haworth Temperance Society was held in 1834 and that in his role as incumbent of the parish, Patrick Brontë was present (48). Barker's biography *The Brontës* states that Patrick Brontë was the

President of the society for three years but does not indicate the dates of his presidency. Barker also mentions Branwell Brontë temporarily serves as the society's Secretary. Thormählen also mentions that "Patrick Brontë and his son Branwell were at one time President and Secretary, respectively, of the local Temperance Society" (832–33). Again, no specific dates are given. The limited information makes for intriguing questions, such as did Anne Brontë herself ever attend any of these temperance meetings? did Branwell's own heavy drinking play a role in why he temporarily joined the society—or, why he dropped his membership? did Patrick Brontë hope to help his son as well as the working-class members of Haworth in starting such a society? when and why did the Haworth Temperance Society see its demise? etc.

9. I am indebted to Thormählen's article "The Villain of *Wildfell Hall*: Aspects and Prospects of Arthur Huntingdon" for first making this connection.

10. As late as the twelfth edition of *Modern Domestic Medicine*, published in 1858, Dr. Graham still advises sufferers of gout to abstain from hard alcohol, without making the connection explicit that alcohol is causing their gout. He writes, "Ardent spirits are altogether inadmissible in every case, and the strong and plethoric should avoid wine. Ale and all the stronger malt liquors must also be forsaken" (463). To support his views, Graham calls upon the expertise of physicians and other prominent men. Concerning "Gout," Graham includes Dr. Budd's insight that "In inflammatory gout, above everything malt liquors should be given up; I have known two or three patients make marvellous recoveries by this simple expedient alone" (463), as well as Sir William Temple's insight that "I have known so great cures, and so many, done by obstinate resolutions of drinking no wine at all, that I put more weight upon the part of temperance, than any other" (footnote 463). Graham also includes Dr. Thornton's more general insight about wine usage, which seems to move beyond advice strictly on curing gout. Dr. Thornton writes, "It would be happy for mankind, if wine were prohibited and only good, perfect beer used in its place" (footnote 463). Graham concludes "Temperance and exercise . . . have often wrought great and salutary changes in the gouty man's constitution" (467).

11. While I have not been able to locate Victorian data giving statistics about the correlation of alcoholism and abuse, current research indicates the correlation is high. In his research on adult daughters of alcoholics, Robert Ackerman reports, "It was found that 31% of adult daughters experienced child abuse, 19% were victimized by sexual abuse, and 38% witnessed spouse abuse in their families. These rates of abuse were three to four times higher than found to occur among women who were raised in non-alcoholic families" (14–15). Ackerman also indicates that 80% were subject to emotional abuse (190). While Ackerman's findings are current and relate specifically to child and

spouse abuse, they confirm that incidence of abuse are dramatically higher within families where alcoholism is present. In *Under the Influence: A Guide to the Myths and Realities of Alcoholism*, James R. Milam and Katherine Ketcham report, "Alcohol is involved in 60 percent of reported cases of child abuse and the majority of cases involving wife beating" (8). Again, while these statistics are contemporary, they confirm the connection between alcohol and abuse.

12. Porter records "It is well-known that the Georgian age prized heavy-drinking as a manly and sociable custom" (385). In *Nineteen Centuries of Drink in England*, French quotes the author of *Reminiscences of Captain Gronow* in his perceptions on drinking habits in place as late as 1814: "A three-bottle man was not an unusual guest at a fashionable table. . . . There were then four and even five-bottle men . . ." (323–24).

13. *Under the Influence: A Guide to the Myths and Realities of Alcoholism* is a good reference guide for the current state of the debates on the hereditary, social, and psychological factors in the origins of alcoholism.

14. McGregor also includes this point in her analysis of *The Tenant of Wildfell Hall*, writing of Helen's inclination to save Arthur as being an inclination which "is widespread among daughters of alcoholic fathers who marry men with drinking problems as they so frequently do" (36). This characteristic—"We either become alcoholics, marry them, or both"—is included among the list of characteristics of adult children of alcoholics given in *The Twelve Steps for Adult Children*, published by Recovery Publications (1987). See "Author's Note" (n. pag.).

15. The early temperance movement's focus on moderation did not condemn all use of alcoholic spirits. Only "ardent spirits" such as gin, rum, and vodka which had been more readily available to the public at cheaper prices with the advent of modern technology were considered off-limits. Both beer and wine were considered health-promoting, especially since beer was seen as a main source of nutrients for working-class laborers and since wine was commonly prescribed by Victorian physicians as cures for a large variety of ailments. Also, the fact that drinking water was often contaminated and unsafe to drink promoted the drinking of beer and wine. Thus, a temperance pledge in the 1830s did not exclude use of either beer or wine; it only promoted a moderate use of them.

16. Charles Lamb's "Confessions of a Drunkard," published in 1822, although written earlier, was one of the few literary explorations available to the reading public on the topic of how extremely difficult it was for a drinker to try to control his drinking on his own.

17. Chapter Two of Harrison's book develops how pervasive alcoholic beverages were to nineteenth-century British culture. For my point concerning the nature of isolation of a nondrinker from the mainstream drinking culture, see Harrison, especially pages 44, 45, and 50.

18. At least one of Lowborough's relapses result in "an apoplectic fit, followed by a rather severe brain fever" (182). Such symptoms indicate the severity of Lowborough's alcoholism. While Lowborough's use of laudanum is never referred to specifically as a cure for his drinking, in light of Macnish's advice about using opium "to cure the habit of drunkenness" (214), it seems significant that while Lowborough is abstaining from drinking spirits, he carries around laudanum with him. Macnish writes, "By giving it [opium] in moderate quantities, the liquor which the person is in the habit of taking, may be diminished to a considerable extent, and he may thus be enabled to leave them off altogether" (214).

19. Trotter's idea that the habit of drunkenness was "a disease of the mind" helped question the role of will power in alcoholism; consequently Trotter is typically considered to be the first to see alcoholism as a disease (qtd. in Porter 390). Porter tries to complicate the perception of Trotter's eminence as the founder of the disease concept of alcoholism in "The Drinking Man's Disease" by reporting how Dr. John Coakley Lettsom had already noted the cycle of addiction involved in drinking (391). Similarly, the American physician Benjamin Rush realized that while drinking began as an act of "free will," it descended into a "habit," and finally became a "necessity" (qtd. in Porter 390). Even with the groundbreaking work of such physicians as Lettsom, Rush, and Trotter, the disease concept of alcoholism was not fully established until much later in the nineteenth century.

20. See Macnish (216–17) and Grindrod (387). Grindrod's *Bacchus: An Essay on the Nature, Causes, Effects, and Cure, of Intemperance* won an award sponsored by one of the many temperance societies as the "Best Essay" on Intemperance for the year 1839.

21. Even though Murdock's *Domesticating Drink: Women, Men, and Alcohol in America, 1870–1940* focuses on American alcoholism later in the century, because of the similarity in the transatlantic concepts of Victorian femininity, her insight still is applicable to Brontë's novel.

22. Helen continues in her belief that it is her responsibility to save her son since his young age makes him dependent upon her for his protection.

23. See MacGregor's article for a fuller discussion of the theme of writing as healing within the novel.

CHAPTER 2   AILING WOMEN IN THE AGE OF CHOLERA: ILLNESS IN *SHIRLEY*

1. This list—"consumption," "decline," and "slow fever"—reads like a list of symptoms for a reason. As R.J. Morris notes in *Cholera 1832*, "The seventeenth-century physician, Sydenham, had laid the foundations of the English tradition of studying and classifying diseases according to their various symptoms" (164). Once the microscope and other modern technology can aid physicians in classifying diseases

by cause, this tradition of classifying by symptoms falls into disuse. Consequently, specific types of fever are now determined by cause. Tuberculosis was originally named "consumption" because of the disease's emaciating impact on the body, i.e., the body was literally "consumed."

2. According to Morris, modern statistics for cholera show that, in reality, without treatment only 40–60 percent of those who contract the disease die from it (12). However, before these statistics could be known, with all of the unknowns involved in the appearance and treatment of this new disease, the panic cholera inspired must have led people in the nineteenth century to fear a much higher mortality rate.

3. See Carol Ann Speth's "Cholera in Early Nineteenth-Century British History and Fiction: The Social and Medical Response" for a sense of the British panic on the pending arrival of the second epidemic. Asa Briggs in "Cholera and Society" notes the path cholera takes in the second epidemic is the same as in the first, reaching Britain in 1848 by way of the Baltic (84–85).

4. It is difficult to find information that corresponds exactly to the dates of Brontë's writing and publishing *Shirley* to be able to place it in the context of the cholera epidemic that was sweeping the nation. Nonetheless, the data available does indicate that by the time Brontë turned over the manuscript on September 8, 1849, cholera had already been present on British soil for a full year. To get a sense of the gravity of the crisis, it is helpful to know that two months later, in November 1849, London alone counted 14,137 dead, almost three times the number of those killed in London in the 1831–1832 epidemic of cholera (Speth 162). Morris tabulates the cholera deaths for all four cholera epidemics in nineteenth-century Britain. For the 1848–1849 epidemic, his figures show that for England and Wales, the 1848 death count is 1908, while the 1849 death count is much greater with 53,293 dead. Scotland combines the two years, giving a range from 6,000 to 7,000 dead (13). These figures indicate that the total death count for the 1848–1849 cholera epidemic is at least 61,201. On the local level, Barker notes, that with "an outbreak of English cholera in Haworth, Charlotte commissioned Ellen [Nussey] to buy her a fur boa and cuffs (in July!) And a shower-bath" (603). The date of Brontë's letter requesting these preventative measures is July 27, 1849. Haworth was not the sole locale hit in the north. Bradford and Leeds were also affected. Barker records that The *Bradford Observer* ran an article concerning the local spread of cholera on September 27, 1849, and the *Leeds Intelligencer* ran two articles, the first on September 22, 1849 and the second on September 29, 1849 (944). The source for the textual information about the dates for writing and publishing the manuscript of *Shirley* is the Oxford edition's "Note on the Text," pages xxvi–xxvii. Barker clarifies that Brontë personally gave the manuscript to James Taylor, from the Smith and Elder firm, who stopped at Haworth en route home to London after a visit to Scotland (604).

5. To make my point more clearly within the chapter itself, I have omitted part of Brontë's phrasing. Brontë's full phrase is "the yellow taint of pestilence" (421). At first glance, Brontë's use of the color "yellow" seems contradictory to the blue-black hues most commonly associated with cholera. The word "cholera" comes from the Greek word "choler," with the OED giving the primary definition of "cholera" as "choler; bile." The OED defines "choler" as "cholera, and including perhaps other bilious disorders." Its parenthetical information "(modern Latin dictionaries say 'jaundice')" make the connection between cholera, bile, and the color yellow. According to the OED, "bile" is considered to be "a brownish yellow color, sometimes passing into green." In the humoral theory of illness, still in use in nineteenth-century England, the term "cholera" became the ordinary name of one of the four humours—sanguis, cholera, melancolia, phlegma—and as such, it was associated with yellow bile. (Black bile was associated with melancholia.) Brontë's choice of the adjective "yellow" carries these cultural connotations now lost with the discrediting of the humoral theory.

6. Morris develops the early scientific debate between miasma and contagion theories concerning cholera's transmission. Morris writes, "By 1848–9, miasma had come to dominate government thinking. It did so as middle-class influence began to take a greater part in government . . ." (183–84). Morris's work establishes the inter-connections among miasma theory, increased middle-class influence, and social reform.

7. A reference to cholera in *Shirley*, which contemporary readers would have missed but which is accessible to Brontë scholars, occurs with Brontë's flash-forward to a visit to Jessie Yorke's grave in a foreign land. Jessie's character was based on Brontë's friend Martha Taylor, sister to Mary Taylor, who died of cholera in Brussels, Belgium in October 1842. According to Barker, Charlotte Brontë visited Martha's grave on October 30, 1842 (404–05). Although no reference to his death is included within the novel, a second close family friend to die of cholera was William Weightman. According to Barker, Weightman contracted cholera mid-August 1842 while attending the sick in the Haworth parish (402–04). Patrick Brontë not only visited him twice daily until Weightman's death on September 6, 1842, but Brontë also officiated at his funeral at Haworth church. Cholera had a real presence in the Brontës' life.

8. Of the scholarly work on the new idea of disease being within man's realm to control through social reform, Frank Mort's *Dangerous Sexualities: Medico-Moral Politics in England Since 1830* asserts the connection between cholera and social reform most strongly. R.J. Morris does not equate the cholera epidemic of 1832 with instant public health reform, since people like James Kay, who, in 1832, could already see that the necessity for social reform to deal with cholera, were in the minority (86). Yet, significantly, according to Morris, "What did develop in 1832 was the medical community study" (186). Thus,

NOTES 149

Morris's argument stresses cholera's impact in creating a medical
community, which in turn created leaders capable of taking the initiative in public health reform a decade later when cholera hit again.
Morris summarizes, "As a source of change, cholera in 1832 operated
in the longer term" (125). Margaret Pelling's *Cholera, Fever, and
English Medicine 1825–1865* discusses cholera's "shock value" role
(4); however, she feels fever, rather than cholera, is the most significant contributor in the change toward public health reform since "the
ordinary fever of the country" was an ongoing condition whereas
cholera came and went, affecting the British nation only four times in
the century with four distinct cholera epidemics: 1831–1832,
1848–1849, 1853–1854, and 1866 (6). Pamela K. Gilbert's "A Sinful
and Suffering Nation: Cholera and the Evolution of Medical and
Religious Authority in Britain, 1832–1866" posits that while the
second epidemic was definitely a battleground for the official discourses of Church and Medicine to interpret the social meaning of
cholera for the nation, that the third epidemic marks a "move toward
conflation of the two discourses" (41) with the "Clergy becom[ing]
the secular go-between of the oracular scientist and the public—and
science becom[ing] the expression and servant of Divine Will" (41).
See Charles Rosenberg's *The Cholera Years* for an insightful explanation of why England was two decades ahead of the United States in
making the transition to understanding cholera as a social factor rather
than a moral affliction.
9. Mort writes, "The choice of miasma theory was influenced both by
the internal logic of medical discourse and by wider cultural and
political considerations. Miasma fitted well with the scientific materialism of early social medicine. At the level of public debate it was
graspable—effluvia could be pointed to and graphically illustrated. But
like the concepts of the eighteenth-century hygienists, miasma also
targeted the *human agents* of infection—now defined as the labouring
classes. The theory was elastic and capable of infinite variation; its envi-
ronmentalist logic ranged from unsanitary conditions to immoral
practices" (italics in original, 23).
10. John Snow's breakthrough in cholera research in October 1849 was
important to national health since, by clarifying that cholera was
water-borne, his work was the first indication that the miasma theory
did not apply to cholera. Although Snow's findings, *On the Mode of
Communication of Cholera*, were first published in 1849, they did not
make much impact at the time. According to Morris, it was not until
cholera's third appearance in 1854 that Snow could apply his theory,
successfully tracing the source of infection to the Broad Street pump
in London's Soho district (208–09). Later, William Farr, convinced
by Snow's theory, applied it successfully in the 1866 cholera epidemic
(Morris 210). Even though Snow's water-borne theory countered
the air-borne theory upheld by miasma, nonetheless, the continuing

efforts to contain and stop cholera still relied on the new idea of social reform. In both readings of cholera prevention, environmental measures of social reform were key.

11. Brontë includes one last authorial address to "Men of Manchester," which exists solely to defend her lifelong hero, the Duke of Wellington, against his contemporary detractors, located predominantly in Manchester and the north of England (636).

12. In their respective illnesses, Robert and Louis Moore are used as contrasts to her heroines. However, few other illnesses affecting Brontë's male characters are given much development in terms of the cultural role at play in these illnesses. Perhaps as an indication of class, the middle-class Henry Sympson is born lame, whereas the working-class Moses Barraclough acquires a wooden leg. Both Mr. Helstone's rheumatism and Mr. Sympson's gout are mentioned but never explored as culturally constructed illness. Mr. Sympson's gout would indicate to contemporary readers that he is a long-term drinker. Potential alcoholism is the most commonly mentioned disease affecting male characters in *Shirley*. Moses Barraclough, Mr. Malone, and Michael Hartley all have drinking problems, with the latter also being considered half-crazed. Mr. James Helstone, already deceased, died of alcoholism. However, Charlotte Brontë's novel, unlike Anne Brontë's *The Tenant of Wildfell Hall*, does not explore the cultural implications of such drinking. The only point in the novel that reaches for this larger picture occurs when Robert uses alcohol to help Mr. Sykes get up his courage for a confrontation with the rioters. With two tumblers of wine and water, Mr. Sykes becomes "at least *word*-valiant" (130). Here, Brontë makes the connection between alcohol and the male need to appear courageous and manly, perhaps an insight she gained through close contract with Branwell's excessive drinking. Again, Charlotte Brontë's focus is much more directly on her female characters' health.

13. The OED notes that "canker" was "formerly, often the same as 'cancer'." It clarifies that "the Latin 'cancer' was introduced about 1600; but 'canker' was used alongside of it till circa 1700."

14. Mrs. Pryor gives her real name as Agnes Grey Helstone, an echo of Anne Brontë's heroine in her first novel, *Agnes Grey*. Whereas Anne Brontë has provided a happy-ever-after ending with marriage and family as a reward for her young governess Agnes Grey, Charlotte Brontë, in detailing the life of Agnes Grey Helstone, has provided a much more realistic portrayal of what a governess's fate would be: ill-health, fears of insanity, and a bad marriage, chosen as a desperate attempt to escape from being a governess.

15. Cauterizing the wound inflicted by a potentially rabid dog with a "red hot iron" was still common practice in the nineteenth century, and recommended as treatment as late as 1878 in the *Lancet* (Carter 69). Shirley's choosing to remain silent may have been in part prompted by

her desire to protect Phoebe since it was a common assumption that killing the dog would prevent rabies in the person who was bitten (Griffin 4). Shirley's lack of faith in modern medicine parallels Emily's, who in her final illness remained adamant that she wanted "no poisoning doctor" (Barker 575). Emily agreed to see a physician only hours before her death, presumably when she knew it was too late for his administrations to make any difference. Shirley's lack of faith is not clarified whether it refers specifically to the lack of a proven medical cure for rabies or to a lack of faith in the health profession in general.

16. Because it was readily available in all Victorian households until the Sale of Poisons and Pharmacy Act of 1868 limited its easy access, laudanum was often used as a means of committing suicide. Laudanum was one of the four favorite household poisons most commonly chosen by Victorian and Edwardian women bent on suicide (Anderson 364 footnote 83). Elizabeth Siddal, Dante Gabriel Rossetti's wife is just one example among many Victorian women who chose laudanum to end their life. Thus, Shirley's request of death by an overdose of laudanum is historically accurate, especially once we consider that laudanum is recorded in the *Lancet* in 1825, 1854, and 1877 as one of the many remedies commonly prescribed for rabies (Carter 73). In addition, the great advantage of laudanum for the purpose of suicide should be considered. Olive Anderson notes "it was notoriously difficult to be confident that death from an overdose of laudanum was deliberate, since the quantity which could be safely taken varied enormously" (185). Thus, Shirley's request for laudanum rather than another form of euthanasia connects a possible "cure" for rabies with her final solution of a dignified death while simultaneously protecting her family from knowing for sure that she deliberately ended her own life.

17. See Miriam Bailin's chapter "Varieties of Pain" in *The Sickroom in Victorian Fiction: The Art of Being Ill*, or her article " 'Varieties of Pain': The Victorian Sickroom and Brontë's *Shirley*" in *Modern Language Quarterly* for a fuller discussion of this idea.

18. In Louis's statement concerning the attack on his brother, "I cannot hear unmoved that ruffians have laid in wait for him, and shot him down like some wild beast from behind a wall," Louis links Robert to the "wild beast," yet the overall portrayal in the novel of the man capable of doing such a deed dehumanizes him rather than his victim (560). Phoebe is the mad dog; Michael Hartley, the madman. In addition to Michael Hartley, only one other lower class character is named as a perpetrator of the local riots—Moses Barraclough. Moses Barraclough is described as a cripple with a wooden leg and Michael Hartley as "half-crazed weaver" (635). Both men are repeatedly described in grotesque terms, with Barraclough's disability and Hartley's drunken excess and consequent half-crazed visions emphasized. Both men are demonized as potential disruptive social forces and are "killed off" by the novel's

plot, Barraclough, figuratively so, since he is transported to Botany Bay. Hartley dies of delirium tremens (635).

19. This lesson can be seen as a milder version of the lesson Rochester learns at the end of *Jane Eyre* where Rochester's blinding and disabled arm teaches him to be a better partner to Jane.

CHAPTER 3   HYSTERIA, FEMALE DESIRE, AND SELF-CONTROL IN *VILLETTE*

1. For the sake of clarity in my argument, I will be referring to Protestantism and Catholicism in broad terms. However, in *Villette*, Brontë addresses religious nuances within Protestantism and within Catholicism. For example, Lucy attends three different Protestant churches in *Villette*. She attends "the French, German, and English— *id est*, the Presbyterian, Lutheran, Episcopalian" (525). Also, the Catholic characters have three different nationalities. Mme Beck is Labasscourrien, Pére Silas is French, and M. Paul is Spanish. Their nationalities give a slightly different slant to the Catholicism in *Villette*. The only overlap Brontë sees between a Protestant sect and Catholicism occurs when she compares the Catholic pamphlet written by Pére Silas to "certain Wesleyan Methodists tracts I had once read when a child" (519). According to Lucy, the Methodists are similar to the Catholics in their both being "flavoured with about the same seasoning of excitation to fanaticism" (519).

2. In *The Professor*, Crimsworth's attack of hypochondria occurs toward the end of the novel. As mentioned earlier, whereas today we consider hypochondria to be an imaginary illness, or more aptly, a psychological disposition to imagined illness, in Victorian times, hypochondria was regarded as chronic illness with symptoms both physical and mental. See Introduction.

3. Illness also affects the narrative in *Villette* in terms of plot. Lucy's social advancement depends largely on illness. Because of her lack of connection, Lucy's advancement in society is not the usual one which grows out of healthy connections with others. Her aloneness creates a situation where her social advancement is largely dependent upon her ability to stay well when others fall ill. First, she accepts a position nursing Miss Maria Marchmont, a rheumatic cripple, whose sickroom becomes Lucy's world for two years. With the death of Miss Marchmont, Lucy takes the radical step of searching for employment abroad at Mme Beck's school in Villette, where she is hired to replace Mrs. Sweeney, an Irish alcoholic. Mrs. Sweeney's alcoholism presents Lucy with the opportunity to become Mme Beck's *bonne-d'enfant*. This is not the only illness which becomes Lucy's stepping stone at Mme Beck's establishment. When Mr. Wilson fails to come to class, Mme Beck fears he is ill. This illness, real or otherwise, opens the door

for Lucy's next job as a teacher. Although not specifically job related, illness also gives Lucy an opportunity for growth when the student Louise Vanderkelhov becomes ill and makes it possible for Lucy to act in the play that the school is performing under M. Paul's direction. Later, when Miss Marchmont's heir suffers from a terrible illness, he sends Lucy Snowe one hundred pounds to right his conscience which she invests in ameliorations for her school. For someone who has not inherited money and social connection, other people's illnesses and her own continued health are of the utmost importance in Lucy's struggle to get ahead.

4. Two of Brontë's letters relating to her growing personal relationship with her publisher George Smith, the model for Dr. John in *Villette*, use this stone metaphor. A letter to Ellen Nussey, thought to have been written on January 20, 1851, refers to a trip down the Rhine that Smith has proposed they take together with his sister. Brontë writes of this trip, "I am not made of stone—and what is mere excitement to him— is fever to me" (Smith 2: 557). The second letter is to George Smith himself, written on April 19, 1851. Earlier Smith had invited Brontë to visit his family in London, an invitation she refused. Once she received a second invitation from his mother, she accepted. Writing of her changed response, Brontë comments, "One can't help it. One does not profess to be made of granite" (Smith 2: 606).

5. Rachel P. Maine's *The Technology of Orgasm: "Hysteria," the Vibrator, and Women's Sexual Satisfaction* is thorough in its research about historical ways in which physicians and midwives relieved hysterical symptoms, predominately in celibate women—virgins, widows, and women involved in religious orders. In addition to manual stimulation of women's external genitalia, movement of the pelvic region was promoted as helping relieve hysterical symptoms. Riding horses and using rocking chairs were among the remedies recommended for hysteria. See Maine's Chapter One.

6. Whereas Brontë uses both the terms "hysteria" and "hallucination" in descriptions of her heroine Lucy Snowe, Lucy herself applies the term "monomania" to Polly when she declares her young friend to have a "monomaniac tendency" (14).

7. See Diane Price Herndl's *Invalid Women* for a fuller discussion of this idea.

8. Arthur Kleinman and Arthur Frank are among the medical anthropologists and medical sociologists who talk in terms of a "body-self" to express this duality. In terms of understanding how illness functions, the concept is incredibly helpful. However, as a cultural theorist of the body, Judith Butler would argue that the distinction is too simplistic, that the physical body is always already cultural (12–13). See Butler's *Gender Trouble*.

9. Even Gaskell, in her role as biographer, chose to skirt the issue of the appeal that Catholicism had for Brontë. In "Two Suppressed Opinions

in Mrs. Gaskell's 'Life of Charlotte Bontë'," Angus Easson includes Gaskell's scored out paragraph that originally addressed this issue. Gaskell wrote and then omitted, " . . . and yet I imagine that part of its vehemence [toward the Catholic religion] arose from the fact that she was aware of her own susceptibility to some of the influences employed by its professors . . . " (qtd. in Easson 282).

10. Perhaps Brontë's choice of the name Dr. John Graham for her fictional physician has greater significance than generally assumed, given the fact that the medical authority in use at the Brontë Parsonage was Dr. Thomas John Graham, author of *Modern Domestic Medicine*.

11. Brontë may have also been familiar with another of Combe's books, *A System of Phrenology*, which goes into great detail about the abilities of each of the different faculties.

12. See Shuttleworth for her discussion of how Combe's use of phrenology shifts focus from Gall's original thesis and the impact of Combe's more optimistic theories on the self-help movement in Britian.

13. Although never described in phrenological terms, as highly intelligent heroines of Victorian novels, George Eliot's Dorothea Brooks and Henry James's Isabel Archer would be likely candidates for having high foreheads.

14. In addition to the courtship between Lucy and M. Paul being a comparison of foreheads, it is a comparison of religions. M. Paul's active need to convert Lucy relates to Catholicism's need for an external authority for approval. Ultimately, Lucy and M. Paul come to believe that the essence of each's religion is the same. In part, it is Lucy's and M. Paul's deprivations based upon religious grounds that bring them together. She has nothing, and what he has, he has given away to the church.

15. With Dr. John as the Protestant representative, Protestantism seems more concerned with self-control as the means for living up to ideals, especially for women, than Catholicism. Dr. John's ideal of the perfect woman controls both Polly and Lucy as they increase their self-control in attempts to please him. Dr. John's compliment to Mme Beck on her "*sang-froid bien opportun*," i.e., her well-timed composure, also connects to this ideal (116). Both Ginevra and Lucy are wise in breaking away from his idealized visions of them. With M. Paul as the Catholic representative, Catholicism seems more nonchalant about self-control. Lucy notes M. Paul does not care about his own "dignity," commenting on his habit of "casting to the winds that dignity and self-control with which he never cared long to encumber himself" (428). Following this value system, M. Paul urges Lucy not to be so concerned about her fear of failure, which he attributes to fears of loss of dignity, as when she refused to write impromptu.

16. Maynard's argument is similar to mine in that he feels it is due to Lucy's emotional confidence that she can now face and accept loss which begins the transformation of the nun from mythical figure of

legend into the actual figure of de Hamal. However, I see more happening here with illness being instrumental in the timing of the nun's symbolic destruction.

17. Indeed, we could speculate that, even in M. Paul's presence, Lucy would flourish fully. After all, M. Paul actively encourages Lucy's development of her faculties throughout the novel. M. Paul encourages Lucy to perform in the play, he tutors her in arithmetic, he pushes her with her French compositions, and he enables her to start her own school.

CHAPTER 4   VAMPIRES, GHOSTS, AND THE DISEASE OF DIS/POSSESSION IN *WUTHERING HEIGHTS*

1. My reading differs from Susan Gorsky's " 'I'll Cry Myself Sick': Illness in *Wuthering Heights*," in two fundamental aspects. First, whereas Gorsky focuses primarily on Cathy's illness, I provide a theoretical framework that encompasses all of the illnesses present in the novel. Second, as I have indicated by placing the term "anorexia" within quotation marks, I read the easy attachment of a modern medical diagnosis to a Victorian ailment as potentially problematic. While any analysis using modern diagnostic terms can offer wonderful insights, it may do so at the expense of important historical dimensions. A greater understanding of the original cultural context of the Victorian texts is always valuable. Consequently, I feel troubled by the ease with which Gorsky claims Cathy is an "anorexic," even though she is following in the footsteps of such feminist critics as Sandra Gilbert and Susan Gubar. [I would also call into question Terry Eagleton's casual reference to Heathcliff's "schizophrenia" rather than exploring Brontë's own term of "monomania" (111).] Joan Jacobs Brumberg's historical analysis of anorexia, *Fasting Girls: The History of Anorexia Nervosa*, is useful here because Brumberg points out that there are two phases within the disease of anorexia. Whereas the second stage where the body, because of the physiological changes involved, begins to refuse food is common in all cases, the first stage of anorexia differs from culture to culture, century to century. This first stage, with its emphasis on the acculturation of the body, explains the difference behind the individual's motives to refuse food in the first place. For example, the medieval mystics' refusal of food differs culturally from modern American adolescent girls' refusal of food. While the various readings of Cathy as anorexic are intriguing, they seem blind to the cultural difference that exists between our current culture and the Victorian era. Also troubling, Cathy's use of "hunger strikes" often becomes exaggerated, blown up into a full-fledged disease. In the novel, Cathy uses her hunger strike for *three days*,

hardly time enough to develop into the chronic life-threatening disease we know as "anorexia." In addition, Cathy's inability to eat is just one aspect of Brontë's description of Cathy's illness, which also includes descriptions of her "brain fever" (104), her "delirium" (100), and her "confinement" due to both pregnancy and "despondency" (105). Building on this tradition, some scholars, such as Katherine Frank, have even made the problematic claim that Emily Brontë herself was "anorexic."

2. In "The Incompetent Narrator of *Wuthering Heights*," Terence McCarthy demonstrates Lockwood is "a thoroughly unreliable narrator" (51) who "passes on a tale he never understands" (50).

3. Of Emily Brontë's characters, only Catherine Linton, following her illness after nursing Linton Heathcliff, shows the internal growth from illness that Charlotte Brontë applauds. Yet Catherine's psychological growth is minimal since it consists only of her new awareness of her vulnerability in a patriarchal household other than her father's.

4. Emily Brontë's poem "The Old Stoic," with its beginning line, "Riches I hold in light esteem;" also emphasizes her disdain of worldly pursuits and privileges (1). In "To Imagination," Brontë writes, "So hopeless is the world without, / The world within I doubly prize;" (7–8). Other poems on the power of imagination, such as, "I'm happiest when most away" and "The Prisoner (A Fragment)" also implicitly critique "the world without." All poems are to be found in Janet Gezari's *Emily Jane Brontë: The Complete Poems*.

5. David Cecil contrasts Brontë's use of the supernatural with Walter Scott's use of the supernatural where the supernatural is at variance with the laws of nature. Cecil writes, "With Emily Brontë it is an expression of those laws" (305). However, whereas Cecil thinks the supernatural "is a natural feature of the world as she sees it" (305), I see the alignment of the supernatural and the natural serving the purpose to point out the unnaturalness of culture. In my reading, Brontë's use of vampires and ghosts, i.e., the supernatural, is an expression of culture's distortion of the natural laws.

6. Frank's romantic reading of Emily Brontë's novel emphasizes that "Love, for her, was essentially an amoral power, like an immutable force of nature. It . . . was no respecter of artificial human creations such as matrimony" (131). If this were true, the artificial human creation of matrimony would not have been strong enough to keep Cathy and Heathcliff apart. In reality, the cultural values inherent in matrimony condemn Cathy and Heathcliff to be separated from each other and to live their consequent lives of self-alienation.

7. Hindley's cultural transformation into a gentleman takes place while being away at school. Nelly tells us that Hindley came back "altered considerably" (36). Part of this alteration is apparent in that Hindley had "lost his colour, and spoke and dressed quite differently" (36) and part of the alteration is apparent in his new insistence that Joseph and

Nelly "quarter ourselves in the back-kitchen," thereby distinguishing them as servants rather than as members of the family (36). With his father's death, Hindley's abusive treatment of Heathcliff intensifies as a result of his newly acquired power within the family.

8. Hareton Earnshaw's greater emotional connection to Heathcliff as his foster-father attests that this pattern of Heathcliff being more emotionally able to share than Hindley extends beyond their relationships to Cathy. It is crucial to note that since Heathcliff's plan is to cut Hareton off from his rightful inheritance, Brontë is pointing to the greater importance of emotional connection over material possession.

9. Of the items Esquirol lists, "fear" and "vanity" are the two not easily identifiable with psychic loss. Yet even "fear" can be seen as relating to psychic loss since fear is brought about by a sense of loss of control over one's ability to deal with the situation at hand. Perhaps "vanity" is also connected to psychic loss through vanity's loss of a true sense of the value of inner worth and beauty through its emphasis on outward appearances and more worldly circumstances.

10. Linda Ray Pratt's " 'I Shall Be Your Father': Heathcliff's Narrative of Paternity" offers an alternative reading of Heathcliff's motives for "collecting" Hareton and Catherine around him to form his family. Pratt writes, "If we read the ending *as Heathcliff's design* instead of his last minute abandonment of his plan for 'revenge,' then he remains the novel's center, and the narrative is his unbroken quest to reunify the Earnshaw family" (italics in original, 17).

11. Terry Eagleton also makes this point, writing "As an extreme parody of capitalist activity, Heathcliff is also an untypical deviation from its norms" (114). Eagleton sees Heathcliff's struggles with the Grange as symbolic of "the contemporary conflict between bourgeoisie and landed gentry" (115). I would agree Heathcliff's position is at the heart of this cultural moment of change; however, in my eyes Brontë's goal is to point out that whether patriarchy's power is in the hands of the landed gentry or in the hands of the bourgeoisie, it is still a system based on dis/possession of women. As the French saying goes, "*Plus ça change, plus c'est la même chose.*"

12. Because middle-class women in the novel are denied the option of work, Brontë emphasizes the "degrading privileges" of women's idleness. Brontë's term, "degrading privileges," originates in her essay, "The Siege of Oudenarde" (Lonoff 68). The patriarchy sets up a no-win situation in which the women's not working symbolizes the man's status but then provides men with the opportunity to condemn women for their idleness. Joseph condemns Catherine for her "idleness," saying, " 'Bud yah're a nowt, and it's noa use talking— yah'll niver mend uh yer ill ways; bud goa raight tuh t'divil, like yer mother afore ye!' " (12). Heathcliff condemns Catherine, saying " 'there you are at your idle tricks again! The rest of them do earn their bread—you live on my charity! Put your trash away, and find

something to do. You shall pay me for the plague of having you eternally in my sight' " (25).

13. Isabella arrives at the Grange with blood streaming down her neck from a battle scene between Heathcliff and Hindley, in which she allies herself with Hindley. Overtly, her battlewounds are the markings of the battle between Hindley and Heathcliff, but they also mark the more hidden battle between Heathcliff and Edgar. After symbolically taking off her wedding ring, Isabella comments on her knowledge that she is the pawn in this latter battle, saying, " 'He'd be capable of coming to seek me, to tease Edgar' " (133).

14. Although Karl Marx's *Capital* was not published until 1867, it built upon ideas already present in *The Communist Manifesto*, which was first published in London in 1848, the year following the publication of *Wuthering Heights*.

15. Brontë and Marx's arguments are similar, even if they focus on different elements within British culture. Brontë's critique emphasizes the power of civilization and culture while Marx's emphasizes capitalism and money. In *The Communist Manifesto* Marx writes about how capitalism has affected the family, stating "The bourgeoisie has torn away from the family its sentimental veil, and has reduced the family relation to a mere money relation" (6). If we apply Brontë's logic to Marx's argument, in Brontë's version, "*Civilization* has torn away from the family its sentimental veil, and has reduced the family relation to a mere *power* relation." Heathcliff's problematic relationships to both the Earnshaw and the Linton families, where he is simultaneously inside and outside of the family, make these power dynamic more visible.

16. As servants, the source of Joseph's and Nelly's physical good health— Joseph's ongoing "rheumatism" is his only health complaint (12) and Nelly's three-week cold is hers (187)—connects to their mutual ability to shift allegiance to new patriarchs. With the patriarchs metaphorically seen as the "head vampires," Joseph and Nelly, in their efforts to do their master's bidding, can be seen metaphorically as "wolves" or "lesser vampires." Heathcliff's reference to Joseph as a "toothless hound" reinforces Brontë's extended use of this metaphor (138). Of the two servants, Joseph changes masters the most easily since he lacks emotional loyalty to anyone other than himself. Self-interest allows Joseph to serve Mr. Earnshaw, Hindley, Heathcliff, and finally Hareton. Nelly is similar to Joseph in her realization that her self-interest is best served by loyalty to her current master. However, Nelly's cold, her only experience of illness within the novel, results after her momentary inner conflict over torn loyalties. Once past the boundaries of the Grange, when Heathcliff and Catherine together ask for Nelly's agreement in allowing Catherine to pay a visit to the Heights, Nelly feels caught in her torn allegiances to her master Edgar and to her mistress Catherine. Nelly's childhood allegiance to

Heathcliff against Edgar may also play a part here. With her feet already chilled and wet, the extended stay results in Nelly catching a cold. Because of their lower class-status, Nelly and Joseph's health could also relate to the greater amounts of physical work they do in comparison to the middle-class men and women they serve.

17. Within the text, Lockwood's dream of ever-increasing violence between men is best represented in the Heathcliff–Hindley struggle where murder and/or suicide become the only two options. When Hindley fails at his attempts to murder Heathcliff, he succeeds at suicide by locking himself in the Heights and "drinking himself to death deliberately" (145). Yet, Heathcliff's death is also a form of suicide because he simply stops eating. In the Heathcliff–Hindley struggle, whether the final choice is murder or suicide, either way, the violence is the fault of a system where power and conflict are directly related to dis/possession. For a more in-depth look at Brontë's knowledge of Victorian legal and cultural practices surrounding suicide, see Barbara Gate's "Suicide in *Wuthering Heights.*"

18. At odds with her culture, Brontë's decision to follow her inner guide is a theme in her life and work. In her poem, "Often rebuked, yet always back returning," Emily Brontë speaks of her determination to follow her own vision, writing, "I'll walk where my own nature would be leading: / It vexes me to choose another guide" (13–14). In the biography, Gaskell writes, "Emily was impervious to influence; she never came in contact with public opinion, and her own decision of what was right and fitting was a law for her own conduct and appearance with which she allowed no one to interfere" (122). Ellen Nussey felt Emily Brontë was "a law unto herself and a heroine in keeping to that law" (qtd. in Frank 115).

19. Mrs. Earnshaw dies in "less than two years after" Heathcliff's arrival (31). Since Cathy was "hardly six years old" when Heathcliff arrives, she is eight years old at her mother's death (29). Dying herself at age 19, Cathy's nightmare in which "the whole last seven years of my life grew a blank!" indicates her father's death occurred when she was twelve years old, four years after the death of her mother (98).

20. Frances has just died when Cathy, age 15, first agrees to marry Edgar. Three years later they marry in the spring when Cathy is eighteen. Cathy dies the following spring. Hindley's death follows Cathy's by six months. These figures indicate that Frances died four-and-a-half years before her husband and that Hareton is four-and-a-half years old at his father's death.

21. Linton is "twelve, or a little more" when Isabella dies and seventeen at his own death (142). Since Heathcliff dies within the year of Linton's death, Heathcliff's death follows Isabella's by five years.

22. My idea of how Brontë's cultural critique overlaps patriarchal domination of women and of nature is echoed in ecofeminist criticism. In "Is Ecofeminism Feminist?" Victoria Davion notes, "ecofeminists

agree that there is an important link between the domination of women and the domination of nature, and that an understanding of one is aided by an understanding of the other" (8). Another ecofeminist, Val Plumwood theorizes that oppression originates in the politics of nature. In "The Ecopolitics Debate and the Politics of Nature," Plumwood develops her point, writing that "The story of the control of the chaotic and deficient realm of 'nature' by mastering and ordering 'reason' has been the master story of Western culture. An examination of this story reveals that this ideology of the domination of nature plays a key role in structuring all the major forms of oppression in the West, which are thus linked through the politics of nature. It has supported pervasive human relations of domination within Western societies and of colonization between Western society and other societies, as well as supporting a colonizing approach towards nonhuman nature itself" (74). While my reading of *Wuthering Heights* focuses on Brontë's representations of illness, I find myself returning again and again to Brontë's insight that in Nature, everything is interconnected. Even though literary criticism exists which deals with the theme of nature in Brontë's novel, I have been unable to find an extended ecofeminist reading of *Wuthering Heights*. Such a theoretical reading of Brontë's novel will prove compelling.

23. Nelly's status as a single woman and her lower-class position does grant one advantage over that of the married middle-class women around her. As an unmarried working woman, Nelly has not had to turn her personal property, however limited, over to the legal use of her husband.

24. Ironically, women, culturally cut off from the possibility of owning land, can own animals, specifically dogs. First, Isabella owns Fanny, which Heathcliff tries to kill by hanging it, and later Catherine is offered a puppy by Hareton. The ownership of horses is more problematic for both generations. For example, Cathy requests her whip because "she could ride any horse in the stable" (29). Yet, when Mr. Earnshaw buys colts at the local fair, he only buys colts for his son Hindley and his foster son Heathcliff. It appears Cathy does not own her own horse. In Catherine's case, whatever the actual legal status of ownership is, Catherine feels her horse Minny is her own since she offers "her pretty birds, and her pony Minny" to Linton as a bribe to get his help in helping her escape from Heathcliff (214). Linton's response— " 'but I told her she had nothing to give, they were all, all mine' "—indicates that Minny is legally Edgar's property and, as such, will pass into Linton's ownership at his death (214).

25. Salleh's 1/0 formula is insightful. She writes, "Eurocentric cultures are arranged discursively around what has standing (A) and what does not (notA). Such a logic gives identity to A expressed by the value of 1. NotA is merely defined by relation to A, having no identity of its own, and thus 0 value" (35). Basically, the 1/0 formula is an equation

that defines man as the norm and woman as "a hole," as "zero" or as "lack" (36).

26. To reinforce that the gender politics within illness continue in the second generation, Brontë creates Linton Heathcliff, the only character in the novel sickly from birth. Linton's "sickly peevishness" is the result of his precarious health (155). Perhaps because he cannot physically compete with healthier males, such as Heathcliff and Hareton, Linton sees his ill-health as giving him a perverse form of power over young Catherine. Linton is constantly cruel to her, often paradoxically complaining that she is the cause of his illness while implying that she is also the cure. Heathcliff capitalizes on this type of rhetoric when he tells Catherine that Linton is " 'dying for you' " (179) and that " 'a kind word from you would be his best medicine' " (180). Yet, because of the power inherent in his male position, even though sick himself, Linton has no empathy for another's illness. Linton follows Heathcliff's advice, saying " 'He says I'm not to be soft with Catherine; she's my wife . . . she may cry, and be sick as much as she pleases!' "(213). Catherine may "be sick as much as she pleases" because illness in a woman demonstrates how fully she is disempowered.

27. Brontë's metaphorical language also codes her references to her female characters' sexuality, including references to pregnancy. For example, when Isabella is in flight, Nelly comments on "your condition" (133). It is not until later in the text that we realize that this reference is to Isabella's being pregnant. Isabella herself tells Nelly about her pregnancy when she asks if Nelly thinks Heathcliff would be content to allow her to "grow fat and merry" at the Grange (133). The only reference to Cathy's pregnancy is a mention of her "long confinement" (105). To Victorian readers, the phrase "confinement" would automatically have carried the connotations of pregnancy. Again, reading as a Victorian reader clued into how sexual information must be conveyed metaphorically, we learn that the period of Cathy's active sexuality with Edgar which results in her pregnancy is triggered by Heathcliff's return. In Cathy's efforts to placate her husband's fears, "she rewarded him with such a summer of sweetness and affection in return, as made the house a paradise for several days; both master and servants profiting from the perpetual sunshine" (79). In some critical readings, such as Pratt's "Heathcliff's Narrative of Paternity," the possibility of Catherine being Heathcliff's daughter is raised. Not only does the physical description of Catherine's light Lintonesque features belie this possibility, but also this acknowledgment within the text of Cathy's sexuality with her husband.

28. In addition to Catherine's feigning of illness, when Catherine is held hostage by Heathcliff at the Heights, the reason given for her not being able to visit her dying father also involves an imaginary illness. Edgar's four henchmen, sent to retrieve Catherine, are helpless in the face of illness when they are told that "Catherine was ill, too ill to quit

her room" (216). According to Nelly, this imaginary illness is strategically created by Heathcliff. Because Catherine successfully escapes
from the Heights to visit her father on his deathbed, Nelly's reading
that this is an imaginary illness seems accurate.

29. Sanger gives a detailed account of the Victorian inheritance laws to
explain the difference between the law of land (real property) and that
of money and goods (personal property) and to describe the law of
entails. I have used Sanger's work as my base to give an overview of
how land is passed on to heirs in *Wuthering Heights*. For more of the
legal details, including the legal terms of the time, such as "owner in
fee-simple," "estate tail," and "tenant in tail," see Sanger (293–94).

30. In the scene where Catherine and Hareton meet for the first time,
Brontë stresses that while the cousins are out on the moors, class does
not become an issue, but when they are once more within the realm of
culture by being indoors, Catherine's class awareness leads to her treat-
ing Hareton with contempt. Catherine complains to Nelly, " 'And he
never said, Miss; he should have done, shouldn't he, if he's a servant?' "
(151) and " 'Mustn't he be made to do as I ask him?' " (151).

31. For example, in "The Incompetent Narrator of *Wuthering Heights*,"
Terrance McCarthy asserts "With Nelly Dean and Lockwood, Emily
Brontë insures the rejection of simple categories by presenting her
story from two distorted viewpoints." McCarthy sees Lockwood's
inability to "get beyond the notions of romance" (55), claiming that
"Lockwood is a study in frailty, triviality, and inadequacy, and Brontë
uses his errors to tell her tale. Throughout, his comments are discred-
ited, and then, in a final piece of irony, the novelist gives him the last
word" (61). McCarthy sees Nelly's unreliability in that "It is her very
involvement with the action which colors and distorts her narrative"
(56–57). While McCarthy comments on the impact of Lockwood's
"romantic" nature and Nelly's "traditional faith" in their reading of
the death of Heathcliff and the three graves, his reading foregoes a
commentary on the lives of the second generation entirely. In "The
Unreliable Narrator in *Wuthering Heights*," Gideon Shunami's focus
is on how the two unreliable narrators's "misunderstanding of the
spirit of the protagonists and the meaning of their actions" ends by
"paradoxically, augment[ing] for us the inner story's credibility"
(468). Shunami does not comment on the contribution the unreliable
narrators make to the novel's ending.

32. Eagleton's interpretation focuses on how the ending relies on the
death of an old class and points toward a new class. Nancy
Armstrong's reading points toward the reinstatement of the past.
Armstrong writes, "While Hareton's rise into power does represent
the reform of an intolerably authoritarian society along more human-
itarian lines, this reform is accomplished by means of a return to the
past which restores the lines of inheritance and reconstitutes the family
as it was prior to Heathcliff's intervention" (372).

33. Newman discusses Hareton's acculturation in different terms than mine. In her discussion of the novel's conclusion, Newman writes of "the domestication (and figurative castration) of a potent male figure (Hareton)" (1036). Newman's terms, "domestication" and "figurative castration," both imply a loss of power in Hareton's transformation. In my reading, Hareton's "acculturation" results in his gaining of cultural power.

34. Johnson explains that gooseberries and currants are related species, having the scientific name *ribes*. He gives a standard recipe for gooseberry wine: three pounds of sugar, four pounds of fruit, to eight pounds of water (179).

35. Charlotte Brontë's letter of December 10, 1848 tells of Emily Brontë's edict that " 'no poisoning doctor' shall come near her" (Smith 2: 152). This letter and others recording Emily Brontë's last days manifest her continual refusal of trying recommended medicines. Because laudanum, a tincture of opium dissolved in alcohol, was the most common form of medicine in Victorian England and because alcohol itself was commonly used as medicine to stimulate the system, Brontë is likely to be equating the "poison" of the "poisoning doctor" with alcohol.

36. Alcohol is also used for medicinal purposes when Linton bids Catherine to " 'add a spoonful of wine' " in his water (182).

37. Given women's complete cutoff from legal rights and property rights during the Victorian period, Brontë's metaphor of ghosts to represent complete dis-possession works well. Now that various legal and cultural reforms have taken place in western cultures, women's total dis-possession is no longer as possible on such a grand scale. I am sure gender-based dis-possession continues to occur even now on to a smaller degree, i.e., partial rather that total dis-possession, or on a more individual basis rather than across all families of a certain culture.

BIBLIOGRAPHY

Ackerman, Robert J. *Perfect Daughters: Adult Daughters of Alcoholics.* Deerfield Beach, FL: Health Communications, Inc., 1989.

Allott, Miriam, Ed. *The Brontës: The Critical Heritage.* London: Routledge & Kegan Paul, 1974.

Anderson, Olive. *Suicide in Victorian and Edwardian England.* Oxford: Clarendon, 1987.

Armstrong, Nancy. "Emily Brontë In and Out of Her Time," *Genre* 15 (Fall 1982): 243–64. Rpt. in *Wuthering Heights: A Norton Critical Edition.* Ed. William M. Sale, Jr. and Richard Dunn. 3rd ed. New York: Norton, 1990. 365–77.

Bailin, Miriam. *The Sickroom in Victorian Fiction: The Art of Being Ill.* Cambridge: Cambridge University Press, 1994.

———. " 'Varieties of Pain': The Victorian Sickroom and Brontë's *Shirley,*" *Modern Language Quarterly* 48.3 (Sept. 1987): 254–78.

Bakhtin, Mikhail. *The Dialogic Imagination: Four Essays.* Austin, TX: University of Texas Press, 1981.

Barker, Juliet. *The Brontës.* London: Phoenix, 1994.

Briggs, Asa. "Cholera and Society," *Past and Present* 19 (April 1961): 76–96.

Brodwin, Paul. "Symptoms and Social Performances," *Pain as Human Experience: An Anthropological Perspective.* Ed. Mary-Jo Dellvecchio Good, Paul E. Brodwin, Byron J. Good, and Arthur Kleinman. Berkeley, CA: University of California Press, 1994. 77–99.

Brontë, Anne. *Agnes Grey.* 1847. Ed. Robert Inglesfield and Hilda Marsden. New York: Oxford University Press, 1991.

———. *The Tenant of Wildfell Hall.* 1848. Ed. Herbert Rosengarten. New York: Oxford University Press, 1992.

Brontë, Charlotte. *Jane Eyre.* 1847. Ed. David Malouf. Oxford: Oxford University Press, 1999.

———. *The Professor.* 1853. Ed. Margaret Smith and Herbert Rosengarten. Oxford: Oxford University Press, 1987.

———. *Shirley.* 1849. Ed. Margaret Smith and Herbert Rosengarten. New York: Oxford University Press, 1981.

———. *Villette.* 1853. Ed. Margaret Smith and Herbert Rosengarten. New York: Oxford University Press, 1990.

Brontë, Emily. "The Butterfly," *The Belgian Essays: Charlotte Brontë and Emily Brontë.* Ed. Sue Lonoff. New Haven, CT: Yale University Press, 1996. 176–79.

Brontë, Emily. "The Cat," *The Belgian Essays: Charlotte Brontë and Emily Brontë*. Ed. Sue Lonoff. New Haven, CT: Yale University Press, 1996. 56–59.

———. *Emily Jane Brontë: The Complete Poems*. Ed. Janet Gezari. London: Penguin, 1992.

———. "The Palace of Death," *The Belgian Essays: Charlotte Brontë and Emily Brontë*. Ed. Sue Lonoff. New Haven, CT: Yale University Press, 1996. 224–31.

———. *Wuthering Heights*. 1847. Ed. Richard J. Dunn. 4th ed. New York: Norton, 2003.

Brumberg, Joan Jacobs. *Fasting Girls: The History of Anorexia Nervosa*. 1988. New York: Plume, 1989.

Buchan, William. *Domestic Medicine*. 1772. Rpt. New York: Garland, 1985.

Butler, Judith. *Bodies that Matter: On the Discursive Limits of "Sex."* New York: Routledge, 1993.

———. *Gender Trouble: Feminism and the Subversion of Identity*. 1990. New York: Routledge, 1999.

Carter, K. Codell. "Nineteenth-Century Treatments for Rabies as Reported in the *Lancet*," *Medical History: A Quarterly Journal Devoted to the History of Medicine and Related Science* 26.1 (Jan. 1982): 67–78.

Cecil, David. "Emily Brontë and *Wuthering Heights*," *Wuthering Heights: An Authoritative Text with Essays in Criticism*. Ed. William M. Sale, Jr. 2nd ed. New York: Norton, 1972.

Clark-Beattie, Rosemary. "Fables of Rebellion: Anti-Catholicism and the Structure of *Villette*," *ELH* 53.4 (Winter 1986): 821–47.

Combe, George. *The Constitution of Man*. 1828. Introduction by Eric T. Carlson. Delmar, NY: Scholars' Facsimiles & Reprints Inc., 1974.

———. *A System of Phrenology*. 3rd ed. Edinburgh: John Anderson; London: Longman, 1830.

Dames, Nicholas. "The Clinical Novel: Phrenology and *Villette*," *Novel: A Forum on Fiction*. 29.3 (Spring 1996): 367–90.

Davies, Stevie. *Emily Brontë: Heretic*. London: The Women's Press, 1994.

Davion, Victoria. "Is Ecofeminism Feminist?" *Ecological Feminism*, Ed. Karen J. Warren. New York: Routledge, 1994. 8–28.

Dickens, Charles. *Hard Times: An Authoritative Text, Contexts, Criticism*. Ed. Fred Kaplan and Sylvere Monod. 3rd ed. New York: Norton, 2001.

———. *Sketches by Boz: Illustrative of Every-Day Life and Every-Day People*. 2 vols. London: Chapman & Hall, 1910.

Dinsdale, Ann. "The Brontës in Haworth," Brontë Parsonage Museum 28 Aug. 1995.

Drinka, George Frederick. *The Birth of Neurosis: Myth, Malady, and the Victorians*. New York: Simon & Schuster, 1984.

Eagleton, Terry. *Myths of Power: A Marxist Study of the Brontës*. 1975. 2nd ed. London: Macmillan, 1988.

Easson, Angus. "Two Suppressed Opinions in Mrs. Gaskell's 'Life of Charlotte Brontë'," *Brontë Society Transactions* 16 (1974): 281–83.

Eliot, George. "Janet's Repentance," *Scenes of Clerical Life*. Ed. Thomas A. Noble. New York: Oxford University Press, 1985.

———. *Middlemarch*. 1871–1872. Ed. Bert G. Hornback. 2nd ed. New York: Norton, 2000.

Fahnestock, Jeanne. "The Heroine of Irregular Features: Physiognomy and Conventions of Heroine Description," *Victorian Studies* 24.3 (Spring 1981): 325–50.

Federico, Annette. " 'I must have drink': Addiction, Angst, and Victorian Realism," *Dionysos: Literature and Addiction Tri-Quarterly* 2.2 (Fall 1990): 11–25.

Foucault, Michel. *The Birth of the Clinic: An Archaeology of Medical Perception*. 1963. Trans. A. M. Sheridan Smith. New York: Vintage, 1994.

———. *Discipline and Punish: The Birth of the Prison*. 1975. Trans. Alan Sheridan. New York: Vintage, 1979.

———. *Madness and Civilization: A History of Insanity in the Age of Reason*. 1961. Trans. Richard Howard. New York: Vintage, 1988.

Frank, Arthur W. *The Wounded Storyteller: Body, Illness, and Ethics*. Chicago, IL: University of Chicago Press, 1995.

Frank, Katherine. *A Chainless Soul: A Life of Emily Brontë*. Boston, MA: Houghton Mifflin, 1990.

French, Richard Valpy. *Nineteen Centuries of Drink in England: A History*. London: Longman, Green, & Co., 1884.

Frost, Brian. *The Monster with a Thousand Faces: Guises of the Vampire in Myth and Literature*. Bowling Green, OH: Bowling Green State University Popular Press, 1989.

Gaskell, Elizabeth. *Mary Barton*. 1848. Ed. Edgar Wright. London: Oxford University Press, 1998.

———. *The Life of Charlotte Brontë*. 1857. Ed. Elisabeth Jay. New York: Penguin, 1997.

Gates, Barbara. "Suicide in *Wuthering Heights*," *Readings on Wuthering Heights*. Ed. Hayley R. Mitchell. San Diego, CA: Greenhaven Press, 1999. 129–35.

Gezari, Janet, Ed. *Emily Jane Brontë: The Complete Poems*. London: Penguin, 1992.

Gilbert, Pamela K. "A Sinful and Suffering Nation: Cholera and the Evolution of Medical and Religious Authority in Britain, 1832–1866," *Nineteenth-Century Prose*. 25.1 (Spring 1998): 26–45.

Gilbert, Sandra M. and Susan Gubar. *The Madwoman in the Attic: The Woman Writer and the Nineteenth-Century Literary Imagination*. New Haven, CT: Yale University Press, 1979.

Giobbi, Giuliana. "The Anorexics of *Wuthering Heights*," *Readings on Wuthering Heights*. Ed. Hayley R. Mitchell. San Diego, CA: Greenhaven Press, 1999. 136–41.

Gissing, George. *The Odd Women*. New York: Macmillan, 1893.

Good, Byron. "A Body in Pain—The Making of a World of Chronic Pain," *Pain as Human Experience: An Anthropological Perspective*. Ed. Mary-Jo

Dellvecchio Good, Paul E. Brodwin, Byron J. Good, and Arthur Kleinman. Berkeley, CA: University of California Press, 1994. 29–48.

Good, Mary-Jo Delvecchio, Paul E. Brodwin, Byron J. Good, and Arthur Kleinman, Eds. *Pain as Human Experience: An Anthropological Perspective.* Berkeley, CA: University of California Press, 1994.

Grindrod, Ralph Barnes. *Bacchus: An Essay on the Nature, Causes, Effects and Cure of Intemperance.* London: J. Pasco, 1839.

Gorsky, Susan Rubinow. " 'I'll Cry Myself Sick': Illness in *Wuthering Heights,*" *Literature and Medicine* 18.2 (Fall 1999): 173–91.

Graham, Thomas J. *Modern Domestic Medicine: A Popular Treatise, Describing the Symptoms, Causes, Distinction, and Correct Treatment of the Diseases Incident to the Human Frame; Embracing the Modern Improvements in Medicine.* 1st ed. (1826); 8th ed. (1840); 9th ed. (1844); 11th ed. (1853); and 12th ed. (1858). London: Simpkin, Marshal and Company.

———. *Sure Methods of Improving Health, and Prolonging Life; or, A Treatise on the Art of Living Long and Comfortably, by Regulating the Diet and Regimen.* London: Simpkin and Marshall, 1828.

Griffin, Brian. " 'Mad Dogs and Irishmen': Dogs and Rabies in the Eighteenth and Nineteenth Centuries," *Ulster Folklife* 40 (1994): 1–15.

Gubar, Susan. "The Genesis of Hunger, According to *Shirley,*" *Critical Essays on Charlotte Brontë.* Ed. Barbara Timm Gates. Boston, MA: G.K. Hall & Co., 1990. 232–51.

Hardy, Thomas. *Jude the Obscure: An Authoritative Text, Backgrounds and Contexts, Criticism.* Ed. Norman Page. 2nd ed. New York: Norton, 1999.

———. *The Mayor of Casterbridge: An Authoritative Text, Backgrounds, Criticism.* Ed. James K. Robinson. New York: Norton, 1977.

———. *Tess of the D'Ubervilles: An Authoritative Text.* Ed. Scott Elledge. New York: Norton, 1979.

Harrison, Brian. *Drink and the Victorians: The Temperance Question in England 1815–1872.* Pittsburgh: University of Pittsburgh Press, 1971.

Helm, W.H. "Tuberculosis and the Brontë Family," *Brontë Studies.* 27 (July 2002): 157–67.

Herndl, Diane Price. *Invalid Women: Figuring Feminine Illness in American Fiction and Culture, 1840—1940.* Chapel Hill, NC: University of North Carolina Press, 1993.

"Hints on the Modern Governess System," *Fraser's Magazine* 30 (Nov. 1844): 571–83.

Hutcheon, Michael. "The Body Theatrical: Embodying the Voice." Opera Incarnate: Re-Viewing the Operatic Body. The Abraham Lincoln Lectures. University of Nebraska Press. Lincoln, Nebraska. 6 April 1999.

Hutcheon, Linda and Michael Hutcheon. *Opera: Desire, Disease, Death.* Lincoln, NE: University of Nebraska Press, 1996.

James, Henry. *Portrait of a Lady.* 1881. Ed. Nicola Bradbury. New York: Oxford University Press, 1998.

Johnson, George William. *The Cucumber and the Gooseberry; Their Culture, Uses and History.* London: Baldwin, 1847.

Kleinman, Arthur. *The Illness Narratives: Suffering, Healing, and the Human Condition.* New York: Basic Books, 1998.

———. "Pain and Resistance: The Delegitimation and Relegitmation of Local Worlds," *Pain as Human Experience: An Anthropological Perspective.* Ed. Mary-Jo Dellvecchio Good, Paul E. Brodwin, Byron J. Good, and Arthur Kleinman. Berkeley, CA: University of California Press, 1994. 169–97.

Lamb, Charles. "Confessions of a Drunkard," in *The Works of Charles and Mary Lamb. Volume I 1798–1834.* Ed. E.V. Lucas. New York: G.P. Putnam's Sons, 1903.

Langland, Elizabeth. *Anne Brontë: The Other One.* London: Macmillan, 1989.

Lashgari, Deirdre. "What Some Women Can't Swallow: Hunger as Protest in Charlotte Brontë's *Shirley,*" *Disorderly Eaters: Texts in Self-Empowerment.* Ed. Lilian R. Furst and Peter W. Graham. University Park, PA: Pennsylvania State University Press, 1992. 141–52.

Leavis, Q.D. "A Fresh Approach to *Wuthering Heights,*" *Wuthering Heights: An Authoritative Text with Essays in Criticism.* Ed. William M. Sale, Jr. 2nd ed. New York: Norton, 1972. 306–21.

Lemon, Charles. "Sickness and Health in *Wuthering Heights,*" *Brontë Society Transactions.* 14.3 (1963): 23–25.

Lonoff, Sue, Ed. *The Belgian Essays: Charlotte Brontë and Emily Brontë.* New Haven, CT: Yale University Press, 1996.

Lorber, Judith. *Gender and the Social Construction of Illness.* New York: Sage Publications, 1997.

MacGregor, Catherine. " 'I Cannot Trust Your Oaths and Promises: I Must Have a Written Agreement': Talk and Text in *The Tenant of Wildfell Hall,*" *Dionysos: Literature and Addiction Tri-Quarterly* 4.2 (Fall 1992): 31–39.

Macnish, Robert. *The Anatomy of Drunkenness.* 6th ed. Glasgow: W.R. M'Phun, 1836.

Maines, Rachel. *The Technology of Orgasm: "Hysteria," the Vibrator, and Women's Sexual Satisfaction.* Baltimore, MA: Johns Hopkins University Press, 1999.

Marx, Karl. *Capital: A Critique of Political Economy.* 1867. Trans. Samuel Moore and Edward Aveling. Chicago, IL: Charles H. Kerr & Company, 1921.

Marx, Karl and Friedrich Engels. *The Communist Manifesto.* London, 1848. New York: Monthly Review Press, 1998.

Mason, Nicholas. " 'The Sovereign People are in a Beastly State': The Beer Act of 1830 and Victorian Discourse on Working-Class Drunkenness," *Victorian Literature and Culture* (2001): 109–27.

Maxwell, Ruth. *The Booze Battle.* New York: Ballantine, 1978.

Maynard, John. *Charlotte Brontë and Sexuality.* Cambridge: Cambridge University Press, 1984.

McCarthy, Terence. "The Incompetent Narrator of *Wuthering Heights,*" *Modern Language Quarterly* 42.1 (March 1981): 48–64.

McNeill, William H. *Plagues and Peoples.* 1976. Rpt. New York: Quality Paperbacks, 1993.

Milam, James R. and Katherine Ketcham. *Under the Influence: A Guide to the Myths and Realities of Alcoholism.* New York: Bantam, 1981.

Mitchell, Giles. "Incest, Demonism, and Death in *Wuthering Heights*," *Literature and Psychology* 23 (1973): 27–36.

Morris, R.J. *Cholera 1832: The Social Response to an Epidemic.* London: Croom Helm, 1976.

Mort, Frank. *Dangerous Sexualities: Medico-Moral Politics in England Since 1830.* 2nd ed. London: Routledge & Kegan Paul, 2000.

Murdock, Catherine Gilbert. *Domesticating Drink: Women, Men, and Alcohol in America 1870–1940.* Baltimore, MA: Johns Hopkins University Press, 1998.

Newman, Beth. " 'The Situation of the Looker-On': Gender, Narration, and Gaze in *Wuthering Heights.*" PMLA 105.5 (Oct. 1990): 1029–41.

Pelling, Margaret. *Cholera, Fever, and English Medicine, 1825–1865.* Oxford: Oxford University Press, 1978.

Plumwood, Val. "The Ecopolitics Debate and the Politics of Nature," *Ecological Feminism.* Ed. Karen J. Warren. New York: Routledge, 1994. 64–87.

Polidori, John. *The Vampyre.* In *Three Gothic Novels.* Ed. E.F. Bleiler. New York: Dover, 1966.

Porter Roy. *Disease, Medicine and Society in England, 1550–1860.* 2nd ed. Cambridge: Cambridge University Press, 1993.

——. "The Drinking Man's Disease: The 'Pre-History' of Alcoholism in Georgian Britain," *British Journal of Addiction* 80.4 (Dec. 1985): 385–96.

——. *The Greatest Benefit to Mankind: A Medical History of Humanity.* New York: Norton, 1997.

Pratt, Linda Ray. " 'I Shall Be Your Father': Heathcliff's Narrative of Paternity," *Victorian Institute* Journal 20 (1992): 13–38.

Rhodes, Philip. "A Medical Appraisal of the Brontës," *Classics of Brontë Scholarship: The Best from 100 Years of the Brontë Society Transactions.* Ed. Charles Lemon. Haworth, West Yorkshire: The Brontë Society, 1999. 129–37.

Rosenberg, Charles. *The Cholera Years: The United States in 1832, 1849, and 1866.* Chicago, IL: University of Chicago Press, 1962.

Sadoff, Dianne. " 'Experiments Made by Nature': Mapping the Nineteenth-Century Hysterical Body," *Victorian Newsletter* 81 (Spring 1992): 41–44.

Salleh, Ariel. *Ecofeminism as Politics: Nature, Marx, and the Postmodern.* London: Zed Books, 1997.

Sanger, Charles Percy. "The Structure of *Wuthering Heights*," *Wuthering Heights: An Authoritative Text with Essays in Criticism.* Ed. William M. Sale, Jr. 2nd ed. New York: Norton, 1972. 286–98.

Scarry, Elaine. *The Body in Pain: The Making and Unmaking of the World.* New York: Oxford University Press, 1985.

Shakespeare, William. *Hamlet*. Ed. G.R. Hibbard. New York: Oxford University Press, 1987.

Shiman, Lilian Lewis. *Crusade Against Drink in Victorian England*. New York: St. Martin's Press, 1988.

Showalter, Elaine. *The Female Malady: Women, Madness, and English Culture 1830–1980*. New York: Penguin, 1985.

Shunami, Gideon. "The Unreliable Narrator in *Wuthering Heights*." *Nineteenth-Century Fiction*. 27 (1973): 449–68.

Shuttleworth, Sally. *Charlotte Brontë and Victorian Psychology*. Cambridge: Cambridge University Press, 1996.

Smith, Margaret, Ed. *The Letters of Charlotte Brontë*. 3 vols. Oxford: Clarendon Press, 1995–2004.

Snow, John. *On the Mode of Communication of Cholera*. London: John Churchill, 1849.

Sontag, Susan. *Illness as Metaphor* (1978) and *AIDS and Its Metaphors* (1988). Rpt. New York: Anchor Books, 1990.

Speth, Carol Ann. "Cholera in Early Nineteenth-Century British History and Fiction: The Social and Medical Response." M.A. Thesis. University of Nebraska, 1979.

Thormählen, Marianne. "The Villain of *Wildfell Hall*: Aspects and Prospects of Arthur Huntingdon," *The Modern Language Review* 88.4 (Oct. 1993): 831–41.

Trotter, Thomas. *An Essay on Drunkenness, Medical, Philosophical, and Chemical and Its Effects on the Human Body*. Ed. Roy Porter. New York: Routledge, 1988.

The Twelve Steps for Adult Children of Alcoholic and Other Dysfunctional Families. San Diego, CA: Recovery Publications, 1987.

Tytler, Graeme. "Heathcliff's Monomania: An Anachronism in *Wuthering Heights*," *Brontë Society Transactions* 20.6 (Fall 1992): 331–43.

Virchow, Rudolf. *Cellularpathologie*. Trans. Frank Chance. New York: Dover, 1971.

Vrettos, Athena. "From Neurosis to Narrative: The Private Life of the Nerves in *Villette* and *Daniel Deronda*," *Victorian Studies* 33.4 (Summer 1990): 551–79.

———. *Somatic Fictions: Imagining Illness in Victorian Culture*. Stanford, CA: Stanford University Press, 1995.

Yaeger, Patricia. "Violence in the Sitting Room: *Wuthering Heights* and the Woman's Novel," *Genre* 21.2 (Summer 1988): 203–29.

INDEX

abstinence, 22, 29, 30
abuse, 15, 20, 22–6, 36–7, 47, 106,
  131, 144n, 145n
Ackerman, Robert, 34, 144n
addiction, 2, 23, 28, 30–1, 36,
  139n, 142n, 143n, 144n, 146n
agency, 14, 48, 51–2, 65, 72–3, 137
Agnes Grey (Anne Brontë), 11, 15,
  20, 22–4, 26, 32–3, 36, 130–1,
  133, 143n, 150n
alcoholism, 1, 15–16, 20–9, 31–4,
  36–7, 116, 120, 125, 130–1,
  133, 135, 140n, 142n, 143n,
  144n, 145n, 146n, 150n, 152n;
  see also intemperance; temperance
Allott, Miriam, 19, 72, 75
anaemia, 139n
anatomy, 9, 141n
Anderson, Olive, 151n
anger, 61, 78, 84
animal propensities, 29, 77
animal spirits, 11, 29, 46
anorexia, 89, 131, 155n, 156n
anxiety, 66
Armstrong, Nancy, 162n
asthma, 2
asylum, 46, 103, 140n
anti-contagion, 10
autopsy, 10

Babbage report of 1850, the, 1–3
bacteriology, 8, 140n
Bailin, Miriam, 44–5, 151n
Bakhtin, Mikhail, 134
Barker, Juliet, 1–3, 39, 51, 143n,
  144n, 147n, 148n, 151n

beer, 144n, 145n
Beer Act of 1830, the, 20, 143n
'Bell, Acton,' 19, *see* Anne Brontë
'Bell, Currer', *see* Charlotte Brontë
'Bell, Ellis,' 93, *see* Emily Brontë
Bepko, Claudia, 33
Bichat, Marie François Xavier,
  8, 140n
birth, 26, 74, 108, 111, 115–16,
  122, 161n
bitter herbs, 90, 126–7
blindness, 130
blood, 16, 79, 92, 94, 97, 99–100,
  104–6, 113, 115–16, 119, 158n
body, 1, 3–6, 8–14, 17, 42, 54, 57,
  59, 60, 65–7, 69, 74, 76, 82, 84,
  86, 92, 95–7, 104, 108, 116,
  124, 130, 132, 135–7, 140n
body-self, 74
Book of Common Prayer, 143n
brain fever, 92, 146n, 156n
breakdown, 13, 63, 71, 83–4, 131
Briggs, Asa, 147n
Brodwin, Paul, 6–7
Brontë family, 2, 129–30
Brontë, Anne, 1, 2, 8, 10–11,
  14–16, 19–37, 129–35, 142n,
  143n, 144n, 150n; *Agnes Grey*,
  11, 15, 20, 22–4, 26, 32–3, 36,
  130–1, 133, 143n, 150n; *The
  Tenant of Wildfell Hall*, 14–15,
  19–20, 24–37, 130–1, 134, 143n,
  145n, 150n
Brontë, Branwell, 2, 9, 15, 28,
  130, 139n, 140n, 143n,
  144n, 150n

Brontë, Charlotte, 1, 2–3, 8–10, 12, 14–16, 39–57, 59–88, 90–1, 93, 95, 105, 130–7, 139n, 147n, 148n, 150n, 156n, 163n; *Jane Eyre*, 2, 60–1, 66, 90, 130, 132–3, 152n; *The Professor*, 12, 61, 130, 136, 152n; *Shirley*, 15–16, 39–57, 59, 61, 73, 105, 130–3, 146n, 147n, 148n, 150n, 151n; *Villette*, 14–16, 57, 59–88, 95, 130–4, 136–7, 152n, 153n

Brontë, Elizabeth, 2, 129

Brontë, Emily, 1–3, 8–9, 11, 14–16, 51, 89–127, 130–4, 141n, 151n, 156n, 159n, 162n, 163n; "The Butterfly," 91–2; "The Cat," 92; "I'm happiest when most away," 156n; "To Imagination," 156n; "The Old Stoic," 156n; "The Palace of Death," 93; "Plead for Me," 94; "The Prisoner: A Fragment," 156n; "The Siege of Oudenarde," 157n; "There was a time when my cheek burned," 127; *Wuthering Heights*, 14, 16, 89–127, 130–2, 134, 155n, 156n, 158n, 159n, 160n, 162n

Brontë, Maria Branwell, 2, 139n

Brontë, Maria, 2, 129

Brontë, Reverend Patrick, 1, 8, 9, 21, 139n, 141n, 143n

Brumberg, Joan Jacobs, 155n

Buchan, William, *Domestic Medicine*, 9, 141n

Budd, Dr., 144n

Butler, Judith, 3, 140n, 153n

cancer, 2, 4, 43, 45

cannibal, 105, 107

Carter, K. Codell, 50, 150n, 151n

cataracts, 130

Catholicism, 16, 59–60, 62–7, 74–6, 79–81, 84–6, 152n, 153n, 154n

Cecil, David, 156n

cellular pathology, 11, 140n

Chadwick, Edwin, 19

charity, 55–6, 157n

Chartist Rebellion, 15, 39

childbirth, 92, 108, 111, 115, 130

cholera, 1, 15–16, 39–44, 55–7, 129, 131, 135, 147n, 148n, 149n, 150n

chronic pelvic sepsis, 139n

Clark-Beattie, Rosemary, 60

Clergy Daughters' School, 2

cold, 11, 20, 48–9, 53, 89, 117, 120, 158n, 159n

Combe, George, *The Constitution of Man*, 77, 79; *A System of Phrenology*, 154n

confinement, 156n, 161n; *see also* pregnancy

consumption, 1–2, 9–10, 15–16, 20, 40, 43, 92, 94, 108, 115, 126, 129–30, 139n, 146n, 147n; *see also* tuberculosis

constitution, 2, 8, 29, 46, 60, 77, 79, 136, 144n

contagion, 10, 42, 55, 148n

convalescence, 42, 54, 74–5, 78, 80, 89, 96, 119–20

corpse, 5, 141n

couverture, 111

cultural conflict, 6–8, 13, 72, 95

cultural constraints, 7, 14, 17, 63, 73–4, 85–6, 95, 97, 131

cure, 9, 22–3, 31, 37, 51, 55, 69, 71, 79, 87, 89–90, 100, 126–7, 139n, 140n, 144n, 145n, 146n, 151n, 161n

Dames, Nicholas, 78, 81

Davies, Stevie, 92

Davion, Victoria, 159n

death, 1–3, 5, 7, 10, 15, 21, 27–8, 31, 35–6, 41–2, 47, 49, 51, 72–3, 87, 89–96, 100–1, 103–5, 107–9, 111–16, 118–20, 122, 124–5, 129–30, 132, 139n, 147n, 148n, 151n, 152n, 157n, 159n, 160n, 162n

Printed in the United States
108303LV00002B/12/A

9 781403 967961